CALLED BY THE DAMNED

WORLD BREACHER: BOOK 2

JALI HENRY

DIVERSE WORLDS PUBLICATIONS

COPYRIGHT

Copyright © 2020 by Jali Henry

All rights reserved.

No part of this book may be reproduced in any form or by any electronic or mechanical means, including information storage and retrieval systems, without written permission from the author, except for the use of brief quotations in a book review.

With thanks to my beta reader, Niqui Merret and my editor-Mum, Charlotte Mbali. My wonderful husband Jai and my two beautiful children, Kaya and Lindiwe. They've given me inspiration, advice, love and lots of time and space to write alone.

GLOSSARY

Sesotho / English
- Dineo/ Gift
- Dumela / Hello
- Haiybo/ Expression of surprise
- Ithwasa/ Physical and mental illness
- Kabelo/ Inheritance
- Kgosi/ Sir
- Lerato/ Love
- Mohlakola/ Eucleia
- Molume/ Uncle
- Morogo/ Type of spinach
- Motsumi/ Seeker
- Naledi/ Star
- Nkhono/ Grandmother
- Ntate/ Father or Grandfather
- Palechee/ A staple maize meal carbohydrate
- Puleng/ Rain
- Sangoma/ Shaman
- Shebeen/ Unlicensed purveyor of alcohol

Tau/ Lion
Thato/ Will
Tokoloshe/ Legendary imp/evil elf

1
THE COUNTESS

∽

The Countess had always hated hospitals and she hated them even more now that she was dead. When she'd been alive, she'd felt a coldness upon entering a hospital; a sense that sadness and death had seeped into the very bricks of the walls, but this had just been a feeling, a sixth sense. It was nothing tangible that could be proven or seen. Now that she was dead, she could see disease dripping down the walls. It congregated in thick sludgy blobs which glooped and bubbled, as it wound its way up and down walls and beneath the feet of unwitting humans who walked around, oblivious to the presence of both disease and the Countess.

She was visiting earth behind the veil, in that place where all material reality had a spiritual double. It was completely beyond the abilities of most humans to perceive anything behind the veil, but it was very real. She sat on a chair in the A&E of Johannesburg General Hospital, waiting for casualties to come in. She'd found this particular hospital to be the most fruitful in terms of soul snatching as there were a lot of gunshot victims who would frequently pass over in distress, unprepared for death. This was the perfect opportunity for her to use their confusion to her advantage and shepherd them over to join her in Hell.

She looked up at the neon lighting, casting a blue tinge across the white walled corridor and polished, grey tiled floors. Even the lighting was depressing, casting a greyish tinge across the faces of people who were already exhausted, anxious or grieving. She crinkled her nose in disgust as a gloop of disease congregated on a light and then dripped down, to land, with a slight plop, on a nurse's shoulder. The nurse continued signing documents and didn't even look up.

The Countess often pitied humans for their lack of awareness; it made them such easy marks; it was almost too easy. As she thought this, she felt a ball of anger gather in her throat. She found it demeaning to be forced into soul snatching her way back to being a demon. She'd been treated appallingly. After everything she'd done for Satan, all the time she'd spent strategising and planning each minute detail of his son, Sehloho's, resurrection - all the sacrifices she'd made. It wasn't her fault that the human host had turned rogue at the last moment. She'd only just made it back through the portal, before it had closed. They'd demoted her, to wicked spirit status, no longer even a full demon, the very bare insult of it! She felt her cheeks get hot with rage as she thought of the Chancellor's words as he'd sentenced her,

I sentence you to be demoted to wicked spirit status and to have no minion slaves nor any privileges of any kind until such time as your status has been revised

No privileges of any kind! She may as well have been demoted back to minion status, the only difference was that she didn't have to serve as a slave to any other damned soul but that was about it. She was more or less a wicked spirit in name only. She'd get back up though, oh yes; she wouldn't lie low and lick her wounds whilst other demons laughed at her behind her back. Oh no, the minute she'd been sentenced, she'd begun to plan her ascent and to that end she'd been spending as much time as possible at this very hospital, waiting for people to die.

The Countess turned her head as the double doors to the emergency drop-off point, burst open and a trolley was pushed out of an ambulance. A couple of paramedics walked briskly by the side, giving their report to the nurses and doctors as the patient lay, unconscious on the trolley. The Countess felt her face crack into a wide grin, this was just what she'd been waiting for: a gunshot victim and it sounded like he had multiple wounds. She followed the trolley down the corridor towards the operating theatre. Her luck would be in today; she could feel it in her demonic bones. As the Countess turned a corner she reared back into the shadows of a wall alcove and withdrew her breath sharply.

Is that Mephistopheles?

She peeked around the corner again, yes, it was him. His thick, smooth, dark hair and ruggedly handsome face was unmistakable. He was also wearing his hallmark black leather jacket, jeans and sunglasses. She inwardly cursed. If he was here, she'd have to give up and go to another hospital. Mephistopheles was regarded, by the whole of Hell, as being the master of soul snatching: she wouldn't stand a chance against him. Plus, she couldn't bear his smug gloating. He hadn't seen her yet. So, if she just crept off, she'd be fine. She turned around and started walking in the opposite direction but then her entire body froze, her shoulders instantly jumping to her ears, as she heard his braying, guttural laugh.

"Well, well, well, if it isn't the Countess. Come to try and soul snatch your way back to demon status have you?"

The Countess relaxed her shoulders, pulling down her cropped, tuxedo jacket as she straightened herself up, whilst trying to salvage as much dignity back from this situation as she could muster. She fixed a smile onto her face, which she hoped conveyed the perfect blend of contentedness, and nonchalance then she turned around,

"Mephistopheles, how lovely to see you, I'm surprised I haven't seen you here before. Is this a regular haunt for you?"

Mephistopheles removed his sunglasses, folded them up and placed them into the breast pocket of his jacket,

"Oh come now Countess, don't think that you can pump me for information. I'm not going to tell you if I come here regularly. I'm not going to give you any tips at all. Everyone knows that I'm the best at soul snatching so now that I'm here, why don't you just run along back to whatever rock you crawled out from under and let the master do his work?" He linked his fingers together and pushed his arms out in front of him, in a gesture of muscle flexing, as his lip curled up with contempt.

The Countess pursed her lips into a tight half-smile of forced politeness. She loathed this male demon. She despised his preening, self-adoring machismo. She'd known plenty of men like him when she'd been alive and she'd found there to be no shortage of these types of men in Hell. Was there no escape from them? From their arrogance, their condescension, their patronising habit of talking over her. Even his good looks were like a slap in her face. Good looks that he weaponised to lure foolish women from their intended heavenly path. Good looks that he now paraded in front of her like a red rag to a bull. She had no respect for him: his tactics were obvious and completely lacking sophistication. Was he successful? Yes, she couldn't deny it but she would never stoop so low as to use her womanly wiles to trick humans into damnation. No, she preferred to use her wit and intelligence to convince them that Hell was actually the best place for them. She'd done this before and she'd do it again now. Hah! She'd show him! However, none of this was revealed on her petite-featured, dark skinned face, she didn't want to give him the satisfaction of knowing he had her beaten or in any way rattled. Looking up at Mephistopheles' smirking, offensively handsome face, she smiled, then said,

"Actually Mephistopheles, I was just leaving. I'm not interested in the weak, gullible souls in this hospital. I prefer a challenge." She turned on her heel and strode off, in just enough time to see the smile drop from his face at the implied insult.

ROUNDING THE CORNER, she assessed her options. This wasn't the only A&E in Johannesburg. Of course, she could leave it for today and go back to Hell Central; perhaps she could try Tijuana tomorrow? She'd been lucky there on a few occasions before. The problem was that it took considerable energy to manifest an etheric form strong enough for humans, near the threshold, or those who had recently crossed over, to see. Going back and forth between Hell and Earth wasn't advisable on a daily basis; it would weaken her to the extent that should a pesky warrior of heaven be hanging around; she could be vanquished and to be attacked on Earth would result in being destroyed forever. This is what had happened to Sehloho in the unfortunate and previously mentioned failed resurrection attempt. He was now thoroughly dead - dead forever with no chance of rebirth in another hell dimension as would be the case had he died in Hell.

She had an idea. She wouldn't go back to Hell yet. There was still the elderly care ward that might be even better. Many of the old geezers were so flattered when someone as youthful and attractive as her talked to them, that they didn't even notice her red eyes. She approached a flight of stairs, gathering up her long, silk skirt as her kitten heels clicked on the steps. Humans passed her on the stairs, brushing past her as if she wasn't there - which of course, to them, she wasn't. She reached the second floor and swept along the corridor to the old age ward. She knew the route well; she'd been here many times before. Reaching the ward, she settled herself on a chair beside the reception team. She'd found it best, in the past, to wait in a central area until medical teams started rushing around in an anxious manner. Then all she had to do was follow them to the source of the panic and wait until the old dear popped off. Pulse rate monitors were very helpful, the sound of the steady beeping becoming at first erratic, before steadying to one monotonous, unbroken tone, was quite literally music to her ears.

A family approached, a mother and father, holding a little girl's hand. The little girl, who looked to be around five years old, was sucking a lollipop and staring at the Countess in a most disconcerting way.

She better not be a clairvoyant.

They were a perfect nuisance. Fortunately, most other humans disregarded them as charlatans and crackpots but every now and then she'd encounter a bothersome clairvoyant who wouldn't let her presence lie and would keep hounding her. The parents had now stopped by the reception desk, leaving the child to wander over to her. She walked over, cocking her head to one side and stopped, uncomfortably close to the Countess' face. *Damnation!*

She was definitely a clairvoyant. She was now staring into the Countess' eyes, creasing her eyebrows as she withdrew the lollipop from her mouth,

"Why are your eyes red?" she asked.

"Didn't your mother ever tell you it's not polite to stare at people?" the Countess replied, ignoring the girl's question.

"But your eyes, they're red?" the girl persisted. The Countess sighed and looked away from the girl, hoping she'd go away.

"Mom! That lady has got red eyes," she walked over and tugged on her mother's shirt, keeping her eyes fixed on the Countess as she did so.

"Mom!..." she tugged.

"Not now darling, we're trying to find out which ward Grandma is in."

The Countess smiled to herself. She could always count on adults to disregard the ramblings of psychic children. Thankfully it hadn't been an adult this time. That time she'd been waiting for suicides on a well known jumping bridge and she'd been approached by the raving homeless man had been most inconvenient. She couldn't shake him off and she'd eventually had to abandon her mission and return to Hell. It was so very tedious waiting for people to die. If only she could give them a little helping hand or better still, murder them. But of course, being non-physical on Earth, she couldn't touch them, only influence them. Finally she saw a group of medical staff mobilise to action as she heard the blessed erratically beeping heart rate monitor of a human about to depart the mortal coil. She followed behind the staff smiling to herself. Yes, she'd be back on top soon and when she was, she'd wipe that smile off Mephistopheles' smug face.

2
GIADA

∽

Giada sat polishing silverware at an ornate antique wooden dining table. She had to admit; working in the Chancellor's household was way better than working in the Countess' household had been. After the Countess had been stripped of her title, the Council of the Seventh Circle had reassigned Giada to the Chancellor's house. He was running the Seventh Circle temporarily until Satan chose one of his sons to succeed Sehloho. The Chancellor was out most of the time and even when he was at home, he preferred the company of his two male minions. This meant that Giada had a large amount of free time, which she chose to spend snooping around his house.

She hadn't yet worked out if she could be brazen enough to skip out entirely and go off and do her own thing whilst he was out. She hadn't yet tested it nor did she know what her new boss' appetite for torture was. He seemed to be a man who was ruled by logic rather than urges but then he was also a very senior government official. You didn't get that kind of power without having done a fair amount of torturing somewhere along the line.

Placing down the last piece of silverware, she went over to the window of the townhouse and looked down at the pathway outside. When she'd first arrived in Hell she'd wondered why demons even bothered having windows in their houses. The windows looked out across the desolate and barren landscape of Hell. The view displayed a sky that was permanently dark red with rolling grey clouds and the odd crackle of lightning. There was no fresh air; the air smelt like sulphur wherever you were. However, now that she'd been in Hell a few months, it was clear to her that the windows were for watching what was going on outside. Or more accurately - who was coming and who was going.

Looking left and right, Giada could see no sign of the Chancellor or either of his other minions so she crept to her favourite room: the study. Entering the oak-lined room she reflected on how difficult it must have been for the Chancellor to get the material over the threshold from Earth to Hell. She wondered how he'd done it and who he'd had to bribe or kill. She ran her fingers across the shelves of books lining one wall from floor to ceiling. Cocking her head to one side, she blew dust away from one of the books and coughed as it tickled her nose. The Chancellor's tastes were eclectic. He had all the classics, Satan's 'Falling from Grace', Mephistopheles' 'How to Snatch a Soul' and even a rare first edition of Baal's 'Demonology'. He also had some riskier texts, which hinted at a streak of rebellion. 'The Gospel of Truth': a heretical biblical text and several autobiographies of famous human dictators. Giada wondered if this was why she liked coming in here - because the Chancellor's books made her suspect that he shared her attraction to the forbidden. He was a man of few words though. Really she hadn't yet worked out what made him tick, other than the obvious taste in young men.

Suddenly Giada heard the sound of a key rattling as someone started to open the downstairs front door. She resisted the urge to look out of the window and instead sped out of the room as fast as her legs could carry her. She plonked herself by the silverware to continue polishing as if nothing had happened. The Chancellor entered the hallway where she sat, flanked by his two minions. Eric and Alonso were both as dim as they were beautiful and Giada had hence nicknamed them 'the Himbos'. As far as she could tell, the only work they were required to do was to share the Chancellor's bed. This made Giada grateful that she was a girl even though it meant that the entirety of the household chores were lumped onto her. The Chancellor had had another female minion maid before her but she'd progressed up to wicked spirit status and so he'd needed a new one.

Giada looked at the Chancellor's stooped posture as he walked over to her. He'd barely made conversation with her in the time since she'd started working here. She felt the hairs rise on the back of her neck as he stood by her table. His keen red eyes watched her through his glasses. She stopped polishing and looked up at him, hesitantly. "Is there something I can help you with, Sir?"

The Chancellor smiled: his smile was of a type that withered almost as soon as it had formed on his face. This gave him the unsettling appearance of always looking like he hated you - perhaps he did hate everyone. "You've been here for some time now haven't you, Giada?"

"Yes Sir. Three weeks I believe."

"And how are you finding it so far?"

Why should he care how I'm finding it? Demons don't care about minions' feelings...

"Fine Sir, I'm adjusting to the new work very well." She felt it wise to suggest gratitude, as she didn't want him to swap her into another demon household which was worse than his. God forbid if she got reassigned to Mephistopheles' home or one of the other pain-inflicting addicted demons.

"Follow me to the study please - I know you like it in there." He gave her a knowing smile. Her mouth dropped open and she felt the blood drain from her face. Was she about to be punished for having gone where she hadn't been invited? Fearing the worst, she followed behind him, dragging her feet as she walked.

. . .

ENTERING the study the Chancellor gestured for her to sit in the large, leather armchair opposite his own. Then he ushered the himbos away with a few flicks of his wrist leaving Giada and the Chancellor alone. She gulped as her mind raced through all the possibilities of his intentions in bringing her in here.

"Don't worry, I'm not going to hurt you," he explained, alleviating her fears somewhat, but not her curiosity. She looked around the room. On the wall behind her chair, a fake fire crackled in the hearth. She must've looked puzzled as she looked at it because the Chancellor explained,

"It gives off no heat. I know it's sentimental of me but I just like the way it looks - it reminds me of my old study back on Earth."

Hmm, interesting, he misses his human life, the same as I do.

"I'm sure you're wondering why I've invited you in here?" the Chancellor continued.

Giada nodded, keeping her head down as she looked at him from under her furrowed brow.

He explained further, "when Clara was promoted to wicked spirit, I didn't want just anyone to replace her. I wanted you specifically and the reason for that is that you used to work in the Countess' household." He paused, looking her up and down as if weighing his words carefully. "You see I now have the great responsibility of governing the Seventh Circle. It is not a position to take lightly as failure will result in at best a demotion and at worst an execution." He stood up and moved closer to the fake fire. He took off his glasses and gazed into the fire. Its orange glow reflected off his grey hair and deep red eyes in a way that made him look especially demonic. "I'll cut to the chase. The Countess is up to something; we believe that she's plotting a coup. Possibly even conspiring with a demon ruler from a neighbouring Hell dimension."

Giada knew it would be better for her to keep quiet, but she couldn't help herself: "How do you know all this?" she asked.

"We have our sources. Wicked spirits, demons, a variety of spies who are loyal to the council and ultimately to Satan whose supremacy is threatened by the Countess' ambitions."

"I see" Giada replied.

He continued: "hence my insistence on getting you as my minion. I predict that the Countess will soon get her demon status back again. This isn't a bad thing as her next move will be to get you back into her household. She can't stand losing and she will perceive me having you here as being a slight to her dominance." The Chancellor looked Giada in the eye, "we want you to be our eyes and ears in the Countess' household. Watch her, follow her, sleep with her if you have to. Do whatever it takes to find out exactly what she's up to."

Giada raised her eyebrows. This was the last thing she had been expecting when he had invited her into his study. "What if I say 'no'?"

The Chancellor replaced his glasses and chuckled softly. "My dear girl, you don't have a choice, especially as now you know too much. If you say no, we will simply execute you and find someone else who is willing to do it. Oh and we'll execute all of your redemption-seeking friends too."

Giada played it cool by shrugging. "Maybe I don't mind execution. I know I'll be reborn in another hell dimension anyway."

"And maybe you're bluffing. You'd rather be here than in any other unknown Hell and besides. We have ways of making the pain before death drag on for an excruciatingly long time. You'll be begging for death over and over again but even then we still won't end it. The last person we executed for not going along with our plans was killed over the course of 6 months. Mephistopheles presided over it - I have video footage if you'd like to see?"

Giada hastily waved her hands in front of her face "No, no, that's okay, I believe you. Okay, if I agree to do it – *if*, that is -what happens when the Countess catches me spying on her?"

"We'll protect you."

Giada raised her eyebrows, "yeah sure and I'm the mother of Jesus - demons lie, all the time. You'll say you'll protect me and then when she catches me I'll be left high and dry and she is not a demon to cross."

The Chancellor chuckled, "you've got some nerve mentioning His name in front of me. I could have you tortured for months for that, you know."

Giada raised one eyebrow at him and folded her arms. She didn't break her gaze for a second.

"That's why you're exactly the kind of person we need for this. You're courageous, Giada, rebellious, a risk-taker. Those are the qualities that make an excellent spy."

"Don't think that flattery will distract me from your lies."

The Chancellor sighed. "Fine, you don't have to believe me but consider this. Who would you rather have running the Seventh Circle? A council of elder demons, hand-picked by Satan himself, followed by one of his sons, who is likely very similar in his leadership style to Sehloho? Or a megalomaniac sorcerer demon, who bears grudges and delights in causing psychological suffering?"

Giada had to admit he had a point. The Countess was a real piece of work and Giada had a lurking fear that she suspected Giada had played a part in the failed resurrection. That meant it was only a matter of time before she would exact her revenge. If she was right then the only thing stopping her so far was her focus on getting her demon status back but as soon as that was in the bag, she'd turn her attentions towards plotting revenge. It was actually in Giada's interests to ally herself with powerful demons who could protect her if it came to that.

"Okay, I'll do it."

"Good. I knew you were an intelligent girl. Now, next steps. Once you're back in her household, simply keep watching her as often as possible. Especially when she goes out for the day. We need to know who she is meeting with and what they are discussing. Then, in due course, we will contact you to arrange a meeting. You must keep this entire operation completely secret - even from your friends in Sinners Anonymous. The Countess has her own spies everywhere and we cannot have her striking first."

Giada nodded, taking a deep breath. This was a lot to take in but she was ready for it. She'd been looking for a way to get back at the

Countess since she'd arrived here. She thought of all the countless humiliations she'd endured whilst working as her maid and then the worst thing of all - the Countess forcing her into eroding a bit more of her soul by sin baiting. Yes, the Countess had it coming all right and Giada was just the minion to dish it out to her.

3
NALEDI

~

Naledi lay, gazing up at Tau's beautiful face as she lay resting her head on his lap. School had started again after the long summer holidays and they were enjoying their lunch break, under the shade of a Mohlakola tree. Tau stroked her face, as she looked deep into his eyes. She had just about got used to the sight of his adult face with both of his eyes intact and no eye patch. He seemed to be calmer now, calmer than he had been since his childhood. It was as if the events of the resurrection had caused a spiritual reawakening. As if everything that he'd found out about his mother, including Motsumi's betrayal of her and Tau's eventual revenge, his death and rebirth, had changed him for the better. He'd started going to church again, she supposed, how could he not? Now that he'd actually died and been to heaven – he could no longer doubt the existence of God. There was a peace and acceptance to his aura, a sense that he had completed his life's purpose. Now he could concentrate on just following what he desired from moment to moment. And what he wanted in this moment was Naledi. He smiled at her, a delicious smile of lazy, contented desire and leaned down for a delicate kiss, which she returned. Whenever she was with Tau, the rest of the world melted away and it was just her and him and eternity. The tranquility of their solitude was broken by Lerato skipping across the field to join them,

"Would you two give it a rest already? Barely a minute goes by without you smooching." Lerato mimed a passionate embrace by wrapping her arms around her torso and twisting her face from side to side in an obscene mimicry complete with sound effects.

Naledi sat up and covered her face with her hands whilst laughing, "Well, if you don't like it you don't have to join us."

"Who else am I gonna hang around with, huh?" Lerato crouched down and attacked Naledi. She pinched her playfully in the ribs until Naledi collapsed with laughter.

"I better head off anyway, I have an assignment to hand in," Tau said. He stood up and brushed grass from his jeans before walking off towards the grey brick school building.

Naledi shielded her eyes from the sun with her arm, squinting at him walking away, as her best friend plonked herself down beside her to take Tau's place.

"I see you still haven't gotten over the novelty of having your boyfriend back then?"

"Lerato, it's like he's a totally new person. Well, not exactly like a totally new person, more like the old person he was before Motsumi abused his mother's trust and stole his eye. He's like how I remember him as a child except now he's a teenager. He's just so contented, I never thought I'd see him like this again."

Lerato smiled, "I'm happy for you... and for Tau, he deserves to be happy, you both do."

Naledi looked down at her lap and felt her eyebrows crease with worry,

"I feel like it's too good to be true though, I don't quite trust it"

"What do you mean?"

"Well, you know what Motsumi is... was like. I can't believe he'd just give up. Even now he's dead, I keep expecting him to come back in some way."

Lerato looked at her as if she was crazy. "Naledi, he's dead. You killed him. Then you watched his body get torn apart by demons. There's no way he's coming back. You're safe, you have to relax and enjoy your life."

"I'm not sure I can"

"That's because you've become used to drama and loss. We all have. Since your parents died, you've been living under the expectation that any day something bad will happen. Then Motsumi came and took you to Hell, quite literally and that increased that feeling."

Naledi sighed and looked up at the sky, "I suppose you're right but what if... I don't know, what if he still has a hold on me? The binding ceremony was supposed to work until such time as I had graduated to become a full sangoma. I never graduated and sometimes I still feel his presence."

Lerato shook her head, "I think it's in your head. He got into your head big time. I'm still not convinced that the binding ceremony was real. He was such a liar, Naledi, a pathological liar almost. He lied and lied and lied. I'm sure he lied to you about that binding ceremony too. He would've done anything to get you to agree to train with him. He was desperate."

They heard the school bell ring indicating the end of lunch and got up to make their way back to the classrooms for their next lesson. Naledi picked up her school bag and walked slowly next to Lerato. She dragged her feet slightly as she walked, reflecting on the conversation they'd had. Was she really free of Motsumi? She couldn't believe he'd just give up and leave her alone. Not even death would stop him from manipulating her if it suited his ends. But then hadn't it all been for the purposes of Sehloho's resurrection? She wasn't so sure, on good days she thought it was all over and she'd never see him again. On bad days, she thought he was incapable of accepting defeat and was probably at this very moment plotting his revenge. Or, if not his revenge, his escape from Hell, which would most likely involve using her powers in some way. She knew there was no escape from Hell for him. He would've gone there as a minion: the lowest of the low. The only way a damned soul could escape Hell would be to get a human to agree to host them. This was only really possible for demons and even then it was rare to find a willing human. The human had to agree they couldn't be forced. A demon could possess a person, against their will, who engaged in witchcraft or spiritual practices whilst under the influence of drugs. But this was not something Motsumi would ever do. She knew that logically this meant that she was free of him but something in her bones made her doubt it.

Perhaps Lerato was right; perhaps she'd spent too long expecting the worst. She'd spent so long looking over her shoulder for the next storm cloud, that she was incapable of relaxing and enjoying the sunshine. Tau had changed: he was happy now, not just happy, he was content and at peace. Perhaps it was time for her to drop her guard and enjoy life as he'd clearly decided to do? But then sometimes, late at night, when she was alone, she thought she could sense Motsumi. She felt him calling to her, summoning her from beyond the grave. He hadn't had a funeral, his body had been torn apart by demons. Perhaps he now wandered just beyond the veil as a ghost? But if that were true, she would've seen him.

Although she'd made great progress at controlling her ithwasa, it still hovered from time to time. When it did, her psychic abilities were greatly increased, especially the ability to see ghosts, angels and demons. If Motsumi called to her, there was one place he called from and that was Hell. Or was this all just in her mind, a part of the 'vivid imagination', which Motsumi had accused her of having? Even her thoughts were not free of him; she was still bound to him. Whether magically bound to him or not, he still had her enchained psychologically. She was entangled to him energetically by the strength of everything they'd been through together.

Kabelo caught up with the girls. Since the truth had come out about him being an undercover angel, sent to Marula to spy on Motsumi,

Lerato's crush had waned slightly but it was still there. In fact, if Naledi didn't know better, she could've sworn that since Lerato's affections had cooled off, Kabelo was paying her more attention. Honestly, boys! They only ever wanted what they thought they couldn't get. Naledi had asked him if he'd be leaving the school now that the mission was complete but he'd told her that he'd been instructed to remain there and await further instructions. There was apparently going to be more work for him in the future and this was another thing that made Naledi anxious. What was it that God knew but was not telling his angels?

"Dumela Naledi, Lerato," he dipped his head and smiled at Lerato, "I wanted to ask you if you'd have time to help me with this history assignment later? Tau has already finished his, but history isn't really my strong point, as you know, I missed all the earlier years."

"Who are you asking, Naledi or me?" Lerato raised her eyebrow haughtily.

Kabelo cleared his throat, "Um, well, I thought, you, because Naledi has to look after Dineo and Puleng…"

In fact Kabelo knew full well that if he asked Naledi to help him then Lerato would look after Naledi's younger sisters for her; they all lived in the same house.

"Plus I wanted to give you something," Kabelo added.

"Ooh! A gift, now I'm interested," Lerato beamed.

"Don't get that excited. It's just something I thought you could use, that's all, but I'll keep it as a surprise."

"Now I'm really interested. I'll do it. Meet you after school and we can walk home together okay?"

"Sounds good"

Kabelo lolloped off, tripping on a broken paving stone as he went. Naledi turned to her friend with her hands on her hips and her eyebrows raised. "How the worm has turned. Now he's pestering you for a date"

"It is not a date!"

"It sounded sort of like one to me."

"Don't be silly. He just wants my help, that's all."

"He could've asked me - or Tau."

"Don't talk nonsense," Lerato rolled her eyes but she was suppressing a smile.

Naledi lifted her hands up, "Alright, alright but you mark my words, he's taken a shine to you."

"Angels don't think like that."

"How do you know?"

"I don't but I'm pretty sure."

"Well I guess you'll soon find out, won't you."

NALEDI SPENT much of the lesson trying to concentrate but her thoughts were still far away. She'd changed. Her experiences in Hell and with the failed resurrection, even the shock of losing Tau and then gaining him back again so quickly. It had all changed her. She felt old beyond her years. She'd felt like that before any of this had begun, but now even more so. It was hard for her to relate to anyone else at school. Most of her classmates were mature as they'd all experienced grief at a young age. Many of them looked after younger siblings or were carers for elderly grandparents. But none of them had travelled the multiverse or defeated demon princes like she had. She felt that she stood several feet above everyone else and this feeling wasn't out of arrogance; it was necessity. She'd had to form a thick protective shell around herself and it was one that could not now be penetrated.

When she'd first met Motsumi, he'd said she needed to toughen up. Well, he had indeed toughened her up. Not in the way that he'd wanted her to but in the way that she'd needed to. She was still the same person but an older, wiser, more cautious version of herself. She drifted into a daydream and felt her ithwasa beckoning at the edges of her consciousness. She could just about sense the reality beyond everyday reality. She could feel the world beyond the veil. Beyond that deeper dimension, she felt Heaven and Hell. If she quieted her mind and concentrated whilst also relaxing deeply, she could almost hear Motsumi calling to her, she could almost smell sulphur and feel heat. With a shock of realisation, she acknowledged that she missed him. She'd hated him so much. She'd killed him. She couldn't forgive him for the lies and manipulations yet he'd looked after her. He'd been the father she'd needed, one that she'd yearned for without even realising it, ever since her own father had died of the epidemic. Maybe she'd yearned even before that. Certainly Motsumi had given her more care and attention than her birth father ever had done. It had been twisted care and attention, care that was self-serving and abusive, but it had still been attention.

Then she couldn't forget that he'd also bequeathed her his entire estate. He'd been smart: he'd instructed the executors of his will to only give her a monthly allowance until she was twenty-one. This allowance meant that she could look after her sisters and Lerato and never have to worry about money for food or clothes or schoolbooks or any other necessities. When she thought of Motsumi, in Hell, being enslaved by a vicious demon, being disrespected and tortured, she felt guilty. It wasn't her fault that he was there. It was his fault. But he had a way of making her feel responsible for him or at least responsible for anything that went wrong. She shook her head and wrenched her attention back onto the lesson. She had to forget about Motsumi and everything he'd put her through. The trouble was, she didn't know if she could.

4

GIADA

~

Giada sat struggling but failing to listen as Motsumi droned on and on and on. He'd arrived in Hell straight after the failed resurrection attempt and had joined Sinners Anonymous because, as he was very eager to tell anyone who would listen, 'he didn't belong in Hell'. Giada understood that she should be extra kind to new SA members and let them share for as long as they wanted but this guy had taken it to the extreme. He was clearly quite deeply in love with the sound of his own voice. He wasn't so much sharing his sins as giving a 'War-and-Peace' length account of his entire life, complete with appendices. Giada stifled a giggle as, looking across the room, she saw that Maureen had given up pretending to listen. She had fallen asleep. Her head nodded on her large bosom. Her cat eyeglasses lay askew on her jowly face, and a small trail of spittle had collected at the corner of her mouth and was now working its way onto her shoulder. Motsumi had just gotten to the part of his life story where he'd sold his soul to Satan in exchange for magical power. To hear him talk, you'd think that he was the victim here, rather than a scheming megalomaniac. All right, so the

Countess had ordered that he be tortured daily as punishment for his failure.

Cry me a river - we all get tortured here.

She'd endured the same thing when she'd first arrived. It was only through careful and constant manoeuvring learnt the hard way, by trial and error, that she wasn't still getting tortured daily now. It seemed to Giada, that Motsumi was the kind of guy who would short-change you and then claim it was your fault for distracting him and then convince you that you hadn't been short-changed after all. She'd had the measure of him the minute she'd met him. After all, it took a manipulator to recognise a manipulator. The difference between her and Motsumi however, was that she knew she was a despicable human being: she'd at least got that far. Motsumi was still very much in denial.

He'd now reached the part, of his spoken-word memoirs, in which he'd convinced a human teenage boy, that agreeing to host Sehloho's resurrection on earth would be a good idea. Only to have that same boy change his mind at the last minute. Giada already knew this part of the story, as she'd been the one to sin-bait the boy - Tau, into killing himself. The boy stabbed himself in the chest, thereby forcing Motsumi to offer his own body as the host. This would've been successful if Naledi hadn't stabbed him to death.

Hmm, Naledi killed him? I wouldn't have thought she had it in her...

Motsumi also confessed that he'd violently extracted Tau's eye, years earlier, to take as payment for curing his mother of Aids. The same mother who died soon after of, you guessed it: Aids. Giada had heard some terrible stories inside the SA meetings but this could quite possibly be the worst. It may even be worse than her own heinous transgression of standing watching whilst her younger brother accidentally strangled himself to death on a curtain chord. Finally, it seemed that Motsumi was wrapping up his soliloquy.

"And so, I find myself here, amongst you, in spite of the many good works I've performed for the community. Did I mention that I took in a home full of Aids orphans? My apprentice, Naledi and her younger siblings and her adoptive sister. I gave them food, shelter, clothing, everything they would need. I did it out of the kindness of my heart, receiving nothing in return for my efforts."

Motsumi sighed and dipped his head down, his eyelids fluttering in apparent sadness, which Giada could tell, was entirely fake. Aaron, the group leader, held his hands up, addressing Motsumi in his familiar Southern U.S drawl.

"You don't need to convince us. We're not judging you, the only one you should fear judgment from is the Almighty."

Giada inwardly scoffed: *Speak for yourself Aaron, I am judging him, and I find him guilty.*

Motsumi gave Aaron the kind of forced smile of politeness of someone enduring a very painful toothache and shuffled back to his seat to the obvious relief of many of the other SA members, a couple of whom sat up straighter in their chairs again. Maureen gave a loud snore, which jolted her awake. Her usual red-veined cheeks became even redder as she smoothed down her purple-rinsed hair and adjusted her plum shirt.

"Would anyone else like to share tonight?" Aaron spread his hands out around the group in a welcoming gesture. There was a lengthy silence during which all the newcomers looked at the floor and those who had shared before looked around the group.

Giada, who had shared before but wasn't about to share again tonight, scanned the room. The group had certainly grown considerably in the past few weeks and she wondered as to the reasons. She'd detected something in the air since Sehloho's annihilation by angels. Minions walked with more of a spring to their step. They went about their work with an attitude of hope. Many of them had had more time off as the demons they were enslaved to had needed to recuperate having been injured during the battle on earth. This atmosphere of slight freedom and new beginnings had manifested in greater attendance at the SA group. Not only that, she'd also heard of other such groups now being held all over Hell Central. She didn't know how long it would last before the demons decided enough was enough and brutally suppressed it. Given that minions could be tortured in Hell for fun, maybe everyone had finally decided to quit complying.

Aaron continued, "well, if nobody else wants to share then I suggest we move onto the final item on the agenda: our exploration of the other Hell dimension."

This was clearly the part of the meeting many people had been waiting for and several minions perked up in their chairs and leaned forward.

"Over to you Giada," Aaron said.

GIADA STOOD UP: she didn't know why but it felt right somehow.

"Thank you Aaron. For the benefit of the newcomers, I'll give a brief summary of events so far. A couple of weeks ago, I was led to the entrance of what appeared to be a portal to another realm, right here, in the Deeper Depths of Hell. I was led there by a parasite, Lucky, which me and Aaron have been keeping as a pet. At first I was excited as I thought it may offer a way out of Hell but my excitement was cut short. It led to another Hell dimension and one which didn't seem much better or worse than this one. This hell dimension doesn't appear to be any of the other seven circles of Hell. My guess is that it's some kind of parallel dimension. In the time since my initial discovery, I've made another two trips. Yesterday I ventured the furthest I've travelled so far.

The Hell dimension appears to be hierarchical in structure, just as ours is. Minions are at the bottom and are enslaved to wicked spirits and demons with demons being at the top tier of society. Their culture seems to be more brutal than ours. They have daily, ritualised torture sessions, which are mandatory for all residents to participate in. They are ruled by a dictator demon called Vassago. Regrettably, I haven't yet found any other portals or anything that suggests we could get to other non-hell dimensions but I'll keep looking."

She sat down again. One of the new minions, a doughy-faced black man, spoke up.

"Have you spoken to anyone there yet? Do they know you're from another hell dimension?"

"I've spoken casually to a few other minions, just to gather information but I don't think they've worked out I'm from another hell dimension. I've kept my head down and shuffled around in the same despondent manner as minions do both here and there and nobody has really noticed me. I would like to get bolder though. I'd like to try and listen in on some of the more senior demons to see if I can discover anything that might be more useful to us."

"Giada, is that wise?" Aaron said,

Giada blinked at him, "What have I got to lose Aaron? I'm already dead... and living in Hell... and getting tortured regularly, how much worse can things get for me?"

Aaron's grey eyes widened, "Oh things can always get worse, believe me"

Giada sighed, "Okay, let's think of the worst-case scenario - someone unmasks me as being from another hell dimension. Then what? They hold me hostage? I have no value here. They could kill me and nobody except for you guys would even notice. I'd simply turn up in another hell dimension."

Aaron rubbed his chin and nodded thoughtfully. "Well at least take one of us with you the next time you go there. Susan, I'm sure you'd like a break from Mephistopheles?"

Susan had looked quite a bit happier in recent days and Giada suspected she may have found a way to escape the PIAD's daily beatings, "Oh no, I don't want to risk it thanks, Mephistopheles has soul snatched a new minion and he's paying me less attention. I don't want to rock the boat and end up getting transferred into a worse situation."

Giada didn't blame her. PIADs were pain-inflicting addicted demons and Mephistopheles had a reputation for being one of the worst. It was highly likely he'd bragged to his other PIAD buddies about how much fun it was to torture Susan. There'd be no shortage of sadists wanting to take her if he decided to swap her.

"Anyone else?" Aaron looked around the room and everyone

avoided eye contact. After a long uncomfortable silence Motsumi spoke.

"I will do it," he said.

"*You?!...*" Giada caught and corrected her look of horror and contempt just in time to change it to one of surprise. "... I mean, you've only just arrived and you haven't yet acclimatised to how life is here. Why would you want to involve yourself in something as potentially dangerous as..."

Motsumi interrupted her, as was his habit. "That is precisely why I want to join you. I have no intention of remaining here for the rest of eternity. You need someone with my superior intellect and experience to guide you towards your goal of heavenly redemption. My understanding is that some of you have had this goal for centuries," he inclined his head in Aaron's direction, "without any progress having been made. It is time for me to take the reins and get this done." A self-satisfied smile slid onto his lips.

Giada did her best to smile as politely as she possibly could but inside she was fuming. She could have punched Motsumi in the face right about now. Just who did this arsehole think he was? He'd come swanning in here, taking over the entire session with his garrulous, self-absorbed ramblings and now he thought he would 'save them all' by solving heavenly redemption for them, as if he was the expert?! He who had just arrived in Hell five minutes ago. He even had the audacity to give Aaron, the leader of this group, and the founder of the heavenly redemption movement, a backhanded insult in the process. The barefaced cheek of the man! As she sat in her chair, her blood boiling in disgust, she heard Aaron utter the words,

"Thank you Motsumi, you are an excellent choice to accompany Giada on her next excursion - for all the reasons you've just mentioned."

Giada couldn't believe her ears. She glared at Aaron then at Motsumi. She was unable to hide her distaste for him. Motsumi's smug smile was being dished out to each member of the group like an old piece of stale Christmas Panettone, being offered to guests at a coffee morning, in late March. She inwardly shuddered but outwardly she said,

"Yes thank you Motsumi." She felt her heart deflating into her stomach as he nodded in saintly acceptance. She now had no choice but to take the odious Motsumi with her the next time she visited the other hell dimension.

5

THE COUNTESS

∽

The Countess sat, tapping her red stilettos on the floor, as she inspected her new minion servant. The girl wasn't as attractive as Giada. She didn't have Giada's luscious, wavy dark hair, doe-like eyes and flawless olive skin but she'd do. The Countess liked her minion servants to be attractive; it helped with disarming male visitors. Giada's good looks had given the Countess an advantage when it came to manipulating other demons.

The Countess had been lucky - extremely lucky. She'd been hanging around the old age ward when a dead human had pretty much fallen into her lap. It turned out that her new minion, who had been a nurse in the old age ward of the hospital, had been severely allergic to nuts and had left her EpiPen at home that day. Just as the Countess had been about to give up and go home, she'd been walking out of the hospital and had spotted the nurse turning blue and grabbing at her throat next to her car. After she'd died, the nurse had told the Countess that somebody walking past had been eating nuts and that had been enough to set her off. Nobody else had noticed the nurse's affliction and she'd passed away right there in the car park.

The Countess had calmly waited, watching as the soul rose out of the body. Then she'd simply convinced the nurse that she was there to lead her to the most amazing afterlife (in Hell but she had left that part out). The girl had hesitated at first, her eyes flicking towards the tunnel of light but the Countess' charms had won out and she'd followed her to Hell. The former nurse's name was Miriam. She had long hair, which hung like a thick black curtain around her face, heavy eyebrows and very red lips. She wasn't traffic-stopping as her nose was a little on the large side but she was attractive enough. At least she had a lovely figure.

The Countess stood up and walked towards Miriam. The girl's lips wobbled. Minions had a most unfortunate habit of fluttering their lips every time they remembered the human sensation of crying - a function that was lost the minute a soul arrived in Hell. The Countess couldn't remember the last time her own lips had fluttered but then the more time souls spent in Hell, the more of their humanity they lost. The Countess had, after all, been a demon for a couple of decades now. Facing the girl, the Countess reached the red nails of her manicured hands towards Miriam's face. Miriam jerked her head back instinctively.

"It's alright, I won't bite," she stroked her face and tucked her long hair behind one ear as she appraised her. The Countess leaned back with her hip to the side as she rested her chin on one hand, nodding slowly.

"Yes, you'll do. You'll do nicely." She walked to the back of the white marbled room and opened a drawer full of toothbrushes. She took one out and handed it to Miriam, fixing the girl with an unrelenting glare.

"Get down on your hands and knees and start scrubbing. There are more toothbrushes in that drawer if this one breaks. You stay down there until I tell you to stop."

Miriam stood still, trembling slightly.

"Do not make me wait, or ask you twice. You miserable imbecile!" the Countess snapped. She'd never been a particularly patient person and her impatience had increased upon her arrival in Hell.

Miriam sank to the floor, faster than butter sliding off a hot knife, and started scrubbing. She flicked her eyes up at the Countess a few times, as she did so, but didn't speak.

The Countess smiled coldly; she loved the feeling of exerting power over others; it made her feel... alive. Of course she wasn't alive but what difference did it make? Her life here in many respects was better than it had ever been on Earth. Now, to get her other minion, Giada, back from that good-for-nothing Chancellor. There was no way that she was going to let the Chancellor keep her. After all the care she'd taken with training Giada up to be a servile, obedient minion. Giada was not particularly loyal but at least she was intelligent and charming in her own way. The truth was, Giada reminded the Countess of herself when she was younger and that was why she liked her. She saw in Giada, a chance to have a real protege to replace the disappointment that Motsumi had become. The Chancellor could not and would not keep her. Not least because the Countess didn't want him thinking he'd got one over on her. She may have been demoted recently but she'd soul-snatched her way back to demon status and before long, she'd be back on top.

The Countess raised her eyes upwards as she mused. It was time for her to make her ascent to the top. She was no longer satisfied with being second in command. She was tired of playing second fiddle to some useless man who was less capable, less intelligent and less ambitious than her. She was fed up of cleaning up the mess made by that man. Sehloho had made countless mistakes. He'd always been too soft and she believed that was at the root of the failed resurrection. If he'd been a tougher ruler, he would've silenced any opposition, banned those ridiculous redemption meetings and increased the minion torture sessions. Her eyes narrowed and she pursed her lips. She suspected that those redemption followers had somehow played a part in the failed resurrection. She couldn't prove it and indeed had no evidence but she felt it in her bones. That would never have happened on her watch. No, if she had been ruler, there would've been no chance whatsoever for woolly-minded, subversive minions to meet unsupervised and conspire against demons.

SHE LEFT Miriam to her work and strode off. As much as she enjoyed watching minions work, she had better things to do. She wanted Giada back. It was a situation that had to be handled delicately though. The Chancellor didn't care about Giada. That much the Countess was sure of. His predilection was towards attractive, young, male minions and he had two of those already, which he hadn't yet got bored of. However, he knew that the Countess wanted Giada and that made her a valuable bargaining chip. What the Countess needed was to make him think that she no longer cared much about Giada, make Giada worthless somehow. She hadn't yet worked out how to achieve this which was why she needed to observe the Chancellor's house. She'd always found in the past that observation led to ideas and the Countess now had all the time in the world on her side, time which she would use to observe, scheme and then bargain.

The Chancellor had always underestimated her, everyone did. She gave an outward appearance of kindness. This was deliberate: demons always mistook kindness for weakness. The Countess was neither kind nor weak, she was cunning and she knew that if others thought her an easy mark, she could pull the rug out from under their feet at the moment they least expected it and that moment had come. She would get Giada back; she would do it in such a way that the Chancellor didn't even know he'd been had until it had already happened.

6
GIADA

∽

Giada was once again on her hands and knees scrubbing the Countess' marble floor with a toothbrush. Just as the Chancellor had predicted, the Countess had come to get Giada back and he'd played hard to get - just so she wouldn't get suspicious. Interestingly, after the deal had been done, the Chancellor had requested Motsumi as his replacement minion servant. Giada had wondered what that was about since Motsumi wasn't particularly handsome nor was he young. She paused as she considered it once more before returning to her work. She didn't have time to dwell on it too long.

As Giada scrubbed, she looked over at the Countess' new minion maid. Miriam didn't seem like the type of girl she'd have chosen as a friend on earth. She was six years older than Giada's human age but it felt more like twenty, so devoid was she of any youthful fun or exuberance. When the Countess had taken her shopping for clothes, out of necessity rather than as a treat, Miriam had chosen clothes reminiscent of a lowly paid corporate office worker. This had led Giada to conclude that the girl was a bland conformist: the complete opposite of her. When the Countess had taken Giada shopping for clothes, she'd come back with a variety of stylish pieces. Tight fitting jeans, elegant scarlet and black tops that suited her olive complexion and a couple of pairs of pumps. She hadn't been offered jewellery but sometimes, when the Countess was out, she snuck into her bedroom and tried on the diamond necklaces and pearl studs that she kept there.

Giada looked over at Miriam, her thick, long hair tied into a messy bun.

I guess I should try and make conversation; maybe she's not as bad as I think.

"So... you were a nurse before all this, huh?"

Miriam stopped scrubbing for a moment. She sat up on her knees and wiped her forehead before giving Giada an expression that could've turned milk sour. Then she resumed her scrubbing.

Sheesh, it's not my fault you got soul snatched Giada thought.

Not one to give up easily, she tried again. "You know, erm, we're actually pretty lucky to have the Countess, there are a lot worse...."

"Lucky?! You think we're lucky? Actually, I can see how you would think that. You deserve to be down here whereas I don't." Miriam's eyes roamed up and down Giada's face whilst her lip curled up in contempt.

"Now, hold on a minute, you don't know anything about me," Giada protested.

Miriam sat up on her knees again, dropping her toothbrush as she folded her arms. She raised her eyebrows and sniffed. "Go on then, explain to me how you ended up here?"

Giada faltered, she still found it extremely painful confessing her sins, "Erm..."

Miriam extended her forefinger and prodded it repetitively in the air towards Giada. "Did a demon dupe you into coming here? Did you miss your chance at an eternity in heaven? Come on I'm waiting." She folded her arms again and leant back slightly.

Giada felt her lower lip trembling as she looked at Miriam's face, which was rapidly turning red as faint whirls of steam rose from her ears. The thought crossed Giada's mind,

She'll make a good demon some day but she kept quiet.

"That's what I thought," Miriam finished before stooping back down to continue her floor scrubbing.

Giada bent down again and resumed her chore. She should just give up. Miriam was clearly still too angry to communicate with. But she'd always had a mouth that didn't know when to shut up. "You know, if you keep going with that attitude, it'll be worse for you down here. Us minions have to stick together, we're the lowest of the low in Hell."

"I'm not one of you Giada. You're a sinner. We have nothing in common."

Giada felt offended but nonetheless pressed on. "I bet I can find one thing we have in common. What kind of music did you like, back on earth?"

"I didn't really listen to music"

What kind of person doesn't listen to music?

"Okay... well, what did you do in your spare time? You must've had hobbies or passions?"

"I didn't have any spare time, I spent most of my time working"

"Did you have a boyfriend?"

"No"

This is like drawing blood from a stone

Giada gave up and with a deep sigh she went back to her work. After scrubbing in silence for a couple of minutes, Giada sensed Miriam's body soften slightly next to hers. Her shoulders sagged and Giada heard a faint squeak come out of her mouth. As damned souls couldn't cry, their lips fluttered or they made moaning or squeaking noises. Was Miriam squeaking with emotion? Giada slid her eyeballs to the side, looking at Miriam without turning her head. She was trying to hide it but it was obvious she was quite upset. Giada hesitantly tried one more thing. "You know, erm, the Countess has some really nice jewellery. When she's out, I often sneak into her room and try it on. Just for fun. Shall we go and do that now?"

"But... but.... What will happen to us if she finds out?"

"How would she? She's not here. Come on, it'll be fun. She'll never know"

Miriam attempted a smile and nodded. Giada got up and dusted off her knees and then extended her hand to help Miriam up. Miriam's hand felt boiling hot. She was still acclimatising to the heat of Hell.

Giada led the way up the grand sweeping staircase and along the rows of rooms to the Countess' bedroom. Giada had always wondered why the Countess needed so many bedrooms. She lived here alone and although she held frequent parties, she never invited anyone to stay over. It was probably just a show of power and wealth. All the doors were identical, painted ivory with ornate gold handles but Giada knew the layout of the house well and stopped at the last bedroom. She opened the door and beckoned Miriam to follow her.

Inside there was a king-size four-poster bed and an antique ivory painted dressing table with a large gold-framed mirror. The dressing table had three drawers, the middle of which Giada pulled open to reveal multiple glass compartments each containing a different piece of jewellery. There were diamonds, sapphires, rubies, pearls, silver, gold. A staggering array and each piece was as exquisite as the last. Giada grinned at Miriam; whose eyes had grown wide. Giggling mischievously, Giada held up a diamond necklace.

"I think this would suit you. You come and sit down here, I'll put it on."

Miriam obediently sat on the silk-covered stool facing the mirror. Giada undid the clasp on the necklace and laid it over Miriam's shapeless shift dress. It immediately made the dowdy outfit look more glamorous.

"You look like Liz Taylor - a young Liz Taylor." She stood back to admire her work.

"Now, for the earrings. The necklace is quite a statement piece. I think the earrings need to be a bit more demure. How about something like these?"

She held up a couple of diamond clip-on studs, arranged in clusters, against each of Miriam's ears. "Yes, they're perfect, put them on"

Miriam opened the clips and put one earring on each ear. Then she got up and looked at herself in the full-length mirror at the side of the Countess' bed. She smiled then the smile withered from her face and her lips began to quiver.

Miriam shared, "I had so much more life to live. I still wanted to meet someone nice, get married, have children, grow old, all the usual." She put her head in her hands and shook her head as if trying to wake from a bad dream. Giada remembered feeling like that when she'd first arrived. Like this was all just a bad dream.

"Listen, Miriam, I know this is hard to accept. I felt the same way when I first arrived, but it's better if you try to adjust."

Giada cocked her head to the side as she looked at Miriam. She wondered if she should tell Miriam about Sinners Anonymous and the regular meetings, she went to every Tuesday night to share her burdens with her fellow damned souls. The meetings weren't illegal, but they weren't exactly encouraged either. It was more that demons turned a blind eye to them. She watched as Miriam sighed and reached one hand up to trace her fingers around the diamonds on the necklace. Her lips were no longer fluttering but she had a look of pain on her face as if she was wrestling with something inside herself.

No, I can't trust her thought Giada.

Even if the SA meetings weren't forbidden, they were a safe space for Giada and one that she couldn't risk jeopardising over someone she'd only just met.

Giada turned her attention back to the drawer containing all the jewellery. "Now, which pieces should I try on today?" She ran her fingers over the tray of glittering beauties before settling on a jade two-piece set of brooch and bracelet.

"Say what you like about the Countess but she does have exquisite taste," Giada pinned the brooch onto her black top, before slipping the bracelet onto her hand. She turned to face the full-length mirror, admiring herself as she held her hair up in a high chignon.

"What do you think?" she looked at Miriam.

Before Miriam could answer, Giada heard the familiar clatter of the front door being opened. Her blood ran cold: the Countess had returned. Quick as a flash, the slipped the bracelet off her wrist. Miriam slipped off the earrings and necklace and replaced both before dashing out of the room, leaving Giada still struggling to remove the brooch.

Damn it! The needle is stuck!

Panic rose in her stomach and she felt slightly dizzy as desperation rose, like a fiery inferno, up her body. Her palms were sweating. There was no way this brooch was going to come off. She thought quickly. Her eyes darted from left to right as her fingers still fiddled with it. Finally, the needle clicked out of the clasp and she slipped it off her top but it was too late to put it back in the drawer. The Countess' footsteps were on the landing, directly outside, and she was turning the knob of the bedroom door. Giada slipped the brooch into the pocket of her jeans just as the Countess opened the bedroom door.

"Giada, what are you doing in here?"

"Erm, I was just dusting. I felt like it probably needed doing."

The Countess' eyes narrowed and she inhaled sharply as if trying to catch a whiff of lies. Like a bloodhound, she sniffed them out.

"Miriam!" she boomed, her voice echoing off the marble in a way that made Giada wince. There was a light pitter-patter of Miriam's feet as she scurried back up the stairs and into the bedroom. Her eyes were wild with fear and she clutched her toothbrush in both hands so tightly that her knuckles had turned white. Her shoulders had risen up near her ears and she trembled slightly.

The Countess folded her arms. "What has been going on in here? Giada thinks she can lie to me but I know I can rely upon you to tell me the truth." She turned to the side and half smiled at Miriam, her deep red eyes boring into the girl's face.

"I... she... she made me do it." Miriam's arm flung out as she pointed at Giada.

Oh Jeez, the first sign of any trouble and she spills her guts.

"Made you do what, Miriam?"

"Your jewellery, we were trying it on but I didn't want to. She made me do it. It was all her idea. I swear."

"Giada, is this true? What is that in your pocket?"

Giada looked down at her snug fitting jeans and saw the brooch bulging obviously in her front pocket. She slipped her hand inside and withdrew the brooch.

"Were you planning to steal that?"

"No! It got stuck on my top. I tried to get it off but I couldn't do it in time and..." her voice trailed off and she sighed.

"I suppose you're going to send me to the torture rooms?"

"I most certainly am... You know Giada, if I wasn't a principal demon and duty bound to torture you for your own good - to keep you in line, I'd be quite impressed. Firstly at your good taste in jewellery and secondly at your attempt at deception." A smile played at the corners of the Countess' mouth and for a second Giada almost thought she'd got away with it.

"But like I said, I'm a principal demon. So, it'll be the disemboweling room for you. Come on, let's go, I'll escort you there myself. I wouldn't want Miriam going soft and letting you go."

Fat chance of that, the little snitch Giada thought. One thing was for sure, that was the last time Giada would ever trust Miriam with anything. She'd been right not to tell her about the SA meetings. As she walked behind the Countess, dragging her feet, she turned around to look at Miriam. She could've sworn she saw a devious smile that the girl quickly wiped off her face and replaced with a look of remorse. There was more to Miriam than meets the eye and Giada suspected that Hell might be the right place for her after all.

7

NALEDI

~

It was Saturday morning and Naledi and Lerato were hanging up clothes to dry on the washing line outside their home. Dineo and Puleng ran around chasing each other and Tau and Kabelo sat on wooden chairs nearby, waiting for their load of washing to finish. After Motsumi had died and Naledi had inherited all his money and his house, one of the first things she'd bought had been a washing machine. As it had been their regular practice to meet up on Saturdays and hang out together at the river, whilst doing their laundry, Naledi and her friends still maintained this habit but now they would meet up at Naledi's house. Naledi and Lerato had agreed to stay in Motsumi's property instead of moving back to her old family home. Motsumi's place was bigger, fully wired with solar panel electricity and fully plumbed into the water mains. It also had enough bedrooms for all of them and it had two bathrooms, which was an extreme luxury in this part of Lesotho. Naledi had moved into Motsumi's old bedroom, which meant she had her own room for the first time in her life, as did Lerato. Dineo and Puleng still shared the room down the hallway.

It was a sunny, windy day and Naledi smiled and sang softly to herself as she pegged a sheet to the line. As the wind blew the sheet back and forth, she saw a figure walking up the hill towards the house. Putting her hand up to shield her eyes from the sun, she squinted and saw the familiar outline of Thato, a girl from two years below her in school. Thato lived in the neighbouring village of Leralleng, with one older brother and a large extended family of cousins, all looked after by their grandmother. The girl was small for her age and had closely cropped hair. Naledi suspected this was because it lessened the burden on her gran of brushing and braiding so many children's heads.

"Dumela Sis' Naledi" she called out as she walked up the hill smiling in greeting.

"Dumela Thato, how is your family?"

"They are well, thank you." Thato smiled weakly, casting her eyes around the group of friends. She cracked her knuckles and shifted from foot to foot, giving Naledi the sense that she had something to say but didn't know how to spit it out.

"Can we go and talk in private?" she said.

"Yes of course, let's go inside." Naledi dropped the vest she'd been holding into the laundry basket and handed the bag of pegs to Lerato who continued without her. She opened the back door and walked through the kitchen, down the hallway and into the living room. Thato followed behind her. When they got to the living room, Naledi gestured for Thato to sit down on the sofa.

"Please take a seat. Can I offer you something to drink? Mango juice?"

Thato nodded and smiled politely and Naledi walked back to the kitchen, reappearing with a glass of juice, which she placed on the small coffee table to the side of Thato.

"Thank you," Thato said as she reached forward and took a sip. It was clear to Naledi that she was stalling for some reason.

"How can I help?" Naledi prompted as she sat down in the armchair opposite.

Thato looked around, "It's nice. This house was your uncle's, wasn't it? Before he died suddenly?"

Naledi shifted in her chair, "yes that's right." She'd told people that he'd passed away while on a business trip to Maseru and that the funeral had been held at his ancestral home near there. This lie meant she wouldn't have the expense and awkward questions, which would come with a local funeral.

"I heard that he was training you to become a sangoma?"

Naledi started to feel uncomfortable, "not really training me, well I suppose he was... it's complicated."

Thato stared at her then her brow furrowed. She picked up the glass of mango juice and gulped it down before wiping her mouth with the back of her hand. Then she took a deep breath and said very quickly, without making eye contact. "I've been called by the ancestors." She looked at Naledi, seemingly to gauge her reaction.

Naledi raised her eyebrows, cocking her head slightly to one side, "oh?"

Thato continued, "I have all the symptoms, restlessness, lack of appetite, seeing visions, dreams. Last night I dreamt of water. I've dreamt of water a few times, of drowning and being submerged. Then I have a constant feeling as if there are ants crawling over my body. It's very annoying. I'm sure I don't have to tell you." Thato started laughing. She looked at Naledi to share the joke but Naledi didn't find it amusing and instead, felt herself get irritated. Thato evidently noticed Naledi's stern expression and stopped laughing abruptly. There followed an uncomfortable silence as Naledi sat looking at Thato, waiting for her to reveal why she'd really come.

"Will you train me Naledi?" Thato looked at her with pleading eyes.

Naledi's eyes grew wide and then narrowed as she scrunched her face up in disbelief. "But I'm not fully qualified. I'm not even committed to the path.... I'm a Christian," she added.

"You can be both a Christian and a sangoma, can't you?"

"I don't believe so, no."

"Then why did you begin training in the first place?"

"I was called just like you were and then... like I said, it's complicated."

Thato looked down at her lap, her jaw clenched a few times and she chewed on her lip as she studied the floorboards. For some reason this conversation was making Naledi feel more and more uncomfortable She wished Thato would just go away. She was asking difficult questions that strayed too close to the secrets Naledi had kept carefully hidden from the rest of the community. Plus Naledi could tell she was the kind of person who would gossip the first chance she got. Moreover, Thato appeared unwilling to give up easily and this made Naledi feel uneasy. She began to feel like a wild animal that was backed into a corner by a hunter.

"Couldn't you just teach me what you know so far?"

"No." Naledi struggled to keep the tension out of her voice.

"Please Naledi, I'm desperate, the ancestors won't leave me alone. I need to start training. I don't know anyone else who can help me."

"*I* can't help you," she snapped, then feeling terrible guilt, when she saw the hurt in Thato's eyes, she softened her voice. "I can't even help myself".

Surely she'll give up now and leave but Thato was like a dog with a bone

"Well, do you know anyone else, who you can trust? What about the person who trained your uncle? Is that sangoma still alive?"

Naledi stood up. She balled her fists tightly at the end of taut arms and her breath was unsteady. "Listen, I can't help you. I can't recommend anyone; I don't even believe in this path. I never wanted it. It was forced upon me. It's actually been one of the most difficult and painful things I've ever had to endure. I almost lost everyone I loved and I failed to qualify in spite of how hard I tried and now you're coming here and throwing it all back in my FACE!" By the end she was shouting. At some point which she hadn't been aware of, she'd moved closer to Thato. She towered over her as spittle flew from her mouth and landed on Thato's nose. Thato lifted a trembling hand and wiped it off. She blinked as her eyes filled with tears. She had such a look of immense disappointment and pain on her face that Naledi felt immediate remorse.

"I... I'm sorry Thato, I didn't mean to…"

"No that's ok. I shouldn't have come here. It was a mistake. I can see that now. I'm sorry, I won't waste anymore of your time." Her voice was cracking with the effort of holding her tears back and she rushed to her feet.

"I'll see myself out." Thato fled through the front door without a second glance and Naledi heard her give a huge sob as she ran. Naledi wanted to run after her but what would she say? Was she sorry? Yes of course. She hadn't meant to get angry. She hadn't meant to hurt her feelings but why hadn't Thato taken the hint and gone away when Naledi had said no? Why had she kept on pushing and pushing until Naledi had snapped? And why had Naledi snapped anyway? It's not as if anything Thato was saying was untrue or hurtful but for some reason it had needled Naledi in a place deeper than her current understanding could reach.

Lerato came in through the back door. "What's going on? I saw Thato running off in tears."

Naledi sighed and sank down on the sofa as she buried her face in her hands and shook her head slightly. "She wanted me to train her to become a sangoma. She says she's being called by the ancestors."

"She's suffering from ithwasa?" Lerato walked over to the window and peered out at the retreating form of Thato.

"That's what she says," Naledi confirmed with a shrug.

"I take it you turned her down?"

"Of course I did. I'm not fully trained nor am I even a willing initiate."

"If you told her that, why was she crying?"

"I handled it badly. I got angry with her"

Lerato blinked at her with a puzzled expression, "that's not like you?"

"I know, I don't understand what got into me. I wasn't even polite."

Lerato looked at her without saying a word. This had always had the effect on Naledi of making her feel like she had to confess whatever was in her heart. The trouble was Naledi didn't know what was in her heart.

"I think I need to go and lie down. Can you tell the others I have a headache?"

Lerato nodded with understanding, "Sure."

NALEDI WALKED to her room and collapsed on her bed. She stared up at the ceiling searching her heart for the source of her outburst. Thato was younger than her and clearly looked up to her. What had possessed her to treat her with such cruelty? It was true that she hadn't chosen the path of shamanism: it had chosen her. However, in spite of her Christian upbringing and her rigid belief that this path was close to witchcraft, she'd found herself enjoying it. It had made her feel more alive than anything she'd ever done before but more than that, it had made her feel powerful and that was the thing she was most afraid of. She'd felt herself getting intoxicated by the power whenever she'd activated her breacher powers.

Naledi looked down at her hands and closed her eyes, feeling for the threads of reality. She took a deep breath, sighing with pleasure as she felt her power responding and crackling at her fingertips. Detecting the presence of the threads, she knew she could tear open a portal right now if she wanted to. And the portal would reveal another dimension of reality behind it. Her breacher power was still there, it always would be - at least as long as she remained a virgin.

Was this how some sangomas got seduced by evil? Was this how Motsumi had been tempted to sell his soul to Satan? Was she heading in the same direction? Was she already doomed in spite of the fact that she'd given up her training?

The truth was, she missed it. She couldn't deny it. She craved it like an addict craves his drug and she knew she wouldn't be able to resist its call for much longer. If she went back to it, no, *when* she went back to it, she wouldn't have any excuses to hide behind. She wouldn't have been ordered by angels to follow the path for a short time for the purposes of stopping a demon resurrection. She would have to face up to the reality that she had wanted it and pursued it in spite of knowing it was wrong and she'd have to face the wrath of God on judgment day when she died. She knew the day of reckoning was coming, that it got closer and closer. Thato's visit had seemed like a harbinger of doom, a synchronous message, pushing her closer to her destiny, a path she'd denied and tried to push down for as long as she could. But now the jack was out of the box. She couldn't hide from it or fight it any longer.

8

GIADA

∽

Giada clambered up rocky enclaves, waving thick green smoke away from her face as her eyes stung from the heat. Having visited this Hell dimension twice before, and being an accomplished con artist, she knew that the best way of avoiding suspicion was to act as naturally as possible. She kept her head down and her strides purposeful. There'd be no creeping, no furtive glances or panicked expressions: she'd just walk as if she belonged here. Motsumi followed behind her, thankfully he'd kept his opinions to himself since they had arrived here. She had, however, had to endure at least twenty tedious minutes of his gabbing, on the journey from Hell Central to the Deeper Depths, where the portal was.

As they approached what looked to be the first of a series of minion dwellings, Motsumi grabbed her and held her back against the wall so that they were covered by shadows. She whipped her head round to give him a look of annoyance but saw his eyes widen as he put his finger to his lips in a 'shushing' gesture. He then pointed ahead of her. Turning her head back in the direction which they'd been walking, she saw the Countess coming out of one of the dwellings. She was walking side by side with another large, muscular, longhaired demon, she didn't recognise. The Countess?! This must be what the Chancellor had been talking about. Maybe this was the neighbouring hell dimension, which she was conspiring with. Giada watched as the Countess and the demon walked briskly down the pathway towards the main cityscape. Giada strained her ears to hear what they were saying. Hopefully she'd catch something that she could report back to the Chancellor.

"If this technology works as well as you say it does, then we should see results within a matter of days?" The Countess asked him

The demon answered her in a deep bass voice. "Yes. My engineers are just ironing out the last few glitches and performing tests before summoning me again for the final demonstration."

"And I take it, I will also be invited to this demonstration."

"Of course Countess, I will send for you."

The demon looked at the Countess, an oily smile on his face as they carried on walking. "Now, I've fulfilled my end of the bargain. It's time for you to fulfil yours..." His voice faded into the distance.

Giada was shocked. Her head spun with thoughts. What bargain had they made? And what was this technology they had been talking about? Was it related to the Countess' ambitions to takeover the Seventh Circle? It must be, surely...

Not for the first time, Giada wished she was here with someone else - or better yet, here alone. She didn't trust Motsumi at all. She had to be careful not to let anything slip that he might use against her. After all, he had been the Countess' acolyte whilst alive, he could still be working for her in secret. All of these thoughts had passed in the few seconds it had taken for the Countess and the other demon to get out of earshot. Looking at Motsumi, Giada widened her eyes, in what she hoped was an innocent expression. "What do you think she's doing here?" she asked.

Motsumi smiled and she wondered if he was smiling because he knew that she was putting on an act - anything was possible with someone like him.

"I have no idea but it's an interesting connection, don't you think?"

"Interesting, yes." Giada kept her expression neutral.

"I wonder if she's here officially on Council business or if she's doing her own thing? If so there'd be plenty of demons in the Seventh Circle who would do good trades for this kind of information." Motsumi touched his fingertips together as he raised his eyebrows.

Giada couldn't help but smile and shake her head slightly in admiration. Barely had Motsumi been in Hell for a month and here he was, already plotting how to advance himself. She wondered why he didn't just sin-bait and get it over with.

"You know you fit in pretty well in Hell," she commented.

"Takes one to know one," Motsumi countered.

Giada narrowed her eyes at him but then she was distracted by another thought.

She looked towards the entrance, to the dwelling that the Countess had just exited.

"Let's see what's in there," she whispered, beckoning for Motsumi to follow her.

Giada edged closer to the doorway. It was really more like a large cave opening. She kept her body flat against the porous, grey rock and when she was right by the opening, she peeked in then retracted her head back flat against the wall again.

"What did you see?" Motsumi asked.

"Nothing. I don't understand it. There are rows and rows of jars. I can't see what's inside them," she whispered.

"There are no damned souls in there?"

"No, nobody."

Motsumi straightened up from the wall, pulling his shirt down as he strolled confidently into the room. Giada followed behind him. The room had rows of shelves, on each wall of the rectangular cave. And a central stone slab in the middle, kind of like an operating table. On each shelf were giant jars, like the type of jars used to hold wine or olive oil back in her human home country, Italy. Giada peered closer at one of the jars, it was a bit dusty. She brushed the dust off and then stood up with a jerk: it contained a human child's arm.

"What the?..." she looked aghast at Motsumi but he didn't seem at all phased by what he was seeing and this bothered Giada.

He knows something.

"What is this place? Why do they have human body parts down here?"

"They are offerings," Motsumi simply said. He picked up a jar to study the contents with as little distress as if he were inspecting a terrarium.

"Offerings? What do you mean?"

"Initiates to satanic cults make sacrifices, killing children often. Then they offer the body parts to the demons whom they summon."

Giada's mouth dropped open. "But... but... how do they get the body parts down here?"

"That is a more interesting question and one which we must get to the bottom of. They either have access to a breacher or they have some other type of technology, which allows transfer of living, physical matter between the realms. If that is the case, that could be just what we need to escape." Motsumi replaced the jar he'd been inspecting and dusted off his fingers on his trousers with a look of distaste on his face.

Oh so now he's disgusted? By dust, but not by severed human children's body parts?!

"I'm surprised they would leave this room unguarded. These types of offerings can be highly sought after by some demons." As if in answer to his comment, they suddenly heard voices approaching. Motsumi urgently gestured for Giada to follow him as he crept out of the cave. Giada took one last look at the gruesome discovery and then followed him. They escaped from the room just in time, flattening their bodies against a shadowed rock crevice, before a couple of wicked spirit guards entered the room to do an inspection round.

Once the wicked spirit guards had gone, they agreed it would be best to head back to the Seventh Circle - they'd seen enough for the day. Motsumi, regrettably, felt confident enough to start talking again.

"How did you end up in Hell anyway?"

"It's none of your business," Giada replied, without even looking at him.

"Come now, you've shared with the rest of the SA group and I am in the group. Why not tell me? We're both damned, I won't judge you."

"I wouldn't care if you did judge me."

"Yes you would."

Giada wasn't having this and she stopped and turned to face him. "You don't know anything about me. We may both be damned souls but that is where the similarity ends. We're not alike. We're not friends. I only allowed you to accompany me here because Aaron wanted me to bring you but don't think that it goes any further than that because it doesn't."

Motsumi raised his eyebrows slightly but said nothing. They walked in silence for a few moments. But as Giada had suspected, it wasn't long before he could no longer help himself.

"Why are you so angry?"

"I'm not angry."

"Yes you are, you're full of anger. What did I ever do to you?"

"Nothing but you sure lied to, cheated and manipulated Naledi didn't you? And Tau."

Motsumi's puzzled expression switched to understanding. "Ah that's right, you met Naledi, didn't you? And now you think you're friends with her?"

"I am friends with her."

"A damned soul? Friends? With a human girl?" Motsumi raised a single eyebrow in an expression of cynicism that infuriated Giada.

She held up her finger to correct him. "A human *breacher* girl - she can come here and visit me anytime she likes."

"And has she?"

"What?"

"Visited you? How many times has she visited you since the failed resurrection?"

Giada felt her brow furrow as she looked down at her feet, clambering over rocks as she panted slightly. She didn't say anything and Motsumi continued. "That's what I thought. She doesn't care about you. Naledi is more self-interested than you would imagine. You don't want to believe that because you want to think that somebody good and wholesome and godly, wants you as a friend. You don't want to see her dark side which is what really makes her friends with you."

Motsumi stopped to catch his breath for a few moments and Giada turned to look at him as he spoke. "You know, you and I are more alike than you think and that's really why you don't like me. You hate yourself, so you hate me."

Giada pursed her lips. "Oh give it a rest, Motsumi. Stop trying to psychoanalyse me. Like I said, you don't know me at all."

"I think you don't know yourself," Motsumi said and Giada felt his words stinging at her like an angry hornet. He certainly knew how to hit where it hurt.

Giada put her hands on her hips. "Why did you really want to come with me today? Was it so that you could prod at my wounds with a red hot poker?"

"No, it's like I said in the SA meeting, I want to help. Not everybody has to have an agenda you know. Just because you do, doesn't mean everyone else does."

Giada rolled her eyes at him, "Right. So says the man who always has an agenda. You're the most scheming man I've ever met in my life."

"So says the one who is herself a schemer." Motsumi half smiled, he was clearly enjoying the verbal jousting and Giada felt that perhaps this was why he'd really come. He'd seen in her someone who was his equal both in terms of intellect and cunning and he wanted to get closer to her. She realised with a shock that he wanted her as a friend but could she really accept someone like him as a friend? Perhaps he was right that they were similar but that wasn't necessarily a good thing in their case. They'd probably be a bad influence on each other. But then again, they were already in Hell, how much worse could it get? Giada looked at Motsumi, a mischievous smile dancing around his lips and she felt herself soften. Maybe he wasn't so bad after all? Maybe he was right that she didn't like him because she didn't like herself? And maybe, the answer towards starting to love herself was starting to accept a despicable person like him as her friend.

Giada was still deep in thought when, rounding a corner, she felt something leap onto her. She yelped in pain as a wet, slug-like entity wrapped itself around her face, suctioning itself to her skin like a leech. She tried to say, 'get it off me!' but the creature was covering her mouth and all that came out was a muffled, 'gaargh!' She grabbed at it with her hands, pulling whilst she staggered around. This seemed to anger the beast and she felt a sudden, sharp pricking sensation to her cheek followed by an immediate whoozy feeling.

Has this thing just stung me?

She felt her legs turn to jelly as her stomach catapulted into her ribs and she melted to the floor in a dead faint.

AFTER SHE'D FAINTED, Giada's perceptions were somewhat muted. She was aware of Motsumi carrying her back to the Seventh Circle. She was sweating profusely, more than usual, and her face felt puffy and sore. He carried her to the Chancellor's house and took her inside, placing her on the floor in the study. Giada fleetingly worried about the impropriety of this and if they'd get into trouble. But by now, she was hallucinating, unable to open her eyes, and lacked the mental capacity to care. After a period of time, which she was in no state to gauge, she recognised the shuffling steps of the Chancellor entering the room. He and Motsumi began talking about her as if she wasn't there.

"How bad is it?" the Chancellor asked.

"It's bad, the hell sprite jumped at her out of nowhere. Completely unprovoked," Motsumi replied.

"That's very unlike them. They are normally timid creatures. An attack is rare, a sting rarer still."

"Agreed Sir. She is one unlucky minion."

Giada heard the Chancellor move closer. He knelt down and lightly touched her face. The minute his finger made contact with her face, she felt as though her skin was on fire and she howled in pain.

"Oh dear, it's very bad indeed."

"Can't you make her better? With your interest in poisons, your books and your extensive collection of toxins in the cellar, surely you have an antidote?"

"I can see why you would think that and if such a thing existed, I would surely have it but a hell sprite antidote has never been discovered."

"What does that mean?"

"I'm afraid Giada will die." The Chancellor sighed, "This is so disappointing. I had such high hopes for her abilities. She was our best asset in bringing down the Countess. Now we will have to wait until we find another minion who can be trusted."

"What about the Countess' new minion?"

"Absolutely not. She's a goody-two shoes. She's the type to follow authority, which means she's just as likely to stay loyal to the Countess as she is to follow our orders. Too risky."

Motsumi and the Chancellor lapsed into silence, leaving Giada to despair over what they'd said.

She was going to die. She drifted into unconsciousness and their voices merged into the dream reality of her nightmares.

9
NALEDI

～

It was the kind of boiling hot day that drained all energy or even the ability to think clearly from Naledi. Sweat trickled down the sides of her face and dropped from her chin onto her textbook. The soft, repetitive scratching of chalk on the blackboard, only added to her drowsiness.

Eurgh! When is it going to be break time?

It was only with an extreme effort of will that she kept her head from lolling onto the desk.

Finally, the bell rang, and Mrs. Gumede let the class out for recess. Naledi dragged her heat-leaden legs to the toilets to freshen up. As she walked, her thighs chafed under her skirt, as they rubbed together. She entered the bathroom and walked over to the row of basins. Bending over she splashed water on her face and looked at herself in the mirror. Her normally large, clear brown eyes were bloodshot. She reminded herself to drink more water in the afternoon. She grabbed a paper towel from her bag and patted her face dry. As she was dabbing the towel around her eyes she stopped suddenly and whipped her body around to face the toilet stalls.

That's odd, I could've sworn I saw someone there?

She turned back and ran the cold tap again, savouring the coolness of the water in her sweaty palms. She bent down to take a sip then gasped as someone grabbed her hair and yanked her face upright. When she looked in the mirror at who had assaulted her, her blood ran cold. She'd recognise that face anywhere. That beautiful bone structure, that smooth, ebony skin, that perfectly applied make up and most chillingly of all, the almond shaped eyes with the bright ruby red irises. It was Motsumi's mentor, the arch strategic principal demon of the Seventh Circle of Hell: the Countess.

"Let me go," Naledi gasped as she writhed around, trying to free herself from the Countess' vice-like grip. The Countess didn't respond, she just kept holding her by her braided bunch of hair extensions, twisting tighter and tighter.

"What are you doing here? How are you on Earth?" Naledi shouted.

Again the Countess remained silent and this is when Naledi started to get suspicious. There was something strange going on here. In the short time that she'd been acquainted with the Countess, she'd never known her to be lost for words. Naledi grabbed the Countess' wrist and tried to pull it around towards her teeth but she wasn't strong enough. The demon's eyes flashed with triumph as, holding Naledi's hair with one hand, she put the other hand into her pocket and withdrew a knife. Naledi screamed and kicked one of her legs back, making contact with the Countess' shinbone with a satisfying crunch. However, this didn't seem to affect the Countess at all. She was behaving as if she was a robot, completely devoid of any sensory awareness or personality. The Countess raised the knife and brought it down towards Naledi's neck in a quick slashing motion. Naledi instinctively ducked just enough that her hair extensions tore off at the roots giving her enough time to crouch down and sweep her leg towards the Countess' ankles. The demon went crashing to the floor, dropping the knife with a clatter. But the Countess barely reacted. Getting up again, she dusted herself off, picked up the knife and advanced towards Naledi, her eyes glassy with fervent intent. Naledi didn't wait to be grabbed again. She bolted for the door, screaming.

"Help! Help! Somebody help me!"

She ran blindly into the corridor. The many other pupils and teachers milling around surrounded her but this offered her little comfort. Her head whipped from side to side, in acute awareness that her attacker was still very much after her. She ran forward, turning her head around in panic, expecting to see the Countess coming out of the toilet after her. Instead, she ran slap bang into Tau.

"Naledi, what's wrong?" He held her firmly by the shoulders.

Naledi could barely speak, she was so terrified, she blubbered and pointed, hyperventilating.

"It's her... there... in the toilets... she... the..."

"You're not making any sense. Who is in the toilets?"

"The Countess. She's got a knife. She's trying to kill me."

Tau's face grew dark. He marched over to the girl's toilets and rapped on the door.

He boomed in a voice several tones lower than normal. "Who's in there? Come out. Or I'm coming in."

A crowd of other school children had by now gathered around them. Nobody really understood what this commotion was about but nevertheless there was hushed silence. Everyone waited to see the drama that they hoped would unfold. There was no answer from the toilets so Tau bashed the door open. He strode inside, watched by the crowd which crept forwards and clustered around the entrance, twittering excitedly.

Inside Tau checked every toilet stall, opening each door but there was nobody there. He came out and pushed his way through the crowd to Naledi. Gathering her up into his arms he whispered, "there's nobody there, Naledi."

"She... she was there, I swear she was. She was there. She had a knife. She tried to slit my throat. You've got to believe me."

Naledi looked up at him imploring him with her eyes. She knew that people often doubted what she saw because of her ithwasa. The mental illness caused hallucinations but was also the source of her breacher powers.

Tau looked down at her, tracing her chin with his thumb. "It's okay Naledi, I believe you." He gave her a little peck on her nose. The crowd started to lose interest at this point and drifted off.

"She must've escaped out of the window or something," Naledi suggested. Tau raised a sceptical eyebrow, "have you seen the size of that window? The Countess is a slender woman but she's not an infant. She couldn't fit through there."

"What other explanation is there?" Naledi pulled away from him and folded her arms as she looked at him. "Unless you don't believe me after all?"

Tau raised his hands. "I do believe you, I promise…. I think we need an expert opinion here. Let's ask Kabelo. He knows far more about this kind of stuff than we do."

KABELO AND LERATO were sitting in the sunshine on the grass chatting. Lerato lay on her back, resting on her shoulders as Kabelo looked over her laughing.

Tau wasted no time in getting to the point. "Guys, something strange just happened to Naledi in the toilets."

Lerato sat up abruptly and Kabelo's smile dropped.

"What?" Lerato asked.

Naledi recounted the terrifying episode with the Countess and how strange she had acted before apparently disappearing.

Kabelo rubbed his chin thoughtfully. "You're saying that she didn't say a word the entire time and this is out of character for her, from what you know?"

"Yes, she looked like her but she didn't act like her, not at all."

Lerato held her finger up, "apart from the homicidal tendencies. I thought that was right up her street?"

Naledi smiled, "you're right, she does have those tendencies."

Kabelo stared into space as he took a deep breath. "It sounds like a tulpa."

"A what?" Naledi asked

"A tulpa. It's a device sorcerers use. It's a thought form, which they imbue with such forceful, negative magical energy that it takes on a solid form and a life of its own. The sorcerer, or in this case sorceress, can then command the tulpa to do her bidding."

"So, the Countess is commanding this creature to kill Naledi?" Tau asked

"Evidently, yes but I'd be worried too if I were you brother. I'm sure the Countess is just as keen on killing you. After all, you both played a large part in the failure of the resurrection."

"That's true, you probably have even more to worry about than Naledi," Lerato added

"Gee, thanks, Lerato, I think I got the idea already," Tau replied.

"I'm just saying," Lerato shrugged, opening her large eyes even wider as she raised her eyebrows.

Tau looked back at Kabelo. "This tulpa, how do we kill it?"

"You can't. As long as the Countess is alive, it will keep trying to kill you. It will only stop if the Countess commands it to, or if she dies."

Lerato held her hand up, blinking rapidly. "Wait a minute, wait a minute. The Countess *is* dead. She's a demon, in Hell. How is she able to make a tulpa?"

Kabelo answered, "The Countess is not dead. Well, she's dead in this earthly dimension, her human life is over but her demon life is not over. She is alive and well and living in Hell. She was a powerful sangoma whilst on earth and her powers have only strengthened with practice and the addition of demonic power, in Hell."

"Then how are we supposed to stop her? How do we kill a demon who is already dead?" Naledi asked. She felt panic rising in her chest at the enormity of what she'd just asked.

Kabelo pursed his lips and narrowed his eyes, "she's a formidable adversary but she's not invincible. Demons can be killed. The problem is that when they are killed in Hell, they simply get reborn in another hell dimension. To kill her, you will have to draw her out of Hell, to another dimension and kill her there. That's what we did with Sehloho. We managed to destroy him completely and forever because we killed him on Earth"

Lerato scratched her head. "The Countess must know that she can be killed by coming to Earth so she's not going to come here is she?"

"She can't come here. The etheric barrier, which protects the realms, doesn't allow demons to inhabit earth in physical form unless a human host whose body they inhabit invites them in. They can visit Earth for short periods of time as spiritual entities but not for long. There are a few locations on earth, which are twilight realms, though: areas where all orders of beings can exist together. Uhuru, valley, where the resurrection battle took place, is one such location, but this school is not."

Tau's expression drifted to the middle distance before he shared another thought, "could there be another explanation? Motsumi is a breacher, right. Could he have breached a portal and that was actually the Countess in the toilet?"

"No. If she tried to come here, she'd turn to ashes. That's what happens when demons try to physically come to earth regions that are not twilight locations. It is true that a breacher could bring her here - she just wouldn't stay alive beyond a few minutes."

"Besides which, how do we even know if Motsumi still has his breacher powers? I thought only humans can have that ability and he's now dead, in Hell most likely." Naledi added.

Lerato had been deep in thought. "Okay. Naledi has breacher powers and the Countess will turn to ashes if she comes to earth. All Naledi has to do is go to Hell and push the Countess through a portal to earth. From demon to ashes!" she laughed as she dusted her hands together.

Naledi groaned, "You make it sound so easy."

"Well, isn't it?" Lerato ventured.

"No! The Countess is very powerful and scheming and slippery. I'd struggle to get near her without her killing me first, especially once I'm on her home turf. And anyway, why am I always the one who has to do the hero stuff? I'm not even heroic."

"You're the breacher, sister. We don't have any magical powers. Although some people say that my voice is magical," Lerato launched into a tuneless rendition of a well-known power ballad.

"Make it stop, please. My ears, my ears!" Tau implored as he clutched the sides of his face, displaying an expression of agony.

"Alright, alright, it's not that bad!" Lerato protested.

"No - it's worse," Tau quipped before she belted him across his chest with her pencil case.

Kabelo spoke. "It's not quite true that Naledi is the only one with special powers. I am an angel after all. I can read thoughts." Lerato blushed and shifted around uncomfortably so he added, "I don't read them all the time, only when I'm invited by prayer."

"How does telepathy help us to take down the Countess?" Tau asked.

"It doesn't but it can be pretty useful. Also there's you brother."

"Me? I don't have any special powers."

"Yes you do. After you died and went to Heaven, you became what we call a realm walker. You can enter any realm you like now without having to die first."

"What?! Seriously?"

Kabelo nodded solemnly, "it's not the same as Naledi's power as she can actually breach portals, however, normally she can't take anyone with her. She could now take you."

"Whoa! That is mind blowing!" Tau made a gesture with his hands indicating an explosion.

"Let me get this straight. Are you saying that I'm now the only member of this friendship circle who doesn't have any magical powers?" Lerato pouted and put her hands on her hips. "That is just so unfair. Although perhaps it's because I'm already so naturally talented."

"Yep, it's definitely because of that," Naledi agreed, half smiling to appease her friend.

Kabelo returned to the problem at hand. "I do think there's something in this idea of killing the Countess, Naledi. You may not feel ready to take her on yet but you may have little choice. Her tulpa will keep coming back and trying to kill you. You can't spend the rest of your life looking over your shoulder."

"But can't you and the other angels help me? Surely you can kill her tulpa?"

"We cannot kill something which is not truly alive. The tulpa is a thought form projection in physical form. We could destroy it, yes but the Countess would just create another one."

Naledi sighed and gathered her knees up towards her chest, tucking her skirt between her legs as she stared up at the blue sky. Had the sun got even hotter or was it the blazing heat of pressure, bearing down on her brain? She realised Kabelo was right: she had no other choice. She had to kill the Countess before the Countess killed her. And there was only one person who could help her achieve this task: Motsumi.

10

NALEDI

∽

Naledi was a little rusty with many of the skills that Motsumi had taught her but she still remembered how to connect with him, telepathically. After school, she settled herself under the acacia tree outside her home. Closing her eyes, she settled her body into deep meditation. Her consciousness descended deeper and deeper, as her breath slowed. Then her physical body became weightless, as if it no longer existed. She was just a soul, floating in the cosmos, surrounded by other souls. At this point all she had to do was use her intention to locate the soul of Motsumi and steer him towards her. Applying the method, Naledi awoke to find herself in an all white room and one which she immediately recognised as being a space and time bubble. Motsumi had used such a device the first time he'd proposed that she train with him to harness her powers and become a sangoma. He'd then taught the technique to her.

Motsumi's head darted from left to right. His eyes flitted towards Naledi and, baring his teeth, he immediately adopted a fighting stance.

"What am I doing here? What do you want?" he snarled.

Naledi stood up and put both arms out in a placatory gesture.

"Molume, I know I owe you an apology…"

"An apology?! You murdered me! In cold blood and then left me to be torn apart by angry demons. I'm in Hell because of you."

Naledi could hardly believe her ears. "That's a lie and you know it. You're in Hell because you tried to orchestrate a demon resurrection which would've brought about the end of the world. Killing you was the only way to stop it from happening and I risked my immortal soul by breaking one of God's most sacred laws. None of that would've been necessary if you hadn't come into my life in the first place."

Motsumi shook his head as he pursed his lips. He paced back and forth with clenched fists. His features switched between pain, loss and rage. "You have no idea do you?"

Naledi felt confused, "no idea about what?"

"Even after all this time, you still haven't worked it out. You still have no idea who I am."

Naledi looked at him with a growing sense of unease building up inside her…. It was as if she was seeing him anew. As she looked, his features reassembled into a younger face, the face of a vulnerable child. A face that she had been powerless to stop herself from saving.

He couldn't be, could he?

Motsumi continued, "yes, that's it. You're starting to remember, I see it in your eyes. You rescued me from certain death and then abandoned me and never came back for me."

Naledi's throat tightened with guilt as the horrible realisation reached its conclusion. "You're the boy who I rescued from Sehloho's first incarnation, in Uhuru valley, one thousand years ago!"

"Yes I am." He reared on her. "Tell me, did you ever think of me again? Even once? I was just a child, I was all alone in the world with nobody to look after me."

"What did happen to you? Was the goat herder kind to you?" Naledi's voice was trembling and she struggled to control her emotions. If she got too upset she'd be propelled back into her body. She willed herself to keep calm and focused on her breathing.

Motsumi's eyes took on a faraway look as he recounted. "The goat herder's sister was the Countess. She raised me as her own. She inducted me into the ways of both light and dark. I never had any choice, I was manipulated from a young age and that was all your fault."

Naledi felt distraught. "Motsumi... I... I am so sorry, I meant to come back, really I did but I was... I guess I was too wrapped up in stopping the resurrection."

Motsumi's face was soaked in sadness. "You know at night I used to stare out over the Uhuru valley, watching, wishing you'd come back for me. The Countess was a cruel mother. She would beat me when she got angry and criticised me constantly. Nothing I did was ever good enough for her. In time I told myself that she made me strong, made me who I am today but really, in my heart of hearts what I wanted was for you to come back for me." He looked her in the eyes. "You were the mother I always dreamed about, the one I always wanted but never had."

Naledi's hand flew to her mouth and she gulped back tears. The enormity of his statement hit her like a forklift truck. Hadn't she felt the same way about him? Didn't she still feel that way about him? He was the father she'd never had but always wanted. The weight of karma dragged at her soul like quick sand, impossible to escape from.

She listened numbly as Motsumi continued. "I progressed in my sangoma training and once I'd learnt how to read the bones, I used my knowledge to come and find you."

"But didn't you realise that if you left me alone and never found me, you'd still be in the past?" Naledi's voice quivered with emotion.

"Of course I did but then I'd also be dead. Plus I was being pushed by a force stronger than what I was able to resist." His eyes darkened. "No man can resist destiny, Naledi. Even though my logical mind was telling me that finding you was folly, that it would set off catastrophic events, I couldn't stop myself."

This was so much more than Naledi had been expecting from this conversation. She felt overwhelmed and struggled to bring her mind back to the purpose of why she'd called him in the first place.

"Motsumi, I'm so sorry. Please forgive me.... Tell me how I can make it up to you?"

Motsumi looked at Naledi and she saw that his eyes were filled with pain and conflict. She felt her heart breaking for the little boy she'd abandoned into a harsh world of evil and sorcery. Motsumi held her gaze. "When I first arrived in Hell, I felt like I never wanted to see you again. I blamed you for everything that had gone wrong in my life," he paused and looked upwards, as if struggling to find the right words.

"And now?..." Naledi quietly urged.

"Now.... It's complicated. I've found that the more time I've spent there, the more I've missed you. I can't explain it Naledi, it feels like you're the closest thing to a mother I ever had and also the closest thing to a daughter. In spite of everything that has passed between us, I can't let you go." He looked deeply into her eyes and she felt the space and time bubble waver as her emotions momentarily got the better of her. She closed her eyes and took deep breaths, steadying the environment once more. She opened her eyes and looked at him again, studying his face as she searched her memories. Now that she'd seen the face of the boy she'd rescued within Motsumi's features, she couldn't unsee it. How could she not have realised before? She'd been so self-absorbed. She felt ashamed and filled with regret over what she'd done. She had to make this right.

"Motsumi, I'm sorry, really from the bottom of my heart. I know my words sound hollow but the depth of my regret is real. I wish I could take back what I did to you." Then another thought occurred to her. "Is that why you were so mean to me, during my training sessions with you?"

He nodded. "I think so. I wanted to punish you. To hurt you as much as you'd hurt me but of course that was impossible..." his voice trailed off as he gave a rueful smile. Naledi rushed to standing and flung her arms around him. She felt his body heave with the effort of trying to keep himself from crying. She'd never seen Motsumi cry before and knew that it wasn't possible for damned souls to do it whilst they were in Hell but what about whilst travelling in their astral bodies? Could Motsumi cry here? She didn't get to find out. Motsumi corrected his face as he pulled away from her.

"Why have you brought me here Naledi?"

"I need your help Molume - I know I have no right to ask but my life is in danger. The Countess is trying to kill me, on earth. Yesterday she sent a tulpa to kill me at school. I narrowly escaped with my life. Please, tell me how to protect myself from her attacks."

Motsumi was silent for a moment. His eyes momentarily flashed with an emotion, which Naledi couldn't read but just as fleetingly, the expression was gone. He looked down at his lap, "You must continue your training with me. The etheric chord, which links us, cannot be broken, not even by death. Completing your training with me is the only way to truly protect yourself from the Countess. She is a powerful sorceress and a demon of high status. Only by you completing your studies and becoming a fully trained sangoma, an adept in full control of your powers, only then will you be free of her....and me."

Naledi bit her lip, "you would take me back as a student, even after everything that's happened? Even after I abandoned you and then murdered you?"

Motsumi sighed deeply and ran the fingers of one hand over his head. "I still think about you, I wonder what you're doing and if you're still practising what I taught you. I know you think of me often. I know you miss me. I know that the connection between us is still as strong as ever. Naledi.... It doesn't matter if I want to train you or not: we are joined together by a bond stronger than human will; we are joined by destiny and we have to heed its call."

"Does that mean you'll help me?" Naledi raised her eyebrows and half smiled at him.

"You understand that if I accept you as a student again, we will have to conduct these training sessions in Hell? We can't train inside these space and time bubbles, they are too unstable and don't allow us to perform any other psychic work at the same time."

"Yes Molume, I understand that..." Naledi smiled at him.

"The Countess is a formidable adversary. You have very little chance of beating her...."

Naledi felt her face drop, "are you saying I have no chance?"

"I'm saying you have no chance without me. With me, you'll be unstoppable." Motsumi smiled and Naledi knew then that he'd do it. Once again, she flung her arms around him. "Thank you, thank you!"

Then she had another thought and dropped her arms.

"Are your powers still active in Hell?"

"The powers that I developed through my years of sangoma training are still active yes, BUT the innate powers given to me at birth, in my human body, namely, my breaching power is no longer active." He sighed and met her eyes, she discerned a look of sincerity such as she had not seen in his eyes previously.

"There's one thing I need from you in return. We need your help Naledi, Giada needs your help."

"Giada?"

"Yes, she has been stung by a poisonous hell sprite. She is dying."

Naledi felt confusion well up inside her, "but Giada's already dead?"

"Indeed she is. She died on the mortal plane but damned souls can also die on the hell plane. They do not escape Hell by doing so, they merely get reborn in another hell dimension, as exactly the same person with all their memories intact. There is nothing to be gained from dying in Hell. She will die within the next two days if we don't find an antidote to the poison."

Naledi studied him carefully, looking for any signs that he was lying. But it was no use, he'd always been such an accomplished liar that even if he was pulling the wool over her eyes, she'd never be able to tell.

"What do you want from me?"

"There is no known antidote for hell sprite venom but really nobody has ever bothered. Souls are cheap in Hell. There is one place however, where we can go to ask where to find an antidote. The source of all universal knowledge: the akashic realm."

"But why do you need me to go there?"

"Actually I can get there alone. The akashic realm is open to denizens of every realm to visit as they wish but the journey takes several days and Giada will not last that long. She is already unconscious and delirious. Plus we have to account for her absence at work to the Countess - she'll only believe an excuse once.

"Who is we?" Naledi asked.

"My comrades in Sinners Anonymous."

Naledi's eyes opened wide. "*You?!* Have joined sinners anonymous?!"

"Why do you seem surprised? You know that I don't believe I deserve Hell."

"You orchestrated the resurrection of Sehloho on earth. You almost caused demon Armageddon and the end of humanity!"

"I was coerced and you know that."

"Coerced by who - the Countess? She didn't force you to offer your own body as a host after Tau had stabbed himself. Motsumi, you sold your soul to the devil and you tried to barter it back by using the entire fate of the world as a bargaining chip. I can think of very few people who deserve Hell more than you."

Motsumi bristled, "I'd forgotten how feisty your true self is. Your words sting Naledi, they do. Anyway, regardless of your opinion on whether or not I deserve damnation…"

"And you do."

Motsumi ignored her, "…all damned souls are welcome at the SA meetings. We all deserve a chance at redemption, a chance to be forgiven."

Naledi couldn't stop one eyebrow from raising as her head cocked to one side in heavy scepticism. "Connecting the dots together, you need my breaching powers to get to the akashic realm immediately?"

"Correct."

"But I'll have to come to Hell first, right? You're trapped there, so if we're to travel to the akashic realm together, then I have to make a detour via Hell."

"That is indeed the case."

Motsumi looked at her, tapping his fingers on his knees. Naledi could tell he wanted to say something else and was trying to find the best way of saying it. What could be worse than asking her to go back to Hell?

"There is something else... the Lords of the akashic demand payment for their knowledge."

"What kind of payment?"

"The last time I went there, I took a human body part."

"A what?!"

"You heard me."

"What human body part?"

Now Motsumi looked around awkwardly. "It was a human eyeball."

Naledi felt rage swell in her chest: Tau's eye! The eye that Motsumi had gouged out of his face when Tau was a defenseless seven-year-old child. He'd used that eye as payment for some type of esoteric knowledge. She felt her breathing increase and the world around her start to fade as her meditating body beckoned her astral form back.

"Naledi, you must stay calm. If you allow yourself to be controlled by your emotions, the adrenaline surge will cause you to rush back to your body. Now, I know this is hard for you. I know Tau is important to you... I know you love him but it all worked out for the best. It was destiny, his and mine. He has his eye back now doesn't he? That was also part of his destiny and he's happier than he's ever been."

"How do you know all of this?"

"I watch you often, as I told you before."

Motsumi continued. "In order for us to find out what the antidote is for Giada, you must bring a human body part with you. We will travel to the akashic realm as soon as you have acquired the necessary payment."

Naledi felt nauseous. "Oh no. Absolutely not. I can't believe you would even ask me to perform such a sick and twisted... such a depraved act. I'm not like you Motsumi. I am not going to kidnap a defenceless child and hack off part of..." She gagged as her hands flew to her face. Her senses distorted slightly as yet again she felt the pull of her inert physical form.

"Naledi, calm down." Motsumi stood up and started pacing around. "There is another way. Just before she was stung, me and Giada visited another hell dimension. When we were there we found a room filled with sacrificial human body parts. You could go there and steal one."

"But isn't the room guarded?"

"It wasn't when we went there. It should be a piece of cake, you just walk in and out."

Naledi had a bad feeling about this. "Is it worth it? I mean, it seems a lot of effort for somebody who is already dead and already in Hell. If she dies she'll land in another Hell, what's the difference?"

Motsumi's mouth dropped open. "Naledi Makwetla, I am shocked that you would be so callous. Giada is making progress in the Seventh Circle, she's already made friends, and she's gaining back her sense of self-worth. I wouldn't say she's happy but she's not miserable. She deserves a second chance."

Naledi narrowed her eyes at him. "Motsumi, are you going soft? You once told me that I should toughen up, well listen to you now."

Motsumi half smiled, "maybe damnation suits me."

"Maybe it does," her eyes twinkled back at him. She'd missed this. She'd missed their conversations, the challenge of his intellect, and the tension of never quite knowing if he was going to put her down or praise her. She knew it wasn't healthy: he was actually abusive or at least he had been when he'd been alive but maybe he'd changed for the better. It certainly seemed as if he had. Perhaps he'd hit his rock bottom when he'd landed in the newly damned waiting room as a permanent resident this time, instead of a passing guest. Perhaps damnation really was the best thing that had ever happened to Motsumi. But she'd misjudged him before, time and again and she knew that if there was one thing Motsumi was good at, it was manipulating her.

Can I trust him?

Was this plan as simple as he said it was? Was his motivation as simple as redeeming himself and getting to heaven someday? She couldn't know for sure and that made this entire plan far too dangerous. She was happy now; she had Tau; she had her friends; she had enough money for food and education; she had a future. She was safe, and her sisters were safe. She couldn't throw it all away in the service of misplaced loyalty to an abusive mentor. The trouble was, she felt like she didn't have any choice. She needed Motsumi's help to defeat the Countess and if his price was her help in curing Giada, she had to do it. She also owed Giada. Her minion friend had helped her to escape from Hell and get back to Earth in time to stop the resurrection and she'd promised she would one day return the favour.

Naledi had made up her mind. She looked at Motsumi. "Okay, I accept your proposal and humbly present myself as your student once more." She bowed her head low in a gesture of respect. When she lifted her head, she caught Motsumi's eyes glittering with triumph in a way that made Naledi feel as though she had just made a pact with the devil.

11

NALEDI

~

Naledi sat in class, twirling a braid around her finger as she reflected on the events of the evening before. She felt a sick knot of anxiety in her stomach when she thought of the fact that Motsumi was once again, back in her life. Even though it had been her who had contacted him this time, she still had a creeping suspicion that she was dancing along to his show tune. It was the same as always. What confused her the most though was that there had been a depth of honesty to their interaction, which she hadn't detected, in her previous dealings with him. Was he telling the truth about his motivation for helping Giada? Or had he simply become an even more skillful liar since his arrival in Hell? Either was entirely possible and she went back and forth over the conversation they'd had, re-examining his every word and gesture, trying to find any clue that would tell her definitively whether or not he was lying.

Motsumi was still pushing her buttons, still holding the strings as puppet master with her as willing puppet. She thought she'd grown mature enough to withstand his manipulations but obviously not as, yet again, here she was stewing over what he'd said and whether or not she should trust him and obey his wishes. She hated that he still had this power over her. Sure, he was her mentor and she'd agreed to train with him willingly as Universal Law dictated. She'd been asked to do it by angels the first time around but if she was honest with herself, she probably would've eventually trained with him anyway, even if there'd never been any demon resurrection to stop.

That was just the way it was between her and Motsumi: he eventually got her to do whatever it was he wanted, and his plans were always malevolent. Surely he couldn't have changed so much in the few weeks he'd been in Hell, as to actually now be acting purely for the benefit of another? Surely not? But then, in Naledi's heart of hearts, there was still that seed of hope. That small kernel of longing for the person he had been when she'd first met him. That kind, selfless, fatherly figure who only had her best interests at heart. Not the manipulative, abusive, liar she'd found him really to be when his mask had slipped.

This vestige of hope was the thing that really kept pulling the strings. It was the thing that made her say, 'how high?' when Motsumi told her to jump. It was the thing that kept her going back for more even after he'd treated her so badly. Hope was the thing that crushed her spirits more than anything. Each time he turned out to have lied to her, and he always lied to her: he always hurt her feelings. She couldn't let him do it again. She had to break this cycle of hope, then betrayal, then hurt, then hope again. Why had she invited him back into her life? Was it really that she wanted his help defeating the Countess or was she was addicted to the drama? Was she dependent on the sick thrill of the rollercoaster of emotions, which he caused?

"Well?" Mr. Pokela stood with his hand on his hip as he raised his eyebrows and looked pointedly at Naledi. "What's the answer?"

Naledi jerked herself upright as her wandering mind shot back into the room. "Um, I'm sorry Mr. Pokela, I didn't hear your question Can you repeat it please?"

"I'm not surprised you didn't hear my question, you're miles away. If you don't pay better attention in my class, you'll never pass the year end finals."

"Yes Mr. Pokela. I'm sorry Sir." Naledi bit her lip, her face glowing with shame at the reprimand. She was aware that all the eyes of her classmates were on her.

Mr. Pokela sighed and rolled his eyes, "I was asking in what year the Boer war officially began?"

Naledi looked down at her textbook, scanning the words for the answer as the silence grew and grew around her and her shoulders rose towards her neck. Beads of sweat broke out on her face.

Mr. Pokela gave up on her. "Anyone else?" he asked, gesturing around the room. Naledi's shoulders sagged with an immediate sense of relief but also disappointment in herself.

Lerato put her arm up and confidently answered, "It was 1899".

ONCE CLASS WAS over Lerato walked out with her. "Naledi, what is up with you today? History is normally one of your favourite subjects."

Naledi looked at her friend as she felt the weight of the world on her shoulders. "I know Lerato, I have a lot on my mind."

"Like what? Is it Tau? Have you two had a fight?"

"No, it's nothing like that. It's worse, much worse."

"Uh oh. Is it demon resurrection worse?"

"Kind of but not quite." She hesitated slightly before continuing. "It's Motsumi, I've decided to continue training with him."

"Say what, now?! Why?"

"It's the only way to protect myself from the Countess. Her tulpa almost killed me the other day. I have to complete my sangoma training so I can finish her once and for all."

They came to the patch of grass outside the school and sat down for recess before the next lesson.

"But why would McShifty agree to train you again after you murdered him?" Lerato still used her nickname for Motsumi even after his death.

Naledi sighed. "Remember I told you that when I travelled a

thousand years into the past with the angels, I rescued a boy but had to leave him in 1970?"

"Yes, you said you felt terrible about it."

"Well that boy was Motsumi."

"No way!"

"Yes way."

Lerato shook her head as if trying to dislodge debris from her brain. "This is hectic. What happened to him when you left him in 1970? Was he well looked after by that goat herder?"

"Not exactly, the goat herder's sister was the Countess. I'm the reason why he got seduced by evil in the first place."

Lerato cocked her head to the side and picked pieces of grass absent-mindedly. "But then... it sounds like he has even more reasons to hate you so I say again, why is he agreeing to train you?"

"It's complicated. He believes we're bound together by destiny."

Lerato raised her eyebrows and gave a smile of doubt.

"I know it sounds crazy but I feel it too. I haven't been able to stop thinking about him or my training. Often when I dream I hear him calling to me. I have this low level grief over killing him. I see his face sometimes, in a crowd of people, when I go into town. Then when I get closer I realise it's not him. I also feel like it's getting harder and harder for me to control my ithwasa. The ancestors are angry that I never completed my training...." Naledi's voice trailed off as she tried to gather her thoughts. "I now realise that I owe him so much. Yes I rescued him from certain death a thousand years ago but then I delivered him into the hands of an abusive woman who made his life hell. I feel like Motsumi needs me to destroy the Countess almost as much as I need to destroy her."

"Has he said that?" Lerato asked.

"Not in so many words but he did say that she was a cruel mother who beat him and was always criticising him."

"Wow! And then he took it out on you as an adult by treating you the same way."

"Exactly."

"This is deep Naledi, this is so deep."

Naledi nodded solemnly, "and there's more."

"There's more?!"

"He agreed to train me again but in exchange he wants me to go with him to the akashic realm to ask the Lords of the akashic where we can find an antidote for Giada. She's been bitten by this poisonous hell sprite thing and will die in the next two days if I don't help."

"Giada? The one who you told me helped you to escape from Hell so that you could get back to earth in time to stop the resurrection?"

"Yes, that one."

"Isn't she already dead though? She's in Hell?"

"Yes but she can still be killed. Then she'd be reborn in another hell dimension which Motsumi says would be devastating to her as it would mess up her chances of redemption - she's part of this movement which believes that redemption is possible for damned souls."

Lerato's eyes opened wide, "This is a lot to take in you know."

"I know,"

"Now I can see why you were so distracted in class." Lerato looked thoughtful. "What is this akashic realm, anyway? Who are the Lords of the akashic?"

"I'm not entirely sure as I've never been there before but Motsumi says they're like the sources of all Universal knowledge. Any being, can go there and ask questions and they'll get a truthful answer, even if nobody on Earth or in Heaven or Hell currently knows the answer to that question."

"This antidote for Giada - it's currently unknown in Hell?"

"Yes, or so Motsumi says."

"But as we both know, he's a pathological liar."

"Yes but I think he might actually be telling the truth this time and if he is and I don't go and help, Giada will die before he's able to get the cure to her."

Lerato looked at Naledi with pity in her eyes, "Naledi, I've told you before, you're too kind for your own good. This is obviously just some ruse of Motsumi's to get you to go to Hell and then exploit you for his own nefarious purposes, whatever they may be. He clearly has a vendetta against you and with good reason by the sounds of it. It could be a trap, he could even still be working with the Countess and luring you to your death."

Naledi lifted her eyes towards the sky as she considered this, "true but then what other choice do I have? I'd have to go to Hell so I can resume my training with him anyway. Plus, if I don't go, the Countess will send her tulpa to kill me on Earth. If I do go, the Countess herself could kill me in Hell. I'm at risk whatever I do. I believe Motsumi is actually trying to turn over a new leaf. Why else would he have joined the redemption group?"

"I dunno, maybe to spy on them and report everything back to the Countess or some other demon," Lerato suggested.

"...Oh damn, I hadn't thought of that....but I believe him this time. After all, I'm the one who reached out to him."

Lerato looked at her with sympathy. "How did you leave things with him?"

"I agreed to his terms. I'm going to breach a portal to Hell tonight and go with Motsumi to the akashic realm."

"And how do you feel about that?"

"Terrified of course!

Lerato sighed and picked at more pieces of grass, "well you could take Tau with you?"

"Yes I could but then we'd both be at risk. The Countess has it in for both of us. I don't want to risk his life as well as my own. I can't lose him again. Part of my wish to kill the Countess is to keep us both safe. It's not just about me."

"Naledi, Tau loves you. You should at least offer him the chance to protect you."

"But how would he help? If the Countess attacked us?"

"He's pretty nimble with a knife. Have you seen him gutting a rabbit?"

Naledi nodded, "you're right about that."

Lerato continued, "look, whether you take Tau with you or not. You have to trust your own abilities. You're a badass!"

"I am not!"

"Yes you are. I mean, shit, you saved the entire future of humanity by slaying a demon-hosting sorcerer. What's more badass than that? You just lack self-confidence but you've got this. I have faith in my girl." Lerato punched her lightly on the shoulder then smiled at her. "You look happier already, I can always tell when there's something on your mind, the circles under your eyes get more pronounced."

"Really?"

"Yes, kind of like a... what is it that Tau calls you? A meerkat? His little meerkat?"

"Hey, shut up, only he's allowed to call me that." Naledi slapped Lerato on her back, playfully as they walked on to their next class. Naledi didn't know what she would find when she got to Hell. She didn't know if she was about to make one of the worst decisions of her life but one thing was for sure, she'd never been able to ignore helping a friend in need and if Giada was indeed as sick as Motsumi had claimed, she'd never forgive herself if she didn't rescue her. Plus she had to face the Countess again sooner or later whether she liked it or not.

12

GIADA

~

Giada walked through a field filled with daisies, the sun was shining and a warm breeze caressed her cheek as strands of her hair whipped across her face, tickling her nose. She wiped the strands away and sat down to enjoy the sunshine. There was something she was struggling to remember but she didn't know what it was. It was something important that nudged at the corners of her consciousness, elusive and just out of reach. Was she supposed to be somewhere? Or was she supposed to meet someone? It was no use, each time she tried to grasp at the memory it slipped away again, like a fish wriggling out of a fisherman's hands. Giada shrugged and decided to just enjoy the beautiful day. She stretched her legs out and leaned back to rest on her hands as she looked around.

In the distance she saw a woman approaching her. Giada lifted her hand to shield her eyes from the sun as she squinted to see who it was. The woman looked very familiar even from far away. Her gait, her posture and her frame; it was a woman who Giada would recognise anywhere. It was someone she'd known her whole life: her mother. A frown troubled Giada's face as she saw her mother get closer and closer and there was that feeling again. What was it that she'd forgotten, damnit! Then as her mother got closer still, Giada saw that there was something wrong with her eyes. Her eyes were a deep crimson red, not the natural brown they had been in life and that's when Giada realised. This was a dream, she couldn't possibly be here, sitting in sunshine, surrounded by daisies. She remembered that she was dead and she was in Hell. Her heart sank as the nagging suspicion that it had been too good to be true, became a reality.

Her mother stood over her now, her red eyes alight with rage, wisps of steam rising out of her ears. It was as if her subconscious mind had conflated her mistress, the Countess, with her mother. In spite of the look of pure anger and hate on her mother's face, Giada couldn't help but feel happy to see her. "Mama!" she said.

Her mother said nothing, she simply stood glaring at Giada.

"Mama, say something," Giada implored yet still her mother remained silent. Waves of anger radiated off her, causing Giada to tremble. "Mama, please say something."

Finally her mother pointed and said three words only. It was the three words that Giada had most feared hearing from her mother's mouth, during the last few years of her life. The words were spoken now as both sentencer and executioner of her heart.

"It was you."

Her mother raised her arm and pointed at Giada and she felt her breath quicken as her heart rose to form a lump in her throat. She was enveloped in grief and regret. It coursed through her veins like cyanide. As she looked at the beautiful field around her, the daisies started to turn brown, curling and dying all around her before disintegrating to dust. The grass underneath her turned yellow then brown then grey and ashen and the wind picked up speed, blowing the dead daisies and grass away. Giada looked up at the sky. The sun disappeared behind thick, swirling, grey thunder clouds which appeared as if from nowhere. Thunder rumbled and lightning crackled. When Giada looked down again every bit of natural beauty had been swept away and her heart filled with grief as she recognised the location that she now sat in. It was Hell Central, her home for the rest of eternity.

Her mother reached forward, bending down to grab Giada's arm and aggressively pull her to her feet.

"Look," she spat. "Look at what you've created. This is your doing and now you will be here until the end of time."

"Mama, no, please don't." Giada pleaded but in her heart, she knew her words lacked conviction. Her mother was right, Giada had caused this. She deserved to be here. Giada had stood over her younger brother, watching as he died. She was the architect of her damnation and she had no defence, no excuse, nothing that could assuage her guilt.

Her mind scrambled for an escape, any release from the pain she now endured. It was a deep, raw, emotional wound that wrapped its tentacles around her core, strangling her just as surely as her brother had been strangled. She clawed at her throat, struggling for breath, feeling herself get faint. She watched as her mother stood smirking at her. She recognised that smirk, it was the same smirk that she, Giada, had given her brother Roberto as his life had slipped away, dangling at the end of that curtain chord. The smirk she'd kept on her face as she'd listened to the squeak of the curtain chord as his corpse spun around and around. Her mother now took it a step further and laughed, a deep, guttural, laugh of torment.

"How does it feel? To be strangled by your own blood? How does it feel, huh?"

Her mother then spat next to her, her lips curled in disgust. Giada felt worse than she'd ever felt but also relieved. She'd needed this condemnation. She'd needed her mother to know the truth but the problem was, this was not real. It was just a dream, the guilt and desires of her innermost thoughts entangled together to form a theatre of the absurd and the tragic. She wished she could really tell her mother the truth. She needed to confess, she ached for it with every fibre of her being. Her guilt consumed her more surely than the hell sprite's venom consumed her and if the poison didn't kill her soon, her guilt would. When she was reborn in another hell dimension, would she still remember her sins, she wondered? Would the memories of her transgressions follow her, ceaselessly from Hell rebirth to rebirth, on and on into infinity? That was what she'd been told to expect.

She felt the dream slipping away from her now. Her eyes flickered open, she murmured,

"Mama."

Someone was standing over her talking, she no longer recognised the voice, her thoughts were so addled by fever.

"She's very close to the end now. We have to get help immediately or we'll lose her," the voice said.

Giada tried to open her eyes wider but all she saw were dark shadows moving around. The venom had ravaged her vision and she was too weak to lift her head or speak.

Suddenly, Giada felt the quality of the air change, a subtle breeze coursed over her face, cooling her raging temperature. She smelt fresh air and wood smoke and grass. This must be another hallucination, a memory of earth but as she thought this she heard a gasp of surprise from one of the male voices.

"What's happening?" the voice said.

"It's a portal, it's Naledi, she's arriving."

The air gathered speed and Giada felt a slight sucking sensation and heard a fizzing pop sound followed by the lighter sounding footsteps of someone of smaller stature.

"Dumela Naledi," Giada heard the joy in, what she now realised, in a moment of clarity was, Motsumi's voice.

"Giada!" Naledi's voice was tight with anguish.

Giada felt a presence at her bedside and a cool hand on her forehead. The sensation was so comforting. Giada felt like crying but being a damned soul, she'd lost her ability to shed tears so all that happened was that she felt her lips fluttering as they always did with intense emotions. Naledi said, "don't worry Giada, everything is going to be okay now. I'm here and I'm going to go with Motsumi to find an antidote for you. We'll make you better, don't worry."

Giada tried once more to open her eyes. She tried to speak to utter the words of gratitude she felt in her heart but all that came out was a strangulated croak of pain. Then once more she felt herself slipping away, slipping into semi-consciousness, powerless against the toxin that wreaked havoc on her system as the spectre of death floated at the corner of her mind's eye. She felt a smile come to her lips though. Naledi was here and she had a chance at survival.

13

NALEDI

Naledi walked quietly along the dark tunnels of the other hell dimension, leading to the room containing the human body parts. She carried a cloth bag, slung over her shoulder, in which to put the stolen body part. She also carried her fighting staff in one hand and a knife, tucked into her bra. She'd decided it was wise to bring weapons. Given that she still had very little training in magic, her fighting skills would be her best chance of survival in the event of an attack by the Countess or anyone else. Motsumi had drawn a detailed map for her and had also performed a cloaking spell to alter her appearance. He'd changed her facial features and given her the partially red eyes of a wicked spirit. His rationale was that it would be easier to lie and avoid punishment if she appeared to be of a higher rank. If he and Giada had seen the Countess here before, they couldn't risk Naledi being recognised and attacked by the demon before Naledi was ready to take her on.

The tunnels were dimly lit by fiery pits which were nestled in between crags of rocks. Naledi's nose tickled with the chemical-like smell, which hung around the air. She reasoned that as she now looked different, the best approach was total confidence. Hence, when she reached the room indicated on the map, she held her head high and strode in.

She breathed a sigh of relief to see that the room was empty and unguarded, just as Motsumi had predicted. Along one wall was row upon row of large glass jars, each containing a gruesome human appendage. She walked closer to get a better look and dusted off the front of one of the compartments. Inside was a small-sized hand. Naledi felt desperate guilt and anguish as she realised that this was a child's hand. She wondered how it had come to be here. Had it been taken from a child who was dead or still alive? Or had the child been murdered for the purposes of this vile sacrifice? She was aware that she was indirectly benefiting from something that had possibly ruined a child's life. Even if the child had been dead when the hand was taken, it was still a terrible thing to do - to offer the hand of some poor family's beloved child's corpse as a demon sacrifice. She shook her head and tried not to think of it. She didn't have time for this and couldn't allow herself the luxury of indulging in sentiment.

Gulping down her guilt, she hardened her heart for the task at hand. Naledi opened the jar and took it, wrinkling her nose in disgust as she dropped the rigid, cold hand into her cloth bag. Suddenly, she heard voices and footsteps approaching. She froze, whipping her head around and inhaling sharply.

Oh no! I have to get out of here.

She closed the jar and scrambled towards the exit, leaping behind a nearby cluster of rocks in the nick of time. As the footsteps got nearer she realised with dismay that she recognised one of the voices. It was the Countess. The other voice was male, very deep and gravelly. From the sound of the footsteps, she thought the Countess and the male were accompanied by at least two other people - possibly minion servants? She wanted to take a look but she couldn't risk being seen. Even though her appearance had been altered, she didn't want to elicit awkward questions that she wouldn't be able to answer.

"Everything is in place Vassago, the Chancellor is currently running things in a shambolic manner. It's the perfect time for your forces to strike and take down the Seventh Circle. The only thing that remains is for the defence shields to be taken down," the Countess said.

"And how do you plan to do that?" replied the male voice.

"I have trusted spies working to secure the codes required to disable the mainframe. Once we have those codes, I'll get a message to you and we will ensure the attack is coordinated."

"I don't like your use of spies and messengers. How do you know you can trust these people? I would prefer it if you came yourself."

The Countess laughed girlishly. "Why Vassago, if you want me to come back here so you can see me again, all you have to do is ask."

"I'm being serious," he replied.

"Don't worry, I kill spies on a regular basis ensuring that none of them are able to talk before they die. The method lacks sophistication but it's effective."

"Hmm, ruthless, I like it. I can see you and I have a lot in common."

"That's why we're such a good team. Once we've taken over the Seventh Circle, we'll be the most powerful demons in all of Hell. Satan won't stand a chance when we move against him."

Naledi could barely believe her ears.

The Countess and this Vassago fellow are planning to topple Satan?!

"Now. I hope I've satisfied your concerns?"

"My *concerns* won't be satisfied until I am ruler of the Seventh Circle."

The Countess wearily corrected him, "*co-ruler*, Vassago."

Vassago laughed awkwardly. "Co-ruler of course, of course."

"I take it the glitch that appeared in the technology the last time I was here has now been fixed and we can at last see a successful demonstration of the machine's capabilities?"

"Yes, I've been assured that this time it will work. Our ability to put damned souls on earth without a host will make all the difference. Satan didn't think big enough but with this technology at our fingertips, after taking over Hell, we can take over Earth and soon the entire universe."

"I've always loved a man with ambition," she replied.

Naledi could hear the amusement in the Countess' voice.

Naledi listened as they walked towards the room she'd just come out of but the absence of any door meant that she could still hear what was being said.

"This is a very nice collection you have here. Plenty of lovely specimens." Naledi could hear the Countess' high heels clicking as she paced up and down the rows of jars.

"Why do you leave the room unguarded though? Are you not worried that somebody will steal them?"

"No, these have no value here, other than what we use them for in the realm teleporter but nobody knows about that technology yet."

"My dear Vassago, they may not have any value here but I can think of plenty of demons in our hell dimension who would love to get their hands on these sacrifices. You must station guards outside immediately or you risk losing the entire collection."

"As you wish." Naledi heard clicking fingers, "Roman, Thumi, from now on you two will remain outside this room as guards."

Naledi sank back against the rocks, no longer listening to what was being said as her thoughts raced chaotically around her head. She tried to absorb the enormity of what she'd heard. The Countess and Vassago were planning to take over the entire universe and they had some kind of realm teleporter technology. A device that made it possible for damned souls to go to Earth without a host. Demons could certainly rule the entire world that way.

This is huge.

Naledi had to stop this from happening but she couldn't do it alone. Could she trust Motsumi enough to tell him? She still wasn't sure exactly what his agenda was and the idea of trusting him with this information gave her a funny feeling in her stomach. She'd tell Aaron. He was a better bet. He was definitely not on the Countess' side. He wasn't on Satan's side either but surely what the Countess and Vassago were planning was worse than having Satan maintain his rule over Hell? She had to get back and fast.

Naledi crept quietly, from rock to rock, keeping low and out of the dim light. Damned souls' eyes were well adapted to darkness so she had to be extra careful not to be seen. As soon as she was out of the guards' sightline, she allowed herself to relax slightly. She was relieved that this part of the plan had been completed. As she walked quickly, she thought more about what else she'd learnt.

The Countess was planning a coup. But was it actually a coup? Since Sehloho had died, who was actually leading the Seventh Circle? Indeed, hadn't the rumour been that while Sehloho had been lying in wait for the resurrection on earth, the Countess had unofficially been running things? Naledi wondered why it hadn't simply been made official as soon as Sehloho had died? She'd have to ask Aaron, when she returned. The politics of Hell was not something she had learnt much about at the induction seminar she'd attended on her first visit here.

What perplexed her the most was that Motsumi had been telling the truth about the sacrifice room. Perhaps he'd been telling the truth about having changed too? Was it possible for people to change that much? She imagined that death would be a transformative experience for anybody's ego but could someone go from being a pathological liar and manipulative, selfish bastard to being Hell's equivalent of a Sunday School teacher? She couldn't shake the feeling that Motsumi was up to something. That was his way: he always had a hidden agenda and this time would be no different. It might be true that he wanted to help Giada. It might also be true that he wanted to protect Naledi and help her complete her training to become a fully qualified sangoma but there would also be some other motive too; something personal that he stood to gain. She just couldn't figure out yet what that could be. Yet again she felt like she was on the back foot with him. They were supposed to be on the same side but Motsumi didn't really side with anyone except himself. She was, once again, following his game plan and taking his orders. But hadn't she wanted it this way?

As she walked she was so deep in thought that she didn't notice the pothole until she'd slipped and tumbled to the side. She fell towards a deep, lava-filled ravine as her fighting staff clattered further down the path out of her reach. Her heart raced as she saw her life flash before her. As she tumbled, her cloth bag caught on a jagged rock ledge, saving her at the last minute. She breathed a sigh of relief followed by a sharp stab of terror as she looked down at the bubbling lava in the chasm beneath her. Falling would mean instant death and she was hanging on by her shoulder cloth bag only.

The extreme heat of the lava caused beads of sweat to break out on her forehead. Taking a deep breath she gritted her teeth and with a colossal effort, she hauled herself up by pulling on the cloth bag strap. She almost made it and then heard a sound, which nearly made her lose control of her bladder: the cloth was tearing. She whipped her other hand onto a nearby rock crevice just in time as the bag tore apart and the child's hand went tumbling into the fiery abyss below.

Shit!

A sickening feeling of fear and failure flooded her stomach. How would they barter with the Lords of the Akashic now? She briefly considered going back but it was impossible now that there were guards stationed outside. Could she make up some excuse? After all, Motsumi had altered her appearance... No it was too risky. She'd just have to go back to the Seventh Circle without it and adjust the plan. She only hoped that she could still get the answer needed to heal Giada. She'd never forgive herself if she let down the girl who had helped her, rescuing her during her darkest hour before the resurrection. Giada had proven her loyalty time and again and now Naledi had to help her in return. Naledi hauled herself up back onto the path, picked up her fighting staff and went on her way.

14

NALEDI

~

Naledi had agreed to meet Aaron and Motsumi at a cave in the Deeper Depths, near the entrance to the other hell dimension.

"Aaron, can I have a word with you alone please?" Naledi said as she approached them.

Motsumi's jaw dropped open as his eyes narrowed, "what do you want to say to him that you can't say in front of your teacher?"

Naledi bit her lip, remembering how jealous Motsumi could be and how much he detested the idea of her seeking advice from other mentors. Her stomach did somersaults as she looked up at him, but she stood her ground. She didn't speak. She simply held his gaze in defiance until he eventually said,

"Fine!" and stormed off.

Once he was clearly out of earshot, Naledi recounted all that she'd learnt outside the sacrifice room to Aaron.

"Well, that explains how they got the body parts down here," he said. "They've got some kind of technology which allows the transference of living tissue between Earth and Hell."

Naledi replied. "The one positive thing is that they've already been testing this and the world hasn't been flooded by demons. Which tells us that this doesn't disrupt the balance between the realms in the same way that a human hosting a demon does."

"You're right, that is a relief." His eyes narrowed, "But if I know the Countess, she won't be satisfied sharing power. This is her play to seize the Seventh Circle throne for herself. She'll ditch that Vassago guy just as soon as she can."

Naledi felt her brow crease with puzzlement, "I don't understand why she needs to stage a coup to do this. Wasn't she already running things behind the scenes anyway?"

"She was but it was never official. Satan is staging a contest between his other sons to decide who will take over the Seventh Circle. Until that has been decided, the council is running things."

"What was the Countess talking about when she said the defence shields would be disabled?"

Aaron explained, "The Seventh Circle has an electrified defence shield surrounding it which stops other hell dimensions invading. The thin etheric barrier that separates the different hell dimensions from one another doesn't offer enough protection because there are so many sorcerers down here who have the power to easily break through. I'd bet you that's what the Countess did to get there in the first place. She used magic to create that portal. Then she simply counted on the aversion most citizens of Hell have to parasites, to stop them from going down to the Deeper Depths and discovering it."

"Why haven't they already invaded? There is already a portal open between their dimension and this one?" Naledi asked

"I s'pose they could but it's a narrow entrance. Only wide enough for one person to walk through at a time. It's not very practical for bringing over an entire invading army."

Naledi went quiet for a moment as she thought. She didn't care that much that the Seventh Circle was going to be invaded by a neighbouring aggressor. But the knowledge was like a bomb detonator against the Countess and it was Naledi's finger that was on the trigger. Assuming of course that Hell viewed treason in the same way that governments on Earth viewed it. She tested her assumption with Aaron. "What would happen to the Countess if the Council found out what she was planning to do?"

Aaron scratched his chin, "she'd be demoted back to minion status and banished to another hell dimension. Then she'd be tortured, for a *looong* time. They can get quite creative with their punishments down here."

Thoughts swirled around Naledi's head. Was this the answer? Simply give the Countess up to the Council and she'd lose her status? But no, her status wasn't what made her dangerous, her magical powers were and those powers wouldn't go away if she became a minion. Getting her demoted would just piss her off and make her even more determined to avenge herself against Naledi and Tau.

Aaron finished his train of thought. "There's no point in reporting her. We don't know who, within the Council, is already on her side. If she's staging a coup, I'll bet she already has powerful collaborators within the Council."

Naledi twirled a braid around one of her fingers. "It's the realm teleportation technology that I'm more concerned about. In some ways it's worse than a demon resurrection. It may not break down the barrier between realms but it removes the need for a human host. It opens up Earth as Hell's playground."

"You're right. That's what we should focus on...." Aaron hesitated and looked at her before asking his next question, "... Naledi, why didn't you want to include Motsumi in this discussion? Don't you trust him?"

"No I don't and you shouldn't either. He might be my mentor but he's duplicitous."

"If you feel that way about him, why did you ask him to train you again?"

"I had no choice. Nobody else can help me to defeat the Countess. I'm worried he might still be working with her and this entire thing is a charade to serve me up to her."

"If that were the case, wouldn't he have done that already?"

"Maybe, maybe not. Motsumi is always one step ahead of me. Maybe he's lulling me into a false sense of security so that the Countess strikes when I'm at my weakest."

Aaron sighed and shook his head. "Naledi, you can't carry on like this. Either you don't trust him, in which case you shouldn't train with him. Or you do trust him, in which case you have to be honest and share your concerns with him."

Naledi nodded. She knew Aaron was right but she had no way of finding out for sure whose side Motsumi was on. If she tried having an honest conversation with him and he was secretly on the Countess' side, he'd simply lie about it and she'd never know until it was too late. She looked up at Aaron. "Do you trust him?"

His face broke into a smile of such sympathy that Naledi felt comforted before he'd even spoken. "For what it's worth, I do."

"Why?"

Aaron's grey eyes grew misty and Naledi wondered which memory he had travelled to in his mind. "I believe in second chances. I don't believe that Motsumi would've come to the SA meetings and shared as honestly as he has been doing, if he didn't want to change."

"But couldn't he just make everything up?"

"He could..... But I've been down here long enough to have a good nose for a liar. Motsumi has been telling the truth at the SA meetings. He's shared some pretty dark stuff. If he was going to lie, he'd leave those parts out. He wants to change, he's ready for it and that makes him trustworthy in my book."

Naledi half smiled at Aaron. She realised she had been scarred by Motsumi's abusive treatment of her whilst alive. Trusting him again after everything he'd put her through was going to take some time and she didn't even know if it was possible. Sure, she'd asked him to train her again and even yearned for it but now she was beginning to have second thoughts. Could she simply put all of his abuse and deception behind her and start afresh with him? Could she take him at his word when doing so meant risking her life? How could she defeat the Countess when she couldn't even trust her mentor?

15

NALEDI

∼

After they'd finished their private chat, Naledi and Aaron went to find Motsumi. He was sitting on a rock brooding as he stared into the lava-filled pits. The orange glow reflected off his dark skin and deep-set eyes in a way that made him look menacing. However when he saw Naledi and Aaron approach, his entire demeanour changed and he broke into a smile of such warmth. Yet again it made Naledi wonder.

Who is the real Motsumi?

He stood up and Naledi felt a knot in her stomach as she anticipated an interrogation about her private chat with Aaron. But instead Motsumi didn't even broach the topic.

"Naledi, I will help you navigate your way to the akashic realm. As I have been there before, you must connect with my consciousness to guide you to the correct location."

Naledi was slightly confused as to why he was so eager to get to the akashic realm so quickly. His sense of urgency evidently surpassed his need to know what Naledi and Aaron had been talking about and this made her even more suspicious about his motives.

There must be something in it for him.

Until Naledi found out what Motsumi's real motivation for travelling to the akashic realm was, she wouldn't be able to trust him. Now wasn't the time for this though. She put the matter to one side as she looked at Motsumi and nodded.

The technique Motsumi was referring to was a simple one, which he'd taught her right at the start of her training. Before they began, Motsumi asked Naledi the one question she'd been dreading.

"Do you have the body part?"

Naledi bit her lower lip and held the cloth bag closer to her chest as if to hide her failure. "No. I did get a human hand but I had a problem on the way back. I almost fell to my death down a steep ravine. The bag tore and the hand tumbled into the pit. It was impossible to retrieve as there was lava at the bottom." She turned the bag inside out and poked her hand through the large hole.

"What? Why didn't you wait until the Countess had gone to go back and get another one"

"I couldn't." Naledi threw her arms in the air in exasperation. "She told that Vassago guy to station two guards outside."

Motsumi sighed and put one hand to his creased forehead. "This is far from ideal."

Naledi felt wretched and threw the torn bag into the nearest lava pit in frustration. "What's going to happen? Does that mean that we can't ask a question?"

"We can ask a question alright but if we ask without giving payment they will take payment from Giada's bloodline."

"What does that mean?"

"I don't know, I've never tested it. I've heard that it's different every time. The Lords of the akashic have their own wisdom and take the payment which makes the most sense to the individual in terms of their karmic destiny."

Naledi looked up at the ceiling. "So our options are: not ask about an antidote for Giada and she dies or ask about one and something horrible happens to her family?"

"That's about the size of it yes."

Naledi closed her eyes and an image of the unconscious Giada entered her mind. She felt sick with guilt. "You two know her better than I do. Which do you think she'd prefer?"

"She'd rather live, no question. I'm not even sure if any of her family members are still alive," Aaron replied.

"Then we ask and trust that it is the right decision for her," Naledi replied.

Motsumi nodded, "if we are both agreed, let's start the process. Naledi, sit by me."

Naledi moved over to stand next to Motsumi and then they both sat down cross-legged on the rough, quarried rock floor. Naledi closed her eyes. First she focused her mind's eye on the room around her. She observed how hard the stone floor felt under her and how the heat of the air tickled her arm hairs. Then she took her focus inwards. She relaxed every part of her body slowly. With each breath, she focused, from her feet, up her back, to her internal organs and finally her head and facial features. Finally she focused on her breathing and cleared her mind. She was now aware of only her breath, as it entered and exited her body. She formed a picture of herself stepping out of her body in her mind's eye and then imagined she was stepping into Motsumi's body.

The connection between them had always been strong and as soon as she merged with him, she felt his consciousness entering hers and a barrage of images flooded her awareness. She saw how to get to the akashic realm. She saw the directions, relative to where they were now and the location. Once she had this in her mind, she felt for the threads of reality around her. Feeling the power crackle at her fingertips, she reached forward and grabbed hold of the fabric, tearing it to create a large portal. Before opening her eyes she was immediately aware of a cold, breeze rushing in from the akashic realm. A dank, slightly mildewed smell filled her nostrils. She opened her eyes to see a world similar in appearance to Hell. It was dark and subterranean but the air was cooler and she detected no smell of sulphur.

Motsumi opened his eyes and stood up, reaching out his hand to Naledi. "Come on, let's go."

He offered no feedback on her merging ability and as usual this annoyed Naledi. She felt that she had done well and she yearned for his praise. Motsumi only ever offered criticism, rarely praise unless he wanted something from her. She took his hand and dusted herself off before following him through the portal. Once they'd got through to the other side, they dropped hands. Naledi saw what looked like a guard, carrying a lantern, standing up ahead to the side of an archway. It looked like the entrance to a large network of caves. Stalagmites and stalactites surrounded them making Naledi aware that there was water here. Did that mean they were on earth? Perhaps deep underground?

"Where is this realm located? Are we on earth?" she asked.

Motsumi shook his head. "This is a non-physical realm. You are able to come here in your physical body because you are a breacher but the only way other humans can travel here is with their astral bodies. This is normally during sleep but some people learn how to do it through meditation too. It's an advanced spiritual practice."

"How did you find out about it?"

"The Countess first brought me here. She taught me almost everything I know."

This came close to the crux of what Naledi feared the most about Motsumi's involvement in all of this. "You said before that she raised you as if she was your mother?"

"Indeed she did."

"Then why are you betraying her? Can't you see that this is why I don't trust you? Surely you still feel loyal to her, however misplaced those feelings are?"

Motsumi sniffed and carried on walking, only turning briefly to check that Naledi was keeping up with his long strides. "The Countess brought me up and it's true that my feelings for her are complicated. But she also led me down a path of darkness, which led to me selling my soul to Satan. She manipulated me. I was young and impressionable, she was my mother or at least the closest thing I had to one. I would've done anything she said. She should've protected me from Satan not advise me to rush into his arms. She is the reason why I'm here and she knows that. There is nothing more important to me than getting to Heaven. That's the reason why I helped with Sehloho's resurrection in the first place. I believed that was my only chance to get my soul back and I hoped that I could still negotiate a place in Heaven by doing good works after that. It backfired spectacularly but my goal hasn't changed."

Naledi nodded. This made logical sense but it still could not completely assuage her suspicion. The problem was that Motsumi had proven himself time and again to be untrustworthy and so now nothing he could say or do could undo that perception she had of him. She'd always be constantly on her guard around him. Constantly waiting for the moment when the truth finally came out. The moment when she would realise, with sinking disappointment, that she'd been used by him yet again.

They approached the entrance and Naledi got a closer look at the guard. He was the strangest being she'd ever seen. He was very tall and standing as still as a statue. He had a collection of features that looked like a mixture of every race of human, but the features were arranged in such a way as to make him look distinctly alien.

"Why does he look so weird?" Naledi hissed.

Motsumi smiled, "there is no point in whispering Naledi. The Guardian can hear with his inner ears and see with his inner eyes. There are no lies that can be hidden from him."

The Guardian moved his head slowly down and rested his gaze upon Naledi. "I am not physical. What you perceive when you look at me is energy beyond that which your human mind can comprehend. It struggles to create an image out of what it perceives which makes me appear strange to you."

Motsumi raised his eyebrows. "He doesn't normally give explanations, he must think highly of you."

The Guardian narrowed his eyes at Motsumi but didn't comment, instead he said, "state your purpose, minion."

"We seek guidance from the Lords of the Akashic."

The Guardian lowered his lantern so that it was level with Motsumi's chest. He sniffed closer to Motsumi and then nodded, closing his eyes briefly in satisfaction.

Hmm, interesting thought Naledi *he can sense lies and he seems fine with Motsumi. Maybe Aaron is right about him having changed after all?*

The Guardian turned to Naledi. "And you human, what do you seek?"

"The same Kgosi, I mean Lord, I mean....Sir?" She felt her cheeks glow with warmth.

The Guardian lowered his lantern once again and this time a small smile played around his lips before he nodded and stood to one side, gesturing for them both to enter.

Naledi used her fighting staff as a stick to guide her steps as she followed Motsumi along the tunnels. The caves were dimly lit from a source she couldn't identify. It was as if when she looked at something, it suddenly got light enough for her to see it but when she wasn't directly looking, everything seemed dark again. It was a strange phenomenon and more than a little disconcerting. Naledi felt a great deal of trepidation at the thought of standing in front of these three formidable, eternal beings, without being able to offer adequate payment for their services. The pathway descended and the deeper they got the more Naledi felt a sense of unease. She couldn't put her finger on it but there was something unnatural about this place. She felt with every fibre of her being that she was in a place which was unsuited to humans.

Everything about the environment was hostile to her physicality. It got colder and colder the deeper they walked. She was shivering and her teeth were chattering. The air also got thinner, until it was an effort, requiring extreme will just to put one foot in front of the other, such was her exhaustion. She didn't get the sense that they were unwelcome here, more that no accommodation had been made for the presence of humans or physical beings in general. And this made sense: breachers were extremely rare after all. At last, after a walk that had felt like a test of endurance, they arrived at a large cavern. In front of them were what looked like three giant statues. They reminded Naledi of the statues she'd seen on the internet of the monoliths that were on Easter Island. Large, oblong heads with wide noses huge closed eyes and ears that stuck out. Motsumi stood before the statues and raised his arms out to the side with his eyes closed in homage. Naledi held her breath as she witnessed subtle movement from the statues. They were coming to life.

16

NALEDI

~

Motsumi stepped forward, "My Lords, we have come to seek your guidance. We wish to consult the Lord of the Present."

The Lord of the Present turned his gaze towards Motsumi, "you may speak, damned soul. Tell me, what knowledge do you seek?"

Motsumi cleared his throat, "nothing for ourselves my Lord. We have a question on behalf of another damned soul, Giada Cantinelli. She wishes to know where to find an antidote to hell sprite venom."

"You must travel to the heavenly twilight realm. Once there you must ask for the witch Tan Ti Han. She is a realm walker and adept healer. Ask her to accompany you back to Hell. She is powerful enough to heal Giada."

Naledi smiled as she felt the tension in her shoulders disappear. This didn't sound too bad, after all, it was a trip that she'd already made once. "Thank you my Lord," she said. The Lord of the present slid back into his position, however the Lord of the Future slid forward and spoke. "She will ask you to do something for her in return. She will ask you to collect water from the pool of vitality and bring it back to her. Retrieving the water is no easy task. In order to get it, you have to battle and defeat your greatest adversary."

Naledi's smile dropped. Did they mean the Countess? That was the only person they could possibly mean as she didn't have any other enemies. As she ruminated on this, the Lord continued.

"You risk your life in fighting her but if you defeat her then you will gain limitless magical powers."

Naledi wrung her hands together. This didn't sound like it was worth it. She owed Giada a debt but she didn't want to lose her life trying to pay that debt back. Surely there had to be another way?

Motsumi looked at her with his eyebrows slightly raised and then back at the Lords,

"I regret to tell you that we don't have payment for the question we asked on behalf of Giada Cantinelli."

"Is that so?"

Naledi let out a short, high-pitched laugh before clearing her throat, "yes my Lord. I apologise, I had some trouble acquiring the necessary payment but I assure you, our intentions are honourable."

The Lord of the Present replied without any emotion. "We are not concerned with your intentions. We are not here to pass judgement only to retain and share knowledge. This is a transactional process and if you have not brought payment for the question then payment will be taken via other means."

Naledi felt anguish grip her chest as she thought of her sisters, Dineo and Puleng. Irrational worries raced through her mind. Surely the payment wouldn't be taken from them, would it? Motsumi had said it would be taken from Giada's bloodline but something about the Lord's response made her feel terrified. She couldn't bear it if she caused her sisters any kind of pain. She looked at Motsumi, but he gave her no smile of sympathy, nothing at all to allay her concerns. He merely kept his chin lifted and his gaze stoically forward. Suddenly she heard a grinding of stone. Dust once again rose, tickling her nostrils, as the Lords moved. They slid backwards into the darkness and closed their eyes, becoming statues once more.

Panic rose up Naledi's body. "What's happening? Why have they gone back to sleep?" she asked.

"Be patient Naledi, let's wait and see. Perhaps they are consulting higher powers. There is much here that is beyond our understanding."

Naledi sighed and wrung her hands. She walked around the cave, kicking small stones that she found along the way to take her mind off her anxiety. Motsumi sat on the floor cross-legged and looked like he was meditating. This made Naledi feel a bit guilty. Perhaps she should be meditating? She sat down next to him, crossed her legs and closed her eyes. She tried to relax her body and focus on her breathing but it only served to amplify how restless her mind was. Was it too late to change her mind about asking the question? Probably not, as the answer had already been given. She wished she could've found out what the price would be before she'd asked though. Nothing was worth harming any of her family for and she was beginning to deeply regret this entire trip. She just kept holding onto what Motsumi had said about the Lords having a wisdom to their decisions that was beyond human understanding. She clung to that, desperately hoping that whatever they decided would ultimately be for the best.

After what seemed like a long time, Naledi heard the now familiar rumbling, grinding sound and she sprang to her feet as the Lords slid forward again. This time the one on the left spoke up.

"We will take payment from the ancestral line of the damned soul, Giada Cantinelli. Now you may leave."

Naledi opened her mouth to speak but she caught Motsumi shaking his head at her out of the corner of her eye and abruptly closed it again. He grabbed her forearm, pulling her back slightly as he bowed and said, "Thank you, my Lords," whilst walking backwards. The Lords slid back into their sleeping position and closed their eyes, becoming inanimate stone once more. Motsumi turned and gestured for Naledi to follow him back to the entrance the way they had come. As soon as they were out of the main cave, Naledi asked him, "Why did you shush me at the end? I wanted to know what they meant by taking payment from Giada's ancestral line"

"Yes, I know you did but I didn't want to risk having them think we'd asked yet another question. The payment isn't being taken from either of our families. Why does it matter what they meant?"

Naledi exhaled loudly as her mouth dropped open. So Motsumi hadn't changed that much then, still a selfish bastard. "It matters, because she's our friend."

"But there's nothing we can do to change the price of our question now and we did it to save her life. Asking more questions would satisfy our curiosity but at too great a cost. In any case, we will find out soon enough what it means."

Naledi wrinkled her nose. This didn't sit right with her but she could see he was right. The most shameful thing had been her instant relief when the Lord had said it would be Giada's family who would pay and not her own. As they walked in silence her guilt grew and grew until she could no longer keep silent. "How much do you know about Giada's family and her relationship to them?"

"Not much. I know she's in Hell because of something that happened between her and her family, which tells me that the relationship was unlikely to have been a good one. But I don't know specifically what happened. I've asked her but she won't tell me. Whatever it is, she's deeply ashamed of it."

That didn't give Naledi any comfort and if anything it made her feel worse. It sounded like Giada had been through a lot during her short life and whatever traumas she'd faced had culminated in her getting damned for eternity. True, she must have done something terrible to end up in Hell but nevertheless Naledi struggled to think of her as a bad person. Giada had only ever been kind and helpful to her. Now, Naledi had paid back that kindness by creating a situation in which someone in Giada's family would suffer in order that she be healed. Surely this would add extra guilt and shame to whatever Giada already felt in relation to her family. Naledi sighed and shook her head, feeling constriction around her throat. She swallowed back her feelings of failure and regret. Naledi's heart sank as she realised that she was still a naive idiot. Still hoping for the best and not anticipating the worst. When would she learn? When would she grow up and realise that bad things happened and often to those who deserved it the least?

Motsumi anticipated her dark state of mind. He didn't turn around but she heard his deep voice ahead of her. "Regret is a waste of time and energy. The past is the past, you cannot change it and beating yourself up will only weaken your self-confidence. You already have a low opinion of yourself and that is the last thing you need when facing the Countess."

Naledi couldn't believe she was hearing this from the man who had done more than anyone else to weaken her self-confidence. Her feelings pivoted from shame to fury.

"Cheap words coming from the man who constantly belittled, humiliated and abused me whilst alive. You never missed an opportunity to beat me down, both psychologically and physically. You were incapable of praise, your feedback was always negative."

"And yet here you are, training with me once more. If I'm such a bad teacher, why are you here?"

"I had no choice and you know it," she spat.

Motsumi continued walking for a few moments before he replied, "If I was rough with you, it was because you were weak and needed to be toughened up. Already your anger and hatred towards me gives you power. You never would've spoken to me like this when we first met."

"Those are excuses, you're trying to appease your guilty conscience."

"Am I? What is the point of a guilty conscience in Hell? You can't see it yet but I'm exactly the teacher you needed and I still am."

Naledi felt herself scowling but she dropped the subject. Motsumi evidently also wanted to move on as he proposed,

"I think we should go to Heaven as soon as possible. I imagine you are weary after the trip here and I don't want you to be too tired to breach a portal back to earth. I suggest you go home and get some rest then we can meet back in Hell this evening and go directly from there to Heaven."

Naledi felt herself scowling as she looked at Motsumi's form striding along the pathway ahead.

"I'm not doing it," she said.

Motsumi stopped and turned around, "what do you mean *you're not doing it?*"

"What I said. This whole thing is getting too risky. You heard what he said, I'll have to face my greatest adversary - that must be the Countess and I could get killed too. I know I owe Giada a debt but not at the expense of my own life. I can't leave Dineo and Puleng all alone in the world."

"But Naledi, defeating your adversary will give you limitless magical powers. Just think about that for a moment. You'd become a qualified sangoma. You'd gain all the powers that would normally take years to attain. It's a once in a lifetime opportunity and I cannot allow you to throw it all away."

"You expect me to risk my life to gain magical powers?! I'm not like you Molume. I didn't come into this willingly. Power doesn't interest me."

"You're lying to yourself. Remember, *you* approached *me* about resuming your training. You missed it and you enjoy it. You're just in denial."

"Why do you care so much anyway? I'm not buying the whole redemption-seeking facade. What is in this for you and this time can you please be honest with me?"

Motsumi stopped and turned around. His eyes searched hers and for a moment she thought that she'd get a straight answer from him for once. But then his body stiffened.

"Did you hear that?" he whispered.

"What?" Naledi hadn't heard anything.

"I thought I heard voices". They were near the entrance and Motsumi crept forward to get a better look. He positioned himself behind a cluster of rocks as Naledi followed him, crouching down behind him. Motsumi peeped up, twisting his body slightly as he craned his head from left to right.

"It's no use, I can't see anything in the darkness but I don't like it. I'm sure I heard voices." He pursed his lips, "I'll go out first, you hang back."

"Couldn't it be just another person coming to see the Lords of the Akashic?"

"Yes it could but we can't be too careful. Like I said, you hang back. You're safe in here, the Guardian prevents anyone with evil intentions from entering."

Naledi nodded and waited behind the rock cluster as Motsumi walked closer to the entrance. She felt a sense of unease that was greater than any possible dangers lurking in the caves. There was so much about this that didn't make sense. For starters, what was a witch doing in heaven? The Lords had said that she sat outside the heavenly gates but surely a witch shouldn't have been allowed anywhere near? Secondly, why was Motsumi so keen on helping Giada anyway? He had nothing to gain by doing this as far as she could see, which made her ultra suspicious. He'd never done anything that didn't further his own ambitions in some way. What was his ambition in Hell? Surely he didn't really believe in the redemption movement? He'd always been a realist, even a pessimist. In fact that was partly what had caused him to sell his soul to the devil. He'd thought it was his best chance of survival and success in a cruel world.

Naledi watched as Motsumi dipped his head slightly on the way out, as a respectful farewell to the Guardian. The Guardian didn't respond nor even turn his head, merely flicking his eyes to the side to watch as he exited the cave. It was only once Motsumi was out that Naledi saw the first lightning bolt crackle towards him.

17

MAUREEN

~

Maureen looked up, over her cat eyeglasses, at the newly damned souls sitting in the waiting room. It had been a relatively slow day and as such it was even more boring than usual. She'd worked here as both administrator and receptionist for the last twenty years. A wicked spirit by the name of Gita had been here before her but she'd been promoted to demon and was now living a life of luxury, at an upscale penthouse, in one of the more fashionable areas of Hell Central. Maureen sighed as she thought of the privileges available to Gita: no work whatsoever; access to any pleasure house she wished; invitations to exclusive VIP events and training sessions and best of all; as many minion slaves as she wanted. If Maureen was honest, she was often tempted by the idea of more sin-baiting. She'd already done enough to be granted wicked spirit status. What harm could it possibly do if she did more?

The problem Maureen had was that she was in a state of limbo. She'd joined S.A and was a regular at the Tuesday night meetings, which Aaron held at a dungeon, in the minion quarters. But her attendance was more due to loneliness than a genuine belief in the cause. She was a cynic, always had been. She simply didn't believe that redemption was possible for damned souls. However, she'd been going for long enough that she had friends there and she hated the thought of how disappointed they would be in her if she resorted to sin-baiting again. Thus, she was at an impasse, a place of stagnation. Unwilling to move forwards and unable to move backwards.

She adjusted her glasses on her nose and looked down at the stack of papers in her hands. She shuffled them in a manner which she hoped intimidated the terrified newbies on the other side of her glass window. She fixed them with an icy glare for good measure. Word had got out about her being a part of S.A and she couldn't have other wicked spirits thinking she was now an easy target. Other damned souls were forever scheming to take her position. Her job, as menial as it was, afforded Maureen a level of power that was difficult to get as a wicked spirit. The arrivals buzzer beeped and flashed red on the wall. A new soul was arriving. A cloud of smoke appeared, some of the other newly-damned souls wafted it away and coughed. Maureen's lip half curled into a rue smile.

They'll soon get used to the smoke.

When the smoke cleared an attractive middle-aged woman stood there. She was slim, with short dark hair and an olive complexion. Her eyes were wide with fear and confusion.

"Where am I? What's going on?" her voice quivered as she spoke.

Maureen was used to this. Without missing a beat, she barked, "name?"

"Sophia Cantinelli. Where..."

Maureen interrupted her, "take a number and sit down."

"A number but?..." the woman's gaze caught the eye of another elderly woman sitting to her right. The woman was vigorously shaking her head with a look of intense warning in her eye. The new arrival clearly knew what was good for her and shut her mouth. She smoothed down her shirt and walked over to the machine dispensing numbers at the far end of the room. Before sitting down she looked at her number then gave one more puzzled glance at Maureen before she plonked herself down on a chair next to the elderly woman.

This was Maureen's favourite part of her job: people watching. She found it fascinating watching how people coped with the shock of arriving in Hell for the first time. Of course, Maureen didn't make it easy for them, why should she? Nobody had made it easy for her when she'd arrived and she wouldn't be doing them any favours by being kind to them. It was best to be as mean as possible and then they wouldn't find the torture, slavery and random punishments that would follow, so difficult to accept. As far as Maureen was concerned, she was a compassionate citizen. Not only was she doing her civic duty but also performing an act of kindness by giving them a small taste of the cruelty of Hell, which would be their reality for the rest of eternity.

The new arrival leaned subtly over towards the elderly woman and spoke in a quiet voice, barely above a whisper. Maureen pricked her ears up to listen.

"Excuse me Madam, where are we?"

The old lady had rosy cheeks and the look of a cuddly grandma who home-baked cookies for her grandchildren every Sunday. Maureen wondered what sin had got her damned but then in her time here, she'd learnt that you never could tell about a person.

"We're in Hell dear," the old lady replied.

"What are you talking about?"

"Hell, eternal damnation, torment, punishment for earthly sins..."

"Yes, yes, I know what Hell is but I'm not supposed to be here"

Maureen rolled her eyes, if she had a minion slave for every time she'd heard that one she'd be a rich woman indeed. The old lady patted the woman on the hand.

"That's what I said when I arrived but I'm afraid there's no way out. At least that's what I've been told. We're stuck here. For eternity."

"But I was in Heaven just a moment ago?"

Now Maureen sat up. This was more than just unusual, it had never happened in the entire time Maureen had worked here, nor had she ever heard of it. The entire waiting room turned their heads to stare at the woman. A buxom, dark-skinned lady leaned forward to peer at her as she spoke. She had a strong Nigerian accent. "What do you mean you were in Heaven just a moment ago?"

"Well, I died, in a car accident, a few months ago and I went to Heaven. What am I doing here now?"

The Nigerian lady's mouth dropped open. She looked at Maureen, "Excuse me. Can you explain this please? Is this normal? Do you get souls arriving here from Heaven?"

Maureen shifted in her seat, suddenly feeling hotter than normal. She turned to one side and moved the desk fan closer to her face. How was she going to handle this? She couldn't let on that she was ignorant of this situation. She couldn't risk losing face or control. She corrected her expression to ensure it was one of complete boredom. "It happens. Now shut up and wait for the induction seminar to begin."

The Nigerian lady didn't seem completely satisfied by her response but she'd already witnessed Maureen delivering a death sting to one of the other newbies who'd asked too many questions. She evidently knew better than to open her mouth again. The death sting was a particularly useful power which wicked spirits acquired upon gaining their status. Maureen could touch her finger lightly on a person's forehead, whilst thinking malicious thoughts and the sting would deliver such an intense burst of pain that the offending soul usually passed out. Demons also possessed this power but they used it seldom, preferring to take souls to the torture chambers and gain pleasure by watching them writhe in pain for days at a time. Maureen liked seeing the complete and abject fear that the use of her power rendered in any newly-damned soul who witnessed its effects.

WITH ORDER RESTORED, Maureen sat back to muse on the situation. She checked her stack of papers. It was a list of damned souls, which was delivered to her every morning directly from the akashic source. She scanned the list of names looking for Sophia Cantinelli. The name wasn't there. This was getting stranger and stranger by the second. Nobody ever arrived without their name being there. Well, that wasn't entirely true, the only other time anybody had arrived without their name being on the list was when the two human breachers, Motsumi and Naledi, had arrived. Maybe this woman was a breacher? She'd said she'd died and gone to Heaven though, why would she say that if it wasn't true? In Maureen's experience, newly-damned souls were far too shell-shocked to even think of lying. But perhaps she was lying? Perhaps she was a breacher and had breached her way to Heaven and then breached from there to Hell?

Maureen looked over her glasses again at the woman. She looked average, there was nothing obviously special about her but then, Naledi and Motsumi had looked pretty average too. If she was right and this lady was a breacher, this could be another opportunity for her and her S.A friends to get out of Hell. After Motsumi had arrived here, that was one less person who could help them to get out so now there was just Naledi. And from what she'd heard, Naledi was on the Countess' death list. Any day now she'd be killed, most likely end up in Hell too if she'd associated with Motsumi whilst alive. Then they'd be shit out of luck. The best thing Maureen could do would be to ingratiate herself to this Cantinelli woman and then she could potentially become the saviour of the entire redemption movement. Maureen put her fingers to her chin as she pondered on the name for a moment.

Cantinelli...Cantinelli...where have I heard that name before?

Maureen had an uneasy feeling in her stomach. She stood up and shuffled to the filing cabinet at the back of her cubicle. Pulling open the bottom drawer she flipped through the files, which were alphabetised by name. There were thousands of Cantinellis but she was looking for confirmation of one in particular. Her finger scanned down before hitting upon the name that she had suspected.

'Giada Cantinelli', I was right.

Could this woman be related to Giada? As far as Maureen remembered, Giada had arrived here a few months ago. She looked at the woman again. She had dark hair and olive skin, just like Giada. In fact there was a definite resemblance to the facial features as well.

Maureen looked up at the ceiling as she tried to remember how Giada had died. Hadn't it been a car crash? That's right, a car crash and her mother had been driving. Maureen dropped her gaze, her breath hitching as she realised with a shock who this woman was: she was Giada's mother. That meant that she wasn't a breacher, she was a soul who had died and gone to Heaven a few months ago and then she'd suddenly turned up here. What on earth could she have done in Heaven that was bad enough to get her damned? Or had she done something? Maybe she'd done nothing. Could this be some kind of glitch in the system? Was that even possible?

That was the problem with Hell, nobody ever explained anything to you. Part of the reason why Maureen had sin-baited in the first place had been to gain access to the extra training sessions so she'd have a bit more information about everything down here. If there was one thing she hated, it was not being in the know. There was nobody Maureen could ask to get the answers she desired. Senior demons like the Countess would probably know but she couldn't risk telling them about this before she knew what it was she was dealing with. Giada was part of S.A and that made her almost like family. Plus, she was currently hidden away, fighting for her life in the Chancellor's cellar. Maureen wondered if she was beyond the point at which she could be told her mother was here and understand it.

She'd heard that Giada was unconscious and close to death. Perhaps that was why her mother was here? Perhaps Heaven had let her come here on some kind of compassionate pass to visit Giada before she died? Maureen shook her head, no, that was a ridiculous idea. After all, Giada had already died on earth and if she died again in Hell, she'd be reborn in another hell dimension. There was no need to comfort her. There was no release to be had from a death which was certain to result in further damnation. No, Giada's mother was here for some other reason. Maureen didn't know what reason it could be but she at least had to tell Giada and the other S.A members. If Giada was about to die, this was the least that Maureen could do for her.

18

NALEDI

~

As the lightning bolt crackled past his shoulder, Motsumi shot back into the cave, flattening himself against a wall. Naledi sprung up from where she had been crouching and leapt towards him but he held her back with a look of urgency. Seeing the look in his eyes, Naledi crept forward, keeping her body flat against the cave walls. Spread around the outer cave were what looked like about twenty wicked spirit soldiers with the Countess at the rear. The principal demon's arms were crossed as she smiled at them. Naledi's head shot back into the cave as she reared on Motsumi, her eyes blazing with anger. "You told her!" she hissed.

"No! I didn't breathe a word, I swear!"

"You're lying. That's why you wanted me to come here. This was a trap. Why did I trust you again? I'm such an idiot!" she slapped both hands against her forehead. It wasn't just the sting of betrayal and disappointment in her own naivety, which had, yet again, let her down. She was heartbroken that Motsumi had lied to her. She'd begun to hope that this time he might have really changed and he'd used that hope. He'd preyed upon her good nature, her tendency to believe the best in people, to serve her up to his former teacher. She felt tears prickle at her eyes as she sniffed away a runny nose. She turned her head away from him. She didn't want to give him the satisfaction of seeing that he'd upset her. She still had her pride.

Motsumi whipped around and grabbed her by both shoulders.

"Naledi, listen, I know what this looks like but you have to believe me. I didn't tell them we were coming here. They must have found out some other way."

Naledi kept quiet as waves of rage radiated out from her skin. The cave no longer felt cold to her. She looked at him, her entire body taut with anger. "How can you expect me to believe you when you haven't been honest with me about your true intentions here?"

Motsumi had an expression on his face like a cornered wild animal, caught in a trap. He put both hands to his face and ran them up and down with a big sigh.

"Alright I'll tell you."

Finally thought Naledi.

"The Chancellor has offered me instant demon status if I orchestrate the assassination of the Countess."

Naledi's mouth dropped open. "All that stuff about wanting redemption was a load of lies was it?"

"No! Demons can still seek redemption. I'm serious about wanting to get to Heaven. It's just that being a demon will make life easier for me here until I achieve that."

Something about this still didn't make sense to Naledi. "What's Giada got to do with that?"

"She's spying on the Countess and feeding information back to the Chancellor. If she dies, we lose one of our main assets in the fight against her."

Naledi narrowed her eyes at him and put her hands on her hips. "You're telling me, I'm here risking my life to save Giada so that you can fulfil the deal you've done with the Chancellor and climb the ranks of Hell?"

Motsumi held his hands up. "Well it suits your purposes too, doesn't it? You need to get rid of the Countess as much as I do. It's a win-win."

"But how do you know you can trust the Chancellor?"

"I don't. But what he's offering me is better than what I've got right now. You don't understand what it's like to be stuck here Naledi. I have to do what I can to survive. Here it's *kill* or *be killed*."

Naledi searched his face. Was he telling the truth? This time she sensed that he was. His motive certainly sounded like the old self-interested Motsumi that she knew so well. But he could still be lying. She bit her lip. Another lightning bolt crackled near their heads and they both ducked down.

Motsumi's eyes were wild with fear. "Look, I've told you the truth. You don't have to believe me but we don't have time for this. You have to get out of here, right now."

MOTSUMI INCHED FORWARD and Naledi followed behind him. He looked at the soldiers and the Countess and Naledi twisted to one side to look at them. Her heart raced as sweat broke out on her forehead.

Is this how I will meet my end? In a cave in another dimension, with nobody who I care about on earth ever knowing what happened to me?

She thought of Tau and her sisters, Dineo and Puleng. She thought of Lerato. Memories of her parents and her life, as a young child playing on the mountain rocks of Lesotho, flashed through her mind. She even thought of her life at school and the community of Marula. Lastly she thought of her parents' last days and how unfair it had been that they had been taken from her so soon.

Why does God allow such suffering in the world?

She realised her brain was doing a recap of her entire life which she'd heard happens just before people die and that made her feel even greater despair. Adrenaline gave way to panic and she began to hyperventilate. Great gasping sobs escaped from her throat.

The Countess' shrill voice echoed through the cave. "You idiots left the portal open. We just walked right through it. You're a pair of complete amateurs." She let out a braying laugh, "you may as well come out now. There's no point in trying anything. We have you completely surrounded."

Motsumi cursed under his breath and turned back to Naledi. "Listen to me, you need to breach a portal back to earth right now."

Naledi felt her lips wobbling. "I... I don't think I can. I'm too upset, I can't concentrate."

"Naledi, you have to. That's why I spent so much time teaching you meditation techniques. It was for moments like this. As a sangoma, you never know when a rival is going to attack you and you can bet it will never be at a time when you're relaxed, so you have to train yourself to reach the stillness in any circumstance."

"I... I haven't been practis..." Naledi stuttered before Motsumi interrupted,

"Get down!" They ducked as arrows began whistling around their heads. At this point the Guardian stepped down in front of the entrance. The arrows punctured his skin and he pulled them out, without injury, as if they were leaves getting in his way. His face was marked by thunderous rage.

"Who dares disturb the sanctity of the akashic realm with petty violence?!" he boomed.

The Countess stepped forward. "Guardian, stand aside, this doesn't concern you."

"It most definitely does concern me, demon! I am the Guardian of the Akashic and I will not allow any arrows or weapons of war to defile the threshold."

The Countess glared at him for a long time with her hands on her hips. Everybody was silent, the wicked spirits looked from her to the Guardian. They were all wondering who would back down first. Eventually the Countess sighed and rolled her eyes. "Very well, we will fall back. But hear this Motsumi - you cannot hide in there forever and your breacher student will not save you. When you emerge..." she held her fist up and clenched it tightly, "...we will destroy you."

Naledi looked at Motsumi, her eyes wide with terror, "what does she mean? Is she going to kill you? Will you end up in a new Hell dimension?"

Motsumi waved his hands up and down in the air in a calming gesture. "Don't worry, I can handle the Countess. She taught me everything she knows which means... that I know everything she knows." His eyes glinted mischievously.

"But I thought you said she was a much better sorcerer than you?"

"She is but I still have a few tricks up my sleeve. Listen, we don't have time to debate this. You have to breach a portal back to earth, right now. I'll meet you back in the Deeper Depths tonight at seven."

"But..."

"Go!"

Naledi looked up at Motsumi. His eyes were full of kindness and she was reminded of when she'd first met him and he'd told her he would like to have a daughter like her. She thought of the time he'd bequeathed his estate to her and told her she was the thing he was proudest of in his life. He'd made plenty of mistakes and sure, she'd hated him enough to end his life but she also loved him. She flung her arms around him, just about registering the look of surprise in his dark brown eyes. Breathing in his familiar smell of wood chips and subtle aftershave, she momentarily thought how strange it was that his human scent had endured even after death. His hands awkwardly patted her back twice before prizing her away and holding her at arms length to get one last good look at her.

"Go" he ordered quietly. Naledi closed her eyes, pulling her awareness inside herself as she focused on her breath and centred her thoughts around the sole purpose of accessing her abilities. As she allowed the darkness inside to envelop her, she became aware of the threads of reality all around her. She reached forward and grabbed at them, pulling them apart to breach a portal back to earth. She opened her eyes and felt her shoulders sag with relief as she saw the green grass at the back of Tau's house and the familiar red painted door. A cool breeze rushed in, tickling her arm hairs and bringing with it the smell of wood smoke from a nearby fire. She turned back to look at Motsumi once.

"Goodbye Teacher," she said, dipping her head in respect. She turned away from him. Once again she didn't want him to see the tears that now poured down her face but this time it wasn't because of pride. It was because she couldn't bare the last thing she saw of him to be his anguish at seeing her tears.

She was just leaping through the portal when she felt a stinging sensation at her shoulder. She cried out in pain and her entire body went rigid. She collapsed on the ground. Her body sang out in a symphony of pain. Raising one shaky hand, she just about had enough strength to close the portal before she passed out.

19

NALEDI

~

Naledi awoke in Tau's bedroom. The sun was going down and she heard the chirruping of crickets in the tall grass outside. The high-pitched whirr of a mosquito disturbed the peace of the room. She slapped it as it landed on her cheek and then winced as a sharp pain surged down her entire arm from her shoulder. She sat up and swung her legs off the bed, wondering what time it was. Walking into the lounge, she found Tau sitting on the sofa reading a magazine. He turned around as she approached. His smile was tinged with a look of concern,

"Hey, you're awake. How are you feeling?"

Naledi's head felt like a herd of buffalo had trampled on it. "Urgh, not great. What happened?" She rubbed her eyes and when she brought her hands away from her face Tau's expression made her stop.

"What?" she asked.

"Your eyes... they're ringed red."

"What do you mean?" Naledi didn't wait for further clarification. She rushed to the bedroom and looked in the mirror. She gasped and her hand flew up to her mouth. Her eyes had a faint red ring around the irises. Tau appeared behind her, looking at her in the mirror. "What's wrong with them?"

"I don't know," Naledi truthfully replied. But what she kept to herself was that her eyes looked exactly like those of a newly promoted wicked spirit. Whatever had happened to her in hell, had changed her in some way. Her mind raced for an explanation. Was it her trip to the akashic realm? Had it cursed her? Or was it the Countess' attack? Could the Countess have used some kind of dark magic against her? Or worse, could she have brought something back with her through the portal? Perhaps she was possessed by a demonic entity? She unbuttoned her shirt and took it off. Then she twisted her body to look at the source of the pain. There was a small, circular wound on her shoulder. There was no blood, it was more like a raw burn of some kind. It was red with a darker red ring around the outside. She looked up to meet Tau's worried gaze.

"Naledi, what happened to you?"

Naledi sighed, "everything went as planned. Me and Motsumi made it to the Akashic realm but then on the way out we were ambushed by the Countess and a load of her armed men. She was hurling bolts of electrical energy at us. I narrowly escaped with my life but just as I was jumping through the portal, I felt something hit my shoulder. I think she hit me with something."

Tau moved closer to inspect the wound. He touched the outside softly and Naledi winced in pain.

"Let's get that cleaned up," he said.

He took her to the bathroom and cleaned the wound. As he did so he looked at her. "Naledi... don't you think this is too dangerous? You almost got killed. Maybe there's some other way you can protect yourself from the Countess and her tulpa?"

"What are you suggesting?"

Tau looked a bit uncomfortable. "Have you thought about asking for God's protection? Perhaps even visiting Father Lekota to get a blessing?"

Naledi immediately felt guilty and she realised the source of his discomfort. He knew that by bringing this up he was insinuating that she'd forgotten about God. As she searched her heart she realised he was right. In her preoccupation with getting back into training with Motsumi and her obsession with beating the Countess, she'd forgotten about the one power she had always turned to in the past. The power that was greater than all others: her heavenly Father. She didn't have to feel guilty though, she could make amends and fix this immediately. A smile spread across her face as she leant forward and kissed Tau. "Thank you, you're right. I'll go and see Father Lekota now." Naledi hurriedly put her shirt back on and walked towards the front door. She kissed Tau goodbye and he stood at his doorway, hands in pockets, watching her as she rushed off.

Father Lekota lived on the other side of the village. As she walked she waved at a couple of neighbourhood children who were playing hopscotch outside their house. She recognised them from Sunday school. Their grandmother sat in a rickety wooden chair watching them play. Naledi knew the old woman's eyes had long since given up. Her stomach sank with guilt as she realised how thankful she felt that her red ringed eyes wouldn't be seen. She didn't want the village gossip mill to be activated. Ever since she had started her sangoma training, people already talked about her in hushed tones as she walked past. Some of the villagers even made the sign of the cross on their chest when she was near.

Reaching Father Lekota's house she knocked on the door. He opened it and gave a wide smile when he recognised her. The smile immediately dropped as he evidently noticed her red ringed eyes and the urgency of her demeanour.

"Naledi - is everything alright?"

"Yes Father. Can I come in please?"

"Of course, right this way." He beckoned for her to follow him to his front room. It was the simple living room of a man with neither a wife nor children. White painted walls were adorned by a wooden cross on one side and a fading black and white family picture on the other side. Naledi glanced at this and saw that it had been taken when he was much younger. On the wall to the side of her was a circular mirror, which Naledi couldn't help but glance in. As she did so she caught a flash of her red-ringed eyes and saw a blush spread across her cheeks.

"Can I get you something to drink?" he asked.

"No thanks, I'm fine"

Father Lekota nodded. "Please..." he gestured for Naledi to sit down on an armchair opposite the sofa on which he sat.

"What troubles you my child?"

Naledi took a deep breath and plunged right in. "I think I need an exorcism."

Father Lekota's eyebrows rose. "And what makes you think this?"

Naledi bit her lip. She wasn't yet ready to divulge everything. In any case, the old man would never believe her so she started small. "I have these red ringed eyes and I just... I don't feel myself. I'm having strange thoughts."

Okay that last part is an outright lie but I think I can fake the symptoms of possession easily enough to get an exorcism performed.

"What kind of thoughts"

"Disturbing... unclean... thoughts that are obsessive and arise as if from nowhere. I'm hearing voices.... Not like the kind of voices I heard during my ithwasa, these are new and sound evil." Naledi studied him, trying to gauge how well her performance was landing.

Father Lekota looked at her for several minutes without talking as he rubbed his grey stubbled chin. Naledi could tell he was reading her and she had a terrible feeling she'd blown it with the last comment about the ithwasa. Perhaps he would think this was just a symptom of her mental illness and send her away. Just as she was thinking this however he said,

"Alright. An exorcism is a good idea." He pushed heavily on the arm of the sofa to stand up, shuffling towards the door with a stooped posture. "I just have to get a few things, I'll be right back. You wait here."

Naledi sat waiting as she heard Father Lekota rustling in another room of the house. She'd never seen an exorcism performed before but she'd heard from friends it involved holy water and was quite a lengthy process. After a few minutes the Father reappeared carrying his holy sacraments, a bible and some holy water. He instructed Naledi to sit on a wooden chair to the side of her armchair. He started praying and as he did, he took out some nylon scarfs and tied her hands to the arms of the chair. Once she was bound he started calling out the demons which were inside of her. Naledi didn't feel anything and sat placidly as the ceremony continued. However, when Father Lekota took out the holy water and flicked it over her everything changed. The holy water felt like acid burning her skin. She howled in pain as it touched her.

"What are you doing to me?" she screamed at him. Father Lekota ignored her and continued chanting, urging the demons to leave her in the name of the Father, Son and Holy Ghost. Again he flicked the holy water on her and again she screamed and writhed in pain. The more she reacted, the more urgently Father Lekota beseeched the demons to leave. The priest clearly interpreted her pain as evidence that she was indeed possessed. Furthermore he seemed to believe that the exorcism was working. Again and again he repeated the agonising process. With each touch of the searing holy water on her skin, Naledi felt not only agony but mounting rage. Eventually she could take it no more. With superhuman strength she ripped her hands from the arms of the chair, tearing the nylon scarves as she stood up and roared. The sound that came from her mouth was an inhuman growl and Father Lekota quailed. He shook with fear as he held a wooden cross towards her.

"Get back demon!" he shouted at her.

Naledi's body was flooded with adrenaline. Without even realising what she was doing, she struck him hard. She watched in horror as his frail body flew across the room, landing in the corner. Naledi's emotions flip-flopped between extreme anger in one moment to shame and regret the next then back to rage. Heat radiated throughout her body and as she looked at herself in the mirror she saw wisps of smoke coming out of her ears. Her mind raced back to the last time she had seen the Countess really angry. Naledi's hand flew up to her mouth as she remembered that the Countess' ears had had wisps of smoke coming out of them too. Her stomach did somersaults as she realised with shock what was happening to her. She was turning into a demon!

20

NALEDI

~

Naledi rushed out of Father Lekota's house without even saying *goodbye*. She was far too upset to worry about social niceties. In any case, the man was clearly too terrified to notice. He'd curled up into a foetal position, cowering in the corner as she rushed past him. She only hoped he wouldn't spread news about her affliction around the entire village. The last thing she needed was a witch-hunt on top of everything else. She had to keep whatever this was from Dineo and Puleng. They had to be protected at all costs. Who could she trust with this? One person sprang immediately to mind.

She raced to Kabelo's house as fast as her legs could carry her. She hammered on his front door in the manner of a debt collector coming to collect a long overdue payment.

"Kabelo!" she shouted.

Kabelo appeared at the door and just behind him was Lerato. She was rubbing sleepy eyes and looking somewhat dishevelled, as she did up the top button of her shirt. Lerato's body snapped to attention as she noticed her friend's panicked expression. Lerato peered closer, narrowing her eyes at Naledi. "Hey, what's up with your eyes?"

Naledi felt her face crumple as her shoulders sagged. "That's what I'm here to talk to you about."

THEY ALL WENT INSIDE and sat down. Naledi filled them in on everything that had happened including the incident with Father Lekota. When she had finished she put her face in her hands and shook her head. Shame radiated through her body at the memory of hitting the kind old man.

"I don't understand what's happening to me. I thought it was demon possession but if it was then surely the exorcism would've worked?" Naledi looked at Kabelo for confirmation.

"You're right. Father Lekota is an experienced priest. There's no way that an exorcism performed by him wouldn't have been successful. I think we're dealing with something else here."

"What could it be? Is it possible that I'm actually..." Naledi hesitated, "turning into a demon?"

Kabelo looked upwards, his chin set as he stared into the middle distance. When he looked back at Naledi his expression was grave. "There is a type of advanced magic that some demons are able to perform. It transfers part of the demon's DNA into another physical being. In this case the physical being is a human - you. It's similar to the technology used in cloning except this is done using magic."

"You think the Countess has used this magic on me?"

"It's the best explanation I can come up with."

Naledi felt like throwing up. "What will happen to me?"

Kabelo paused and looked at her, his eyes heavy with sympathy. "You'll eventually turn into a demon. I don't know how long you have but I do know that once the transformation is complete, it is irreversible."

Naledi's jaw dropped open, "but... but I thought demons couldn't exist on Earth in physical form?"

"You're right, they can't. If the transformation reaches it's completion whilst you're here, you will disintegrate. You'll also lose your breacher powers and won't be able to survive by breaching a portal to Hell."

"What?!"

Kabelo continued, "your best option for survival is to go to Hell and stay there."

Naledi could scarcely believe what she was hearing. "But I don't want to survive as a demon! I want to find a way to reverse this thing. Do you know how I can do that?"

"Killing the demon who put the spell on you is the only way to reverse it. But this has to happen before the transformation is complete, in order for it to work."

Lerato stood up and took a step closer to Naledi, peering into her eyes. "I see a thin red ring around your eyes. Didn't you tell me that the Countess' eyes are completely red?"

Naledi answered, "yes. Wicked spirits have thin red rings, like how my eyes are now but once they are full demons, their eyes turn completely red."

"So the ring around your eyes will grow larger, until they are completely red. Is that right?"

Naledi nodded glumly.

"In that case, you can use your eyes like an egg timer. You have to kill the Countess before the egg timer runs out."

Naledi put her head in her hands once more. She felt like the bottom had just dropped out of her world. Tears pricked at the corners of her eyes but they didn't fall.

Am I already losing the ability to cry?

She stood up and started pacing. Pins and needles ran up and down her arms and legs and she wondered if it was the effects of anxiety or further physical transformation. Or was she just being paranoid? This was the last thing she needed. She'd only recently learnt how to control her ithwasa but she knew that stress caused relapses. As she struggled to calm her nerves by taking deep breaths, she felt her perception of reality wavering. Some colours became muted, others became brighter and she sensed the vague outlines of spirits hovering just outside of her perception. Her breathing increased involuntarily. She stood up and shook her hands whilst still taking deep breaths. Lerato rushed to her side and enclosed her in a squeezing bear hug. "Don't panic Naledi. You can beat her. You beat her before and you'll do it again."

"I didn't beat her before." Naledi's voice sounded ragged and whiny to her ears. "I stopped the resurrection by killing Motsumi and she crawled back to Hell."

"But you were badass enough to take on Motsumi as he was hosting a demon prince. You can take her on. You can and you will destroy her."

Naledi felt the cold hand of despair clutch at her throat. When she spoke again, her voice cracked. "I'll have to stay in Hell. How will I explain this to Dineo and Puleng? What will I eat and drink? Where will I sleep?"

Lerato interrupted, "hey, hey. Calm down. We can tell Dineo and Puleng you're going away for a couple of days to visit relatives. Just put on some sunglasses so your eyes don't freak them out."

Kabelo added, "if your DNA is already changing, it's likely you no longer need food and water. Why don't you try now? Try drinking some water and see how you feel."

Naledi walked robotically to the kitchen and poured a glass of water from a jug sitting on the counter. She took a sip. It was the strangest sensation. It felt like she didn't want to gulp it. It was almost like she had an aversion to swallowing it. It was weird as she hadn't noticed herself not being able to swallow her saliva but the water just wouldn't go down. She spat it out in the washing up bowl beside the jug.

"You're right, I can't swallow it."

"Couldn't you stay with Motsumi in Hell? Or one of those Sinners Anonymous people you're friendly with?" Lerato suggested.

Naledi considered this, "I suppose so. I think that's the least of my concerns anyway. I have to focus on killing the Countess, and fast."

She looked at both of them, "I wish I could take you both with me."

"Why don't you take Tau with you?"

Naledi thought about this for a moment. "No, I can't. He might be a realm walker but he doesn't have any other special powers. Plus he's human so he needs food and water. I don't want to put him in danger."

In truth Naledi knew that her feelings for Tau would make her weak. The Countess was out to get Tau just as much as she was out to get her and Naledi didn't want to have the added pressure of protecting him. In order to beat the Countess she had to harden her heart and make herself as ruthless as the principal demon was. That was the only way she'd beat her. There was no room for human compassion or the vulnerability that came with loving someone.

THEY ALL AGREED that time was of the essence. Naledi borrowed a pair of dark glasses from Kabelo and they walked home to give the excuse to Dineo and Puleng. Her younger sisters handled it better than Naledi had been expecting and only Puleng looked at her strangely. She asked why she hadn't seen her in those sunglasses before. Naledi lied, claiming she had a headache. Then Lerato distracted them by offering to take them to the shop for ice cream. After they'd left Naledi tried to get a little rest. She knew that her breacher powers had to be replenished, before she attempted to breach a portal back to Hell, but she was too wound up to sleep properly. After lying on her bed for a couple of hours, during which her mind ran amok with obsessive thoughts, she gave up. It was futile. How could she sleep when she knew that every second on Earth brought her closer to her death? Naledi got up and summoned her powers, opening a portal at the side of the room. She smelt sulphur and felt hot wind and ash blow towards her. Unlike the other times when she'd breached a portal though, instead of fear, she felt comfort.

With a sinking heart she realised it was the feeling of a demon returning home to Hell.

21

NALEDI

∽

Naledi arrived in Hell several hours before their agreed meeting time so Motsumi was nowhere to be seen. Also, it was only once she'd arrived that she remembered she didn't know the outcome of his battle with the Countess. Had he survived? She shuddered and clasped her upper arms in spite of the heat. How would she face battling the Countess if she no longer had the guidance of Motsumi? She wandered around the Deeper Depths, hoping to find Aaron. He was the only person she felt she could trust. He'd taken the rap for her when she'd almost been caught spying on the Countess. And she knew that he was often on rock collection duty down here. After walking for a few moments, she spotted his crouching figure. He was sifting through a pile of rocks, dropping some into a metal bucket at his side and tossing others away. He had his back to her and only turned around as the sound of her footsteps disturbed him. He broke into a smile and stood up as he recognised her. The smoke must have obscured his vision at this distance so he hadn't yet noticed her eyes.

"Naledi! It's good to see you again. We weren't expecting you here this early."

She walked closer to him. When she was a couple of feet away his smile dropped. His chin dipped as he looked at her, from under a furrowed brow.

"Naledi?..." he angled his body away as if he didn't trust what he was seeing.

"It's okay, it's me," Naledi said. "I know my eyes don't look human. It's a long story."

Naledi sat on a rock next to Aaron and told him her sorry tale. When she'd finished Aaron replied.

"Whoa! You really do have to kill the Countess now. Your life depends upon it."

"That's right and I have no idea how much time I have left. Days? Hours?... It's terrifying." Naledi gulped and shook her head sadly.

"Do you know where I can find Motsumi? Did he survive the Countess' attack?"

"He did and I know where to find him. But I don't think you should go walking around. The Countess has spies everywhere. We'll have to hide you. You wait down here and I'll go and get Motsumi."

Naledi nodded and sat down as Aaron walked briskly off in the direction of Hell Central.

AFTER WHAT SEEMED LIKE AGES, in Naledi's state of agitation, she breathed a sigh of relief as she saw Aaron returning. Then her eyes scrunched up in puzzlement as she saw that he was accompanied by not only Motsumi but also a couple of other ladies.

What are they doing here?

She recognised one of the women as being the wicked spirit who administered the newly-damned waiting room. The way in which her short, purple-rinsed hair matched the colour of the thread-veins around her jowly face, was unforgettable. Naledi's enduring memory of that lady was of her touching a newly-damned man's forehead.

This had caused a blood-curdling scream of pain to emanate from his mouth before he'd passed out.

ONCE THE FOUR of them reached her, Motsumi stepped forward, a sheepish look on his face. "Aaron has explained everything to us. Allow me to introduce you to the others. Motsumi gestured to the wicked spirit administrator from the newly-damned waiting room, "This is Maureen." The lady dipped her head slightly as she adjusted her cat-eye glasses on her nose and smiled. "And this is Susan." Susan smiled and waved, bopping from foot to foot in the manner of a five year old who'd just heard the music of a nearby ice cream van. Susan had red hair, large green eyes and a pale, freckly complexion. She reminded Naledi of a woman who starred in an American soap opera which Tau often watched. Motsumi explained further, "they are fellow members of Sinners Anonymous." He looked at Naledi, apparently to gauge her reaction before continuing. "I had to give them a report of what we learnt at the Akashic realm. When they heard there was a heavenly twilight realm, they begged to accompany us. You don't mind do you?"

Naledi looked at Aaron, Susan and Maureen. She couldn't think of any reason why they shouldn't come. After all, Motsumi was a damned soul and he was coming. She didn't know the women but, if Motsumi and Aaron trusted them, then she would too. She smiled at them reassuringly, "no, of course not," she replied. Then she looked again at Motsumi. "What happened between you and the Countess? How did you get away from her?"

Motsumi shrugged, "I defeated her. She was injured but she'll regenerate quickly. I think her pride was more damaged than anything." Motsumi fidgeted slightly and Naledi wondered if he was being truthful. What reason would he have to lie about this? She studied his face closely but his features remained as impassive as ever. Naledi reminded herself that he was the smoothest liar she'd ever met. If he was being dishonest, she'd never know. She brushed the thought from her mind and turned to the others. "Has Motsumi told you what is involved in this trip? Who we need to find and the trial it will entail for me?"

The others nodded. Aaron in particular looked rather pale, nervous even. It occurred to Naledi that this was a big deal for him. He'd been in Hell for over two hundred years and now, for the first time, he was leaving. Susan on the other hand was brimming over with excitement. "Just tell us if there's anyway in which we can help."

Maureen chimed in. "Yes, we're trying to turn our lives around - better late than never, right?"

Susan's smile dropped. "*You're* trying to turn your lives around." She gestured at Aaron, Maureen and Motsumi. "I'm trying to get back to my rightful place in Heaven."

Maureen rolled her eyes. "Yeah, yeah, you were soul snatched, we get it." She looked at Naledi, "she never misses an opportunity to remind us that we're sinners but she's here by accident."

Susan shrugged, "well I just think it's important to clarify. It's not that I think I'm better than anyone else here but..."

"You do *so* think you're better than us," Maureen shot back.

"No I don't," Susan protested.

"Ladies, please! Can't we just focus on the matter at hand?" Aaron implored. He sighed wearily and shook his head in a manner which illustrated that he spent too much of his time breaking up squabbles between these two.

MOTSUMI SPOKE UP, "let's not waste anymore time. Naledi, if you please..." he put one arm forward for her to open the portal. Naledi inwardly bristled. Motsumi put on a good show of caring about her and Giada but she knew he was only concerned with securing his demon status. She kept these thoughts to herself though. It would do her no good to antagonise him when she needed his help with defeating the Countess. She turned her thoughts inwards, closing her eyes as she began to summon her powers. She was relieved to feel the familiar crackle of energy as she stretched out her hands and felt for the threads of reality.

At least I still have my breacher powers - for now.

Next she focused her attention on the heavenly realm and when she was certain she'd got the location right, she tore open a portal. She heard a gasp from Susan as she opened her eyes. Brilliant gold light shone into the Deeper Depths and Naledi held her hand up to her face to shield her eyes. The smell of honeysuckle and jasmine filled the air. She felt a light breeze and a perfect temperature caress her skin as she stepped through the portal. Motsumi and the other SA members flanked her. Naledi looked up ahead and saw a line of people queuing in front of the balding man who she now knew was Saint Peter. She and Motsumi had travelled here once before when he was teaching her how to harness her breacher powers but they hadn't been allowed through the heavenly gates. She looked at Motsumi. "How should we approach this? Do we just ask around for Tan Ti Han?"

Motsumi shrugged, "I suppose so".

They walked up to the queue and started asking the souls who stood waiting there. Nobody knew what they were talking about and one or two of them were visibly freaked out by Maureen's red-ringed eyes. "I should've warn sunglasses," she hissed under her breath. Naledi was glad that hers were less noticeable. They decided it was best to wait in line and ask Saint Peter, he was bound to know.

"Tan Ti Han? Sure, she sits in a dimension that is just a few degrees below ours."

Naledi blinked at him as if he was speaking in Greek. "Sorry Saint Peter but I don't understand."

He smiled at her. "You have to sit in meditation and then this reality will shift and you'll see her."

Naledi scratched her head. "But doesn't that mean some of us won't see her?"

"Maybe, it depends how well-practiced you are at meditating. Now if you don't mind, I have work to do here." Saint Peter gestured for them to move to one side as he ushered forward the next heavenly admittance.

Naledi huddled closer to the others. "Actually, it doesn't matter if we can't all see her. All we're doing here is finding out where the pool of vitality is. Why don't the rest of you go and explore whilst I try and find her?"

They all agreed and the other SA members wandered off whilst Motsumi stayed by Naledi. They both sat down and entered into deep meditation.

As Naledi calmed her mind she said an affirmation, stating her intention to meet Tan Ti Han. Presently, she heard an alluring female voice laughing. Naledi opened her mind's eye and saw a woman sitting cross-legged in front of her. The woman was much younger than Naledi had been expecting. Indeed, when the Lords of the Akashic had said *witch*, Naledi had expected a hideous, toothless old crone. This woman was nothing of the sort. She was beautiful and looked only a few years older than Naledi. She had lustrous dark hair, in two long plaits which hung down to her tummy. Feathers adorned her hair and scarification markings were arranged in symmetrical patterns on her face. She wore a suede bralet and knee length suede skirt, both embroidered with floral designs. In one hand she carried a short stick with a bird's wing tied to it. Around where she sat, crystals were arranged in a circle. The woman smiled at Naledi and she felt herself burst with joy.

"I am Tan Ti Han - the one you seek. You are Naledi, the breacher." Her voice was husky and inviting.

"How did you know?" Naledi replied.

"I know everything that I need to know at any given time." She paused and cocked her head to one side. Her keen eyes twinkled with a depth of knowledge such as Naledi had not encountered before. "You're wondering how it comes to pass that I, a witch, am able to reside in a heavenly realm? You're wondering why I'm not in Hell?"

Naledi felt herself blush as she looked down. "Yes" she said, feeling relief that Tan Ti Han had voiced her question so she wouldn't have to.

The reply was not what Naledi expected. "You are so blinded by bigotry. It's a shame as you have such potential, but your upbringing has made you blinkered to the spectrum of good and evil, which exists in all dimensions. Not all witches are evil you know."

Naledi thought about this for a moment. "By that logic not all angels are good" she said.

"Amen," Tan Ti Han replied. "Satan was an angel, was he not?"

Naledi couldn't fault this logic. As much as she wanted to continue this fascinating conversation she had a job to do. She was mindful of her companions waiting for her and of Giada on her deathbed.

"If you know all you need to know, then you must know what I come to ask of you?"

"Indeed I do. You wish for me to heal the minion Giada Cantinelli." Tan Ti Han smiled at Naledi. "But are you ready for the trial you must undertake for me in return?"

"I am ready."

"We shall see." The witch looked intently at Naledi. "Your affliction is not your biggest problem right now."

Naledi felt her face curl up into an expression of disbelief but she kept quiet and listened further.

"Your bigger problem is that you don't see the opportunity within it..."

"Opportunity?"

"...Your problem is linked to your bigotry. You must embrace your shadow to defeat the Countess. Accept all sides of yourself, dark and light and you will be invincible."

Naledi tried to keep an open mind but inside she felt herself scoffing. It was the kind of hooey nonsense she often heard charlatan traditional healers, giving to gullible believers. The kinds of people who had no power or training but took your money and offered you 'advice' with no real substance.

Tan Ti Han laughed and Naledi had a horrible suspicion that she'd read her thoughts but the witch had the good grace not to say anything. Changing the topic Tan Ti Han said, "the pool of vitality resides in the shadow realm. It is only accessible by means of ancestral magic. You must summon the help of your ancestors whilst in the heavenly realm and then, with their help, you will gain access to the realm. Once there, you will face your greatest adversary."

"How do I summon the help of my ancestors?"

"You connect with them in meditation and prayer, as with angels."

Naledi laughed slightly awkwardly. "Can you give me any advice on how to overcome my adversary?"

"No I cannot. This is a challenge that is highly personal and only you will know how to conquer her. What I can say though is that if you fail, she will kill you. That is why I asked if you were ready."

Naledi felt the blood drain from her face. This was immense pressure. Her life hung in the balance and she had no idea if she was ready or not. How could she know she was ready when she didn't yet know what or who she would be facing? There was no way she could prepare for such a challenge. Her only hope was that the challenges she'd faced in life up until now had been sufficient preparation. She gulped back her fears and thanked Tan Ti Han. "Can I come and visit you again?" she asked. She didn't know why but she felt drawn to this witch and wanted to continue their conversation.

"Not only can you come and visit me again, you will have to." Tan Ti Han looked knowingly at Naledi but didn't expand on what she meant and as Naledi started to ask, the witch faded. The meeting had come to a natural conclusion. She would now face the pool of vitality and the trial that accompanied it, whether she was ready or not.

22

NALEDI

∽

Naledi walked through mist as she pushed through a thicket of bushes. It was dark and silent except for the crickets chirping and bull frogs croaking. This realm seemed so much like Earth but there was something slightly off about it. Not something she could name but something that she sensed. When she closed her eyes and breathed deeply, her inner sight perceived her companions from Hell waiting for her in the heavenly twilight realm. She saw Motsumi sitting in deep meditation so that he could watch her progress and intervene if necessary.

Naledi's ancestors had transmitted telepathic visions revealing the location of the pool of vitality to her. It was in a non-physical realm and she'd had to travel here in her astral form, with her body still sitting in meditation in Heaven. She now followed the path as it stretched downhill. Looking up at the night sky she smiled as shafts of light, cast by the beautiful full moon, shone across the glade. At her ears flitted delicate fairies, chattering with curiosity and at her feet scurried gnomes and the occasional tokoloshe. She gritted her teeth and tried not to succumb to fear at the strangeness of the realm.

After about ten minutes of walking, she came to the location. The pool was in front of her but there was an impenetrable force field stopping her from accessing it. This was as expected - the ancestors had told her she would only gain access once she'd defeated her adversary. She looked around amongst the trees for a suitable fighting stick. It was all she knew how to defend herself with. Once she'd located a sturdy looking staff, she assumed a fighting stance. She placed her left foot forward and right foot back with knees slightly bent and she held the staff in a position of readiness. Her eyes flicked from side to side. She tensed at every slight noise of which there were many. The seconds ticked by. She could hear her heart pounding and she tried to steady her breathing. Naledi decided to practice a few stick fighting moves whilst she waited. She thrashed her stick from side to side. Warming up and releasing nervous energy, she expelled explosive sounds from her mouth and shook her hands out.

What was that?

Hearing a stick break, she whirled around to see who was coming. Straining her eyes in the darkness, she made out a figure moving through the thick bushes. The figure stepped into the clearing and raised her head. Naledi gasped and staggered back with shock. The person who had appeared was her exact double. She was the same height, she wore the same clothes - she even had the same body language. Looking at herself was the most surreal experience Naledi had ever had. Her doppelganger also carried a fighting staff. As Naledi inspected it, the stick looked exactly like the one she'd just found among the trees in the clearing. It was beyond spooky. Her adversary stood facing her with her eyes closed. Naledi took a step forward intending to attack first but at that moment her adversary's eyes opened. The deep, pure red eyes took Naledi's breath away. She gasped and staggered backwards as fear began to overwhelm her. She was looking at herself in demon form. Split-second thoughts raced around Naledi's head

Is that me in the future? Am I destined to lose and become a demon?

It was her greatest fear and worst nightmare come true and she felt both weak and nauseous. Her instinct told her to run away as far and as fast as possible. She realised her hands were shaking and she felt herself swoon. As the world started to dim she sank down to the ground and put her head between her knees. Looking back up at her own demon form, her adversary threw her head back and roared with laughter. Raising the fighting staff in the air in victory as she spat on the floor near Naledi. Her eyes were filled with scorn and her lip curled in contempt.

I can't do it. I can't, thought Naledi.

Naledi had neither the strength nor the will to get up from the ground. She felt darkness enveloping her soul and she wished her mom was there to comfort her. A large tear rolled down her cheek and she wiped it away. Then she heard a familiar voice inside her head. It was Motsumi. He was remote viewing her in his meditative state.

Get up Naledi. Get up and fight! Your life depends upon it.

His voice penetrated her veil of fear and she gritted her teeth. She shook her head and blew out air from her lips as she gathered her courage. She counted out loud,

"One, two…" and before she said three, she sprang up, sweeping her staff upwards to make contact with her adversary's chin. The demon turned her face with lightning speed and Naledi missed. Undeterred, she tried again, now swinging her staff in a rapid figure of eight to confuse the demon before twirling around to hit her back. This time she hit her target but her enemy spun around and whacked her across the face. The sting of the staff was like a red-hot poker and Naledi was surprised by how much it hurt considering she wasn't in her physical body. She recalled a conversation with Motsumi in which he'd explained that the mind is a powerful thing. If she was in her astral body, she would still feel physical pain, as the mind would make it so. She could also still be killed.

Coming back to the present moment she changed tack. She dropped her staff and charged forward, roaring a determined battle cry. Barrelling into the demon's torso, she dragged her down to the ground. Wrestling was not something she was trained in but she knew she had little chance of defeating a demon at night by stick fighting. Their eyes were way better at seeing in the dark. Perhaps her chances would be better at close combat. The ground was slightly wet and soon they were both covered in mud. Naledi grabbed fistfuls of the demon's hair, pulling at it with one hand as she tried to gouge out her eye with the other. She tried to choke her but found her hands were too slippery both with sweat and mud. Her adversary punched her in the eye and Naledi cried out in pain as stars blossomed in her vision. She felt something trickle down the side of her face and wondered if she was bleeding.

Is it possible for me to bleed in my astral form?

Naledi rolled out of the way, grabbing her fighting staff again as she scrambled to her feet. She had no idea what to try next as she stood there panting. She bent to rest one hand on her knee, supporting her weight against the fighting staff. Sweat dripped from her forehead. She struck out once more with her fighting staff. Remembering what her great grandmother had taught her about guarding her left, she tried to hide her *tells*. She was determined not to give the other fighter an advantage. However it was no use. Naledi's adversary anticipated her every move and bested her at every turn. With growing dismay, Naledi realised there was no way she could beat this demon. How could she beat herself when she knew her every move? She and her adversary were too evenly matched, it was impossible.

Then, just as she was starting to lose hope, she heard Motsumi's voice once more.

Stop trying to beat her with physical strength. She is you. You know your own weaknesses. Your psychological weaknesses. Use those against her.

Naledi listened as she fought. Their sticks clashed, meeting strike for strike in the moonlight as a cuckoo called in a tree above. The problem was, Naledi didn't really know herself; she was still finding herself. Wasn't that what this challenge was all about? Wasn't that why she was here fighting herself in an astral realm, armed with only a stick and a bunch of damned souls as companions? Naledi sprang up again, leaping into the air as she aimed the pointed end of her stick at her adversary. The demon dodged out of the way and Naledi tripped and staggered forwards. In a second, her adversary was on top of her. The demon jumped onto her back, wrapping both legs around her middle. She wrapped both hands around Naledi's neck and began to throttle her.

Naledi grabbed at her adversary's hands but the demon's grip was too strong. Flailing her arms out to the sides, Naledi tried to find purchase by pressing her thumbs into her adversary's eyes. The demon jerked her head back and tightened her grip on Naledi's throat. Naledi felt panic rise in her chest as her vision began to blur. With mounting desperation, she realised she was about to pass out. She'd lost and would now die in the shadow realm, all alone. Nobody on Earth would ever know what had happened to her.

In those final moments she thought of Dineo and Puleng and of Tau. Tears rolled down her face and onto the hands of the demon. Just as she was about to pass out, she sensed someone else nearby. The demon's hands released from her neck and Naledi fell to the floor, gasping for breath as she rubbed her neck. Looking up she saw her saviour. It was Motsumi. Naledi was surprised at the feeling of joy she felt at seeing him there. It was like the feeling she remembered experiencing as a young child whenever her father had returned home for the day.

He cares about me!

He bashed the adversary out of the way then offered a hand to Naledi.

"Come on let's go!" he shouted urgently. Naledi didn't wait to be told twice. She scrambled to her feet and sprinted off with him. The adversary didn't pursue them and, as they slowed to a walking pace, Naledi wondered about this.

"Why isn't she following us?"

"I believe she is just a device to protect the pool of vitality from those who are not yet ready for the gifts it brings."

Naledi felt her heart sink. "So I'm not ready yet."

"Apparently not."

She sighed, "but how are we going to heal Giada?"

Motsumi turned around to look at her, "I think we can do a deal with the witch. Let me negotiate with her. I'm good at that."

NALEDI AND MOTSUMI made it back to the heavenly realm where they were reunited with their friends from Hell. After breaking the news to everyone that Naledi had been unsuccessful, they sat in meditation to connect with Tan Ti Han. Once they were in her presence Naledi kept quiet and let Motsumi do the talking.

"You've failed, as I suspected you would and now you've come here to beg for my help anyway," the witch said.

"No, not beg. I have a proposition which I think you will find appealing."

Tan Ti Han raised her eyebrows at him then laughed as she looked at Naledi. "He's a confident one, isn't he?"

Naledi didn't answer but dipped her head to hide the slight smile she failed to suppress.

Motsumi pressed on, undeterred. "You come back with us to Hell Central and cure Giada. Then Naledi will come back here at a later date and defeat her adversary and give you the water, from the pool of vitality, which you desire."

Tan Ti Han had an expression on her face as if Motsumi had just offered her a handful of 'magic' beans in exchange for her prize cow. "What kind of an offer is that? Naledi might not even survive long enough to ever make good on the deal."

"That maybe so but how often do you get an initiate passing by here? There are very few who are able to travel to the shadow realm as easily as Naledi can. And you obviously don't want to go yourself or you wouldn't have asked us. It could be centuries before you get another chance to get this water." Naledi could see that Motsumi was studying Tan Ti Han's face closely and was surprised to see that the witch was seriously considering it.

"Alright. I accept." She fixed Motsumi with a glare before

extending her forefinger towards him. "But if you try to swindle me out of what I'm owed, I will curse you with a demonic illness far worse than you can imagine."

Motsumi shrugged, "fair enough."

A thought occurred to Naledi. "Tan Ti Han. Are you able to reverse the Countess' magic and make me fully human again?"

The witch's features softened with compassion. "I'm afraid not. You will have to kill her or you will become a demon."

Naledi sighed. She'd exhausted all her options. She felt the inescapable conveyor belt of destiny moving her closer and closer to a fight that she could not escape and scarcely hoped to win.

23

GIADA

∼

Giada was lost, staggering through a desert. The searing heat of the sun beat down on her bare shoulders. She tried to cover them with the rags that she wore. Her lips were cracked and painful. Her throat was parched. She was so thirsty. She'd been walking for days and could find no relief, no water anywhere. If she didn't find water soon she would surely die. She could hardly open her eyes. The light of the sun, reflected on the desert planes was dazzling. Lifting her arm to shield her vision from the blinding brightness, she felt her shoulders relax as her knees gave way with relief. It was an oasis. She was saved! She rushed forward, bursting with happiness as her legs sank into the sand with each step. She waded through the sand but with each step that she took, the oasis seemed further and further away. Her face crumpled with despair as she realised it was just a mirage. But wait - there was someone in the distance. She recognised the figure, someone she'd known her whole life.

No, it couldn't be, could it? Surely not?

She ran, this time more sure footed as the sand seemed to harden.

It pushed her onward, closer and closer to the woman who approached her. A familiar voice called her name, giving her comfort and joy. It was her mother and she was calling her name, softly at first and then with more urgency.

"Giada... Giada...Giada it's me, wake up, Giada"

Her mother reached forward and held a cold flannel to her face. Giada sat up abruptly, waking from the dream she'd been in.

For a moment Giada didn't know where she was. Looking to the side of the make shift bed she was lying on, she recognised her mother's face immediately and smiled. In that same instant, she remembered that she was in Hell and she was dead. She felt her smile drop. She recoiled with fear and panic. What was her mother doing here? She patted herself down, recalling her poisoning. Was this another hallucination brought on by the toxin? Was she still dreaming? She'd been close to death. She'd expected to die.

It feels real...

She saw the faces of her friends from Sinners Anonymous around her bed. Aaron, Maureen, Susan, Motsumi and also Naledi. There was another young woman there with long plaits who she didn't recognise. The woman whispered a few things that Giada couldn't hear to Motsumi and Naledi and then walked through a portal at the side of the room. Naledi closed the portal but stayed in the room.

What is going on here?

Giada's head hurt and she struggled to get her thoughts clear as the effects of the hell sprite venom worked its way out of her system. Then it all came back to her. Naledi had arrived to save her.

Aaron stepped forward and crouched down by her bed. Just behind him, her mother stood, anxiously looking at her. "Giada, I know this is confusing," Aaron began. "We travelled to a heavenly realm and Naledi brought back a witch to heal you. She's the lady who you just saw leaving, a very talented healer called Tan Ti Han."

Giada felt her eyebrows crease. "But how did she get here if she was in Heaven?"

Motsumi explained. "She's a realm walker - a being who can enter any realm, Earth, Heaven or Hell."

Giada looked again at her mother. The confusion on her face must have been obvious. Maureen looked at Aaron. Some type of unspoken agreement passed between them and she stepped forward and knelt by Giada's bed. Aaron stood up and stepped back.

"Giada, your mother turned up at the newly-damned waiting room earlier today. I recognised her surname and saw the family resemblance. I realised who she was and brought her here."

Giada was so overwhelmed. She was still weak from the ravages of the venom but she sat up and rubbed her bleary eyes. Her mother stood looking at her. She wrung her hands as her face creased with worry.

"Mama?" Giada murmured.

Her mother rushed forward and knelt by her side in front of Maureen. She traced a finger over the side of her face, tenderly tucking a wave of hair that was stuck to her face, behind her ear. "I'm here my bambina."

"It is really you?" Giada croaked.

"Yes it's really me, amore."

"But... did... did you die?"

Her mother's face softened with such love and compassion, Giada felt her lower lip begin to tremble.

"Yes I died. We were in a car crash, do you remember? Is that when you died too?"

Giada nodded. She looked down and felt both her lips now quivering uncontrollably. Her mother dipped her head down too and put one hand under Giada's chin to lift her face up.

"Hey, hey, it's okay Giada. I'm here now." She leant forward and enclosed Giada in a hug. Giada felt such love radiating from her mother, she wished she could cry. She felt her entire body shaking with relief, remorse but also joy. Positive and negative emotions bombarded her one after another. Her mother was here. She'd wished for this to be true from the moment she'd arrived in Hell. But also, her mother was here - what had she done to end up in Hell? What sin had her mother possibly committed? Giada frowned. This didn't make sense. If she'd died at the same time as Giada, where had she been for the last couple of months? Giada reluctantly pulled away from her mother's embrace.

"Where've you been? All this time? I've been here but you... were you in another part of Hell?"

Her mother's eyes shifted from side to side before she answered quietly. "No. I was in Heaven."

Giada sat up abruptly. "Heaven? Then how come you're here?"

Her mother looked up at Motsumi and Naledi, opening and then closing her mouth. Naledi and Motsumi exchanged a glance and Motsumi stepped forward. His nervous grin was that of a man who had just entered an antique shop only to knock a priceless vase onto the floor.

"Allow me to explain. You see, we wanted to make you better but until now there has been no known antidote for hell sprite venom. We travelled to the Akashic realm to secure an answer from the Lords who reside there. They are the source of all universal knowledge. They told us that the witch, Tan Ti Han, could cure you."

Giada still didn't understand how this had caused her mother to be damned. Motsumi continued, "regrettably, we were unable to source adequate payment for our question. The Lords require a human body part for each person whose question they answer. Failure to pay results in payment being taken from the subject's ancestral lineage. In this case the Lords decided to take payment by decreeing that your mother be sentenced to an eternity in Hell."

At this, both Giada and her mother whipped their heads up to face him, "*an eternity?!*" they chorused.

"I'm afraid so." Motsumi's sombre expression highlighted the gravity of the situation.

Giada looked at her mother whose mouth had dropped open. Her mama started gasping and stood up, reaching out her hand to paw at the nearest person, which, in this case, was Aaron. "I can't breathe... I think I'm going to pass out."

"Just sit there," he gestured to the edge of Giada's bed. "Put your head between your knees."

Giada's mama did as instructed and her breathing began to calm down. After a few seconds she lifted her head again. Her face was red and blotchy. She looked at Giada, her face contorting with rage.

"You bargained my life in eternal bliss to spare your own miserable life in Hell?" she spat.

"No! No Mama, I didn't bargain anything, I was unconscious. I didn't know what they were doing."

"Lies! You've always been a deceitful little brat. You just take and you take and you take and now, even in death you..." she raised a hand to strike Giada but Motsumi lunged forward and grabbed her hand.

"Madam, Giada is telling the truth. None of us had any idea this would result in your damnation. You have to believe us. We acted with the best of intentions. You may think that Giada's life in Hell is worth little but believe it or not, she's relatively happy here. If she had died she would've been reborn in another hell dimension, one which would likely have been far worse."

"How can it get any worse than Hell?" Her mama's eyebrows rose up in an expression of incredulity as she gesticulated with her hands.

Aaron stepped forward. "Giada is on a redemption path. We believe that we can and will be granted access to Heaven some day. You can join our movement too, any damned souls are welcome."

"But *I* am not a damned soul! I was in Heaven, living a life of perfection and happiness."

"Perhaps that was a poor choice of words but you're still welcome. We meet every Tuesday night. Giada can tell you more."

Giada's mother swore in Italian. "This is preposterous. Isn't there a way I can speak to someone to get out of here?"

Susan piped up. "That's exactly what I said when I first arrived here. You see, I'm not supposed to be here either. I was soul-snatched. That's when a demon visits you at the moment of death and dupes you into following him to Hell instead of Heaven."

Giada's mother stared blankly at Susan so Motsumi explained further. "Just to clarify, what Susan means. No. There is nobody you can talk to. Once you're here, you're stuck here."

Giada's Mum started shaking, her chest heaved and her face grew redder. She rushed at Giada, roaring, "Raargh!" Climbing onto Giada's bed, she scrambled on top of her. As she straddled her, she started throttling her. Giada tried to push her off but she was still too weak.

Her mother spat in her face, incandescent with rage. "You good for nothing piece of.... You've ruined my life! You were worthless while you were alive and now you're even less than worthless. How could you? How could you do this to me?! I'll kill you!" Her face contorted into a rictus snarl. "I'll kill you!"

Aaron and Motsumi rushed forward and pulled her off as Giada coughed, recovering her breath as she rubbed her sore neck. Her throat felt raw and tight but more than that her heart was breaking from her mother's hateful words. Memories of many such moments of cruelty came flooding back. Her Mother's unrealistic expectations of her. Her mother's disappointment that she wasn't more like her brother. Her mother's abandonment of her as soon as her precious jewel and favoured child, Roberto, had arrived in their life. She'd always been a cruel woman. Heartless, cold and vindictive. It was no wonder that Giada had turned out the way she had and Giada now struggled to remember why she'd yearned for her mother since her arrival in Hell. She'd wanted the unconditional love of a mother but her mother's love had never been of that type. It had always come as part of a package laden with spite and carelessness. She'd never been good enough for her mother. That had become even more apparent as soon as there was a 'better' child with which to compare her unfavourably. Indeed there was something almost ruthless about her mother, a quality that she shared with the Countess. Maybe that was why she had settled into the Countess' household so seamlessly. It was the same kind of Hell as the one that she'd endured whilst at home. In spite of these thoughts of judgement towards her mother, a deep pain gripped Giada's heart. She still wanted her mother to adore her, as she had done when she'd been a young child. She still sought her approval and her acceptance. She still wanted to please her. More than redemption, more than God's love, more than anything.

Giada wanted her mother to love her.

24

NALEDI

∼

After her failure at the pool of vitality, Naledi's already shaky self-confidence plummeted. Giada suggested that Naledi bunk in the same dungeon as her. A bed had recently become available as one of the other minions had progressed onto wicked spirit status and moved out. Actually 'bed' was too kind a word for it. It was a stone slab with no blankets or pillow. Not that you would need blankets in the searing heat of Hell. Motsumi performed a cloaking spell to alter Naledi's appearance. This would keep her safe from the Countess until she was ready to take her on. All Naledi wanted to do was curl up into a ball and lick her wounds for a day or two but Motsumi insisted they continue training.

"We don't have time to nurse your wounded pride Naledi. It's in all of our interests that you become powerful enough to beat the Countess."

Naledi had lost her temper at that point. "Why do I always have to be the one with my life on the line? Why can't you kill her?"

Motsumi had rounded on her, his eyes blazing. "I am not a breacher anymore or have you forgotten? You're the only one who can kill her, she has to be pushed onto Earth by a breacher. Your life is on the line, not mine. Any day now you will turn into a demon and then you'll be stuck here for eternity."

You only care about your stupid demon promotion anyway!

Naledi wanted to say but she gritted her teeth and held her tongue.

MOTSUMI HAD INSTRUCTED her to meet him back at the Deeper Depths the following day to recommence their training. Walking through the extreme heat, beads of sweat broke out on her upper lip. She tried to hold her nose to avoid the foul-smelling sulphurous smoke. Even though she'd been to the Deeper Depths several times, she still hadn't gotten used to how scary the many parasites were. They now shrieked and swooped above her head as if taunting her. After a few minutes of walking, she arrived at her destination. It was the same series of dark caves in which they'd met the day before. Motsumi was already inside and shone a torch light in her direction as she entered. The torch was probably unnecessary as Naledi's red-ringed eyes were better at seeing in the dark. But she was touched at his considerate gesture nonetheless. After a cursory greeting, he started the lesson. He placed the torch on the floor to provide dim lighting for the cave. As he did this, Naledi settled herself on the floor, cross-legged. Motsumi paced back and forth with his hands clasped behind his back.

"You have mastered the basics of meditation and your skill as a breacher cannot be disputed," he began. "Now you must master the other 7 skills of the adept. Skill one: knowledge of past lives. Skill two: healing. Skill three is visions of other dimensions. This is close to the skill you already possess as a breacher so we will skip this for the sake of expediency. Skill four: suspension of gravity. This includes the ability to walk on water, flying and levitation. Skill number five is immunity to pain - I believe Aaron has already mastered this so he will be teaching you this module. Skill six is control of the elements. The Countess is especially proficient at this so it is important that you master it to a high level. With this skill, you will be able to control earth, air, fire, water and electricity. The final skill, number seven, is wish-fulfilment or manifestation. This is the ability to call into being whatever your heart desires. With this skill you can move mountains and build empires but in your case, you could create monsters to battle against the Countess, for example."

Naledi felt helpless as she listened to him. How would she even remember all this, let alone learn how to master each skill?

Motsumi walked closer to Naledi, oblivious to her concerns. He bent down so that his face was inches away from hers. "You have such great potential Naledi. I see it in your auric field, more so now that I am dead. Preparing to battle the Countess is part of your destiny. If you work hard and apply yourself, you will become the greatest sangoma the world has ever known."

Naledi felt his words penetrate her heart like an arrow. She hadn't sought this path, it had sought her. She had been resistant at first but now it called to her as surely as a mother hen calls to its chicks. This is where she belonged and she could see no other way to proceed in life except by means of this path. The realisation of this both startled and terrified her. It was at odds with everything she had been taught as a Christian. What did following this path mean for her soul in the afterlife? But equally, what would abandoning this path mean for her safety in this life? This was her dilemma. She felt guilty about ignoring the warnings of her Christian upbringing about sorcery and witchcraft. Yet, she also had to protect herself. In her opinion, God wasn't protecting her or her loved ones to the level that she needed. She felt guilty even articulating these feelings internally - as if she was committing blasphemy. The conflict in her heart was further fuelled by Nkhono. She had looked up to her great grandmother so much. Whilst she'd been alive, Nkhono had told her that this path was good and pure and right. She'd said it was the way of her ancestors, part of her heritage and to deny it was wrong. Nkhono had taught her that it was the white man who had brainwashed their people into believing that the bible was right and belief in magic and the ancestors was wrong.

Naledi was so confused at this point, she no longer knew who to listen to or who to trust. But she knew one thing: what was in her heart. Her heart cried out for this path. It called to her as she awoke and was the last thing on her mind before she slept. She could no longer ignore it. Ignoring it before had driven her crazy and accepting it had saved her from life in a mental institution. She had to at least explore where this path led. If she was going to pursue this path, she would give it her all and do her best to excel. She forced her thoughts back to the present moment as Motsumi asked her,

"Do you have any questions before we begin?"

"No, Molume."

"Good." Motsumi smiled, putting his arms behind his back. "Onto the knowledge of past lives then."

THE LESSON entailed going on a mental journey. It reminded Naledi of the time she had journeyed into her body to view her internal organs during one of the very first lessons she'd had with Motsumi. This time however, she was guided to imagine some kind of flying beast. She'd been surprised to see a phoenix, its large red feathers, shining iridescent in the Lesotho sunshine. It pecked at the ground, moving its head in the same jerky fashion as a pigeon. She couldn't recall ever having seen an image of a phoenix in any book or TV show so she was confused as to how she even recognised it. Motsumi explained that she'd met this bird in previous lives and he was her regular companion. She had ridden on him before through the multiverse to view past lives; to meet beings from other dimensions and so many other journeys that they had made together. As he explained this, Naledi felt a warm feeling of affinity stir up in her heart. She walked forward to stroke the wings of the giant bird. He was warm and soft and made a gentle cooing sound.

The phoenix turned its head and looked at her in the eye and in this same moment she felt it transmit its thoughts. It was reminding her of its name: *Moeti*, which meant *traveller* in Sesotho. Moeti dipped his head down and Naledi climbed on his back. She clung onto the feathers around his neck as he pushed off from his feet. He flapped his great wings and rose into the air. As he flew, wind rushed past Naledi and she flattened her chest flush against his back. She had the sense that she was flying through a place similar to the time and space bubbles which Motsumi had often spoken to her from, arresting her from her nightly dream time. They flew beyond space and time, arriving at a land which was familiar yet far away. A place from her distant memories, before she was born, in a previous life. The life which was the most important for her to heal from in order to progress forward to the next skill set.

OVER THE NEXT FEW DAYS, Naledi journeyed to her most formative past lives. She remembered lives in which she'd been male, lives in which she'd been other races, from other countries. Lives in which she'd been rich and lives in which she'd been poor. She'd been a servant, a slave, a rich baroness, an emperor. Each life taught her something about her current life: why she feared certain things; why she had aches and pains in certain parts of her body and why her personality was shaped the way it was. Some of it was from this life and Moeti also showed her these things, early childhood memories which she'd entirely forgotten but which were poignant and essential to her journey and learning at this point in her life. The lessons left her pensive and profoundly changed. It was like ten years of psychotherapy distilled into a few days. A crash course in self-development.

AFTER HER FOURTH day in Hell, Naledi lay on her stone bed, staring at the stone ceiling of the dungeon. She missed Tau so very much. She wished she could see him or even just hear his voice. Her friends in Sinners Anonymous had made sure they kept her existence here a secret. As far as all the other minions were concerned, she was just another minion on the up. She was soon to be promoted to wicked spirit as they could see from her red eyes. She tried her best to blend in without drawing attention to herself. In spite of her friends here doing their best to keep her spirits up, she felt lonely and increasingly desperate. As she lay there she wondered what Tau was doing at this very moment. She decided it was a good opportunity to practice her remote viewing.

Naledi closed her eyes and focused on her breathing as she got an image of Tau in her mind's eye. She was able to connect with him quickly and the thrill of success brought a smile to her face. She saw Tau sitting on his sofa, whittling a piece of wood into an animal. Around the sofa were placed other wooden animals he'd obviously carved earlier. He would probably take the carvings to the main road and sell them. Naledi felt her smile deepen as she watched him work. He was oblivious to her presence but that made him even more enchanting to look at. The familiar outline of his jaw and hunch of his posture gave her a small taste of home. There was a knock at Tau's door and he stood up to go and see who it was. Naledi watched him walking to the front door.

A HOODED FIGURE stood at the doorway with her back turned. Naledi instantly got a queasy feeling in her stomach and her muscles tensed.

Something is not right here.

The woman turned around and Naledi's heart jumped into her mouth. It was the Countess' tulpa. It had come back to kill Tau just as she had feared. The tulpa withdrew a large machete from inside her cloak and advanced towards Tau, grinning maniacally. Tau staggered backwards, stumbling over the wooden carvings as he went. The tulpa slashed at him but he dodged out of the way, at the same time crouching to pick up his whittling knife. It was pitifully small compared to the tulpa's machete. Naledi felt her heart thumping as she clenched her fists. She had to help Tau. Without even thinking of what the consequences would be for herself, Naledi got off the bed and summoned her powers. She breached a portal back to Earth and into Tau's house.

Tau's eyes grew wide as he saw her appear. The tulpa had him cornered by the kitchen. As Naledi entered, the creature turned around and grinned devilishly, switching its focus from Tau to Naledi. The tulpa strode forward, machete outstretched, as it came towards her. This gave Tau enough time to open a kitchen drawer and get out a kitchen knife. Naledi was relieved that at least this now made the fight fairer, but the creature was coming towards her and she had no idea how to fight it. Tau apparently had the same thought and he charged forward, leaping on top of the tulpa as he slashed his knife onto the creature's neck. Blood spurted from the wound but this didn't seem to slow it down. It twisted around and slashed at Tau's leg. He leapt off just as the blade sliced the front of his thigh. Tau cried out in pain

"Tau!" Naledi cried out, reaching her arm out to him. He limped as blood trickled down his leg, spreading out across his faded khaki trousers. The tulpa's head jerked towards Naledi and it started advancing in her direction. Tau was not giving up. He gritted his teeth. "come on then, let's do this!"

Naledi briefly reflected that she had never found him more attractive than in this moment. But she didn't have time to dwell on it. She scrambled backwards, tripping over a wooden chair, which she then grabbed and held in front of her as a makeshift shield.

Tau limped forwards, slashing his knife from side to side as he neared the tulpa. He didn't take his eyes off her for one minute. The creature was not to be easily bested. She leapt towards him in a suicidal manner. Tau's knife made contact with her shoulder, but it made no difference, she ignored the blood that splattered on the floor from her arm. Naledi watched in horror

She's going to kill him. I can't lose him again!

The thought shocked her into a moment of clarity and instinctively she held up her hands. As she did so, she felt the familiar electrical crackle of her powers. She felt for the threads of reality and tore them open then thrust her hands forward and pushed with all her might. The tulpa went tumbling into another dimension of reality and Naledi closed the portal up immediately and then slumped onto the floor, closing her eyes as she exhaled deeply. Tau rushed to her side and knelt down, cocooning her in his muscular arms. All at once the emotions that she had been holding back since the Countess had cursed her, came crashing down onto her. Her loneliness in Hell; her disappointment of her failure at the pool of vitality; and the enormity of the task that lay ahead of her. She burst into tears, dissolving into his arms like sugar in hot water. Tau didn't say a word but merely stroked her hair, comforting her with his physical presence. Through her tears, a flame of hope ignited inside of her as she had one thought:

I can cry, that means I'm still human!

AFTER THE FIGHT with the tulpa, Naledi knew that she should go back to Hell. She knew she was endangering her life by staying on Earth but she just couldn't face it. She wanted to forget about her worries and be a regular teenager spending time with her boyfriend. She wanted to feel normal for just one night. Tau offered to sleep on the sofa so that she could have his bed but she didn't want to be alone. She was too scared the tulpa would come back during the night and slit their throats as they slept. She didn't share her worries with Tau as she didn't want to give him nightmares but she didn't have to. She knew he had the same concerns. His furrowed brow and the wild, glassy sheen to his eyes told her that he was just as scared as she was.

Settling into his arms, in his bed, they both stared at the ceiling. He stroked her arm and neither of them felt like talking. As much as Naledi knew she should stay awake and on her guard, she was exhausted after having expended her breaching powers to destroy the tulpa. In spite of her best efforts to stay awake, she soon drifted off to sleep. Her sleep was restless and filled with disturbing and vivid dreams. In one of these dreams, all her teeth fell out. She tried desperately to put them back in but without success. She wept in the dream when she realised her efforts to reinsert the teeth were futile and she woke with tears at the corners of her eyes. Drenched with sweat she went to the bathroom to splash her face with water. Once there she saw her reflection in the mirror and she gasped. The full moon shone through the thin curtains, illuminating her face. The thin red line around the irises of her eyes had grown thicker.

25

GIADA

∼

After Tan Ti Han's healing session on Giada, she regained strength quickly and within a couple of days she was back to full strength. In spite of how strained Giada and her mother's relationship was, Giada managed to get her a permanent position working on the minion laundry team. Her mother had protested at first but Giada and Aaron had convinced her that this was the best place for her. She'd be less likely to be subjected to the regular beatings and torture sessions than if she were a maid. It also meant that Giada could visit her regularly although Giada had kept that part to herself.

Giada made her way down to the Deeper Depths where the laundry rooms were located. Clouds of thick black smoke obscured her vision and she coughed, wafting it away. Narrowing her eyes Giada located the laundry rooms. The entrance had a heavy metal door with a rubberised handle. It reminded Giada of the door to the walk-in fridge in her Aunt Stefania's restaurant, back in Rome.

Inside, plumes of steam and humidity replaced the smoke and dry heat of outside. Rows of sheets and other items of laundry hung from racks over tables set with detergent and scrubbing trays. Large tubs of steaming water on the floor contained soaking clothes. Giada knew that it was well within the technological capabilities of the Seventh Circle to provide washing machines and dryers but demons preferred to make jobs as difficult as possible for minions.

The wet floor was slippery and it would be easy to fall over if she wasn't careful. Giada walked gingerly between the rows of dead-eyed minions scrubbing monotonously at underpants and socks. She looked up to see a wicked spirit overseer. He stood on top of a large metal cupboard, holding a whip and pacing back and forth, as he fixed his steely gaze on each of the workers. Giada put her head back down quickly, trying to blend in with the other workers. She spotted her mother behind a mountain of damp clothes, which she was hanging up on a large rotating washing line. Giada wandered over, suddenly feeling the urge to put her hands in pockets, which were regrettably not there today. She was wearing a pair of pocketless slacks instead of her usual jeans. Instead Giada swung her arms back and forth. "Buon Giorno Mama" she greeted her mother in Italian. Then immediately felt silly for having used the formal term for 'good morning'.

Her mother looked up and her face soured when she saw Giada, "is it?" she replied.

Giada smiled nervously and pressed on. "How are you getting on here so far?"

Her mother pursed her lips, "as well as can be expected." She picked up a top and shook it out before pegging it to the line.

"How about the other minions - have you talked to any of them? What are they like?"

"They're okay, they're terrified and overworked, as you'd expect." Her mother didn't make eye contact and carried on with her work methodically.

The conversation was futile and Giada realised she'd never achieve any depth to the relationship with her mother unless she broke first so she took a deep breath. She looked up towards the ceiling before rushing her next sentence out in one long torrent.

"Look Mama, I know you're still angry and I can understand why you blame me. I just want you to know that I'm really sorry about the way everything turned out. If I could take it all back so that you were in Heaven again I would." She looked down to see her reaction. Her mother continued pegging a pair of trousers to the line. Her face was set in a mask of hostility. Waves of silent rage radiated out from her. Giada watched her jaw clench involuntarily. It was clearly taking all of her mother's will to reign in her anger. If Giada pushed her even slightly, she would explode with the strength of a volcanic eruption. Giada considered pushing her that tiny bit further. It would clear the air and get the resolution which she had been seeking by coming here. But was she ready for that? It would surely result in a confrontation but then their relationship was so bad. Would it make any difference? As she stood, silently brooding, watching her mother work, the decision was taken away from her.

"What are you still doing here?" her mother asked.

"I... I was hoping we could... talk."

There was a moment of silence before her mother spoke. Her eyes went misty as she gazed into the middle distance. "You know, after Roberto died, for years I..."

Giada interrupted, "oh here we go, as usual you can't let a single conversation pass by without mentioning your precious golden child Roberto." She spat out his name as if there was ash on her tongue.

Her mother's face went puce with rage. "Well he's not the one who went to Hell after he died, is he?"

The cruel taunt stung Giada worse than if she'd been slapped in the face. She shouted at her mother. "You always loved him more than me. You didn't even try to hide it. Most parents at least have the decency to pretend to love each child equally but you and Papa never even bothered." She hadn't been aware of taking any steps forward but suddenly she realised her face was inches away from her mother's. "I just want to know: what was so terrible about me, huh? What was so unlovable about me that even my own mother rejected me?"

Her mother's voice softened, "there was nothing terrible about you, Giada. Roberto was just younger and needed more help with things. We didn't love him more than you, you were just more capable than he was."

To Giada this excuse seemed hollow. It was a poorly devised alibi, trotted out to a policeman, who has just caught you with a body in the boot of your car. Her mother could lie to her all she liked but Giada knew the truth. She knew how she'd been treated, what she'd endured. Roberto had been their favourite, plain and simple.

Her mother continued, "For years after he died, I wished I could join him. I used to wonder if he'd gone to Heaven; if he still thought about me; if he missed me as much as I missed him. Then when I got to Heaven, he was waiting for me. He was so happy. Life there was perfect. I never knew it was possible to feel such endless love, such bliss. Then in the middle of another perfect day, there I was tending to my strawberry crop and the next thing I knew I was here. Snatched away in an instant, without warning."

Ah yes, your strawberry love affair - no wonder I could never stand the smell of them.

"What do you expect me to say Mama? I've already said I'm sorry. This wasn't my choice. You act like I want to be here."

"Why are you here anyway? I know you were a difficult child but eternal damnation?... How does it work here? Do you get to find out what sin got you sentenced?"

Giada swallowed, her mouth had suddenly gone very dry. "No, it doesn't work like that. Nobody tells us anything. I don't know for sure what sin or sins got me damned."

Her mother's eyes narrowed, "but you have an idea, right?"

Giada didn't say a word but felt heat rise to her face as her eyes darted around to look anywhere but into her mother's eyes.

AT THAT MOMENT the wicked spirit overseer barked at them. "Hey you two, do you think this is some kind of coffee morning meet up? You're not here to chat. Get back to work!" He cracked his whip menacingly making Giada flinch.

"I better go. I'll come back as soon as I can." She rushed out of the laundry without so much as a second glance. She was hugely relieved that the conversation had been forced to end when it did. What had been her agenda in visiting her mother? Did she want to confess that she'd allowed Roberto to die? What did she hope that would achieve? Her mother already disliked her intensely, confessing would only turn a generalised distaste into unbridled hatred. Or did she expect her mother to forgive her? Her mother hadn't yet forgiven Giada for landing her in Hell so how could she expect her to find forgiveness in her heart for her son's sort-of murderer? Or maybe she'd hoped that her mother would confess that she'd always loved Roberto more than her? There was just so much between them that was unsaid. Their relationship was comprised of little packages of pain. An assortment of Pandora's boxes, locked away in secret drawers that could never be opened. The pain smothered any memories Giada had of the good days. The days before Roberto had been born. Although she had a vague recollection of having been adored once upon a time, it was so very distant. It felt more like a dream or a film she'd watched when very young.

I should leave Mama alone for a while

Was that the voice of reason or of fear? Where her mother was concerned, Giada couldn't trust her own perception. She became totally irrational.

STILL WALKING through the Deeper Depths, she decided to stop by Aaron on the way back to the Countess' house. Her boss was out for the day so she knew she could stay out a little longer without getting into trouble. She found him crouched down, picking through rocks which he was dividing into different buckets based on size. There was no wicked spirit overseer here as they'd long since given up sending a guard to watch Aaron. They knew he'd continue working without supervision. It was also no fun whipping him as he didn't react. He had an unnaturally high pain threshold.

He stood up, wiping sweat from his brow when he saw her approach. "Hey Giada, how you doin?"

"I'm feeling much better thanks. I just went to visit Mama."

"Oh yeah? How's she adjusting?"

"Not great... it's a big shock and she still blames me."

Giada recounted the entire conversation she'd had with her mother to Aaron and he listened intently. When she'd finished he looked at her with his hands on his hips. "You know what I'm going to say, don't you?"

Giada bit her lip. "I have to tell her the truth about Roberto's death."

"You have to Giada. I know it's hard. I know you don't even like talking about it with us sinners let alone your own mother. She's the one who you hurt the most. But confessing to her is the only way you're ever going to move past this."

"I don't think I can though. I feel like... maybe that was my intention in going there today. Like I wanted to tell her but chickened out at the last minute. I can't imagine a time when I will ever not chicken out."

Aaron nodded, sighing deeply. "I understand. You're not ready yet but you never can guess when you will be ready. It might take weeks, years or it might happen in an instant. Spiritual change can come at any time," he clicked his fingers. "Like that monkey you' been carrying all these years suddenly leaps off your back. See, right now, you're still feeding the monkey. Every time you decide to lie to your mother or conceal the truth from her, you feed it. You have to stop feeding it, you have to let it go. Truth is the only way."

Giada paced back and forth, covering her face with her hands. "I can't though. What if she doesn't forgive me?"

Aaron nodded, "that's a risk you have to take. She may never forgive you. It's not about her though. Confessing is part of making amends. You need this for your soul, regardless of whether she forgives you or not."

Giada felt distraught. Her lip quivered, "she already hates me..."

Aaron placed a hand on her shoulder, nodding sympathetically.

"Just keep coming to meetings. Keep working the program. Stay away from sin-baiting and pray. Ask God to help you - to give you courage to confess. Sooner or later, you'll be ready. It's gonna happen, I promise you."

She sighed and nodded. Giada knew he was right. She had to find the strength to tell her mother the truth. It had been eating her up for years. Confessing was the only way she'd ever find peace.

26

GIADA

~

Giada sat in the Chancellor's study waiting for him to enter. After visiting her mother, she had been on her way back to the Countess' house when he had summoned her. She tapped her feet, nervously on the floor. As she had not progressed her spy work at all since the last time she'd been here, she was expecting a roasting.

The Chancellor entered, looking at her over his glasses before swiftly closing the door. "I assume you know why you're here?" He raised his eyebrows and put his hands behind his back as he hunched over her.

Giada immediately went on the defensive. "I have been unwell and..."

"I am aware of your hell sprite poisoning but you've been better for two days now and in that time you have failed to report anything to me. That tells me that you've made no progress."

Giada blinked "Well, I wouldn't say I've made no progress..."

"Ah so you have got some information on the Countess' movements, have you?"

"Erm... not exactly."

The Chancellor sighed and removed his glasses. He breathed on them before rubbing the lenses with a corner of his shirt. "May I remind you that you do not have a choice in this matter. I will not tolerate failure. I expect you to return to me with some hard information by the end of today or I will report you to Satan." He fixed her with a cold stare. "I'm sure I don't have to tell you that the repercussions of that will be severe."

Giada shuddered. Getting reported to Satan was a one-way ticket to a permanent spot in the First Circle of Hell. She'd been told by Maureen that the torture rooms there were worse than anyone could imagine. How could it get any worse than skin-flaying, she wondered?

"I understand, Sir. And I'm sorry. I'll make sure I get something concrete to give you by the end of the day." She held her head up as she looked at him but she bit her lip. Following the Countess meant most likely going back to the other Hell dimension. Just a few days earlier she'd been attacked and almost lost her life when she'd travelled there. She didn't feel ready to go back so soon and that was why she'd been putting it off. The Chancellor didn't care about this though. All he cared about were results.

Her thoughts were disturbed by the Chancellor. "And another thing. I'm going to grant you temporary demon status."

Giada's head whipped up to face him. "What? Why?"

"The extra powers that you'll have as a demon will enable you to defend yourself, if you get into any trouble again."

"But then my eyes will be red, I won't be able to work in the Countess' home anymore."

"Yes you will. Here." He dropped a set of contact lenses into her lap. "Wear these at all times. Put them in now. When you leave here, I will activate your new status and your eyes will be red."

Giada wished she could ask how the status change took place but she knew this was a well-guarded secret, only revealed to Satan's closest allies.

The Chancellor was still looking at her and she realised he was waiting for her to thank him. "Thank you, Sir." She swallowed and managed a weak smile.

He took a step closer to her, his red eyes glowing. "Do not fail me Giada." Then he looked away. "You're dismissed."

Giada got up. Her legs felt shaky and she realised that she'd been expecting so much worse. That was the thing about Hell. She never knew when she was going to get tortured and the fear, added to the trauma of past torture sessions, hung over her constantly like a cloud of toxic radioactivity.

LATER THAT DAY, after the Countess left the house, Giada told Miriam that she was running an errand before skipping out to follow her boss. She hoped that the snitch believed her. Having Miriam as part of the household could not have been more inconvenient and Giada cursed her bad luck.

Giada crept along the dark tunnels of the Deeper Depths following the Countess. Being a principal demon, the Countess was particularly good at seeing in the dark, and she also had keen hearing so Giada stayed way back. It seemed the demon was on her way to the other Hell dimension, just as predicted. She suspected her boss was going to meet Vassago. If so, Giada wanted to stay longer this time, to hear more of what they were planning.

As the Countess rounded a corner, Giada stumbled slightly on a rock. She flattened her body behind a dark crevice and held her breath as she heard the Countess' footsteps stop. Giada dared not look but she sensed that the demon was looking around - her suspicions had been raised.

Maybe I should just turn back?

Giada was torn between fear of getting caught and fear of angering the Chancellor any further. He was running out of patience and his initial threat to simply kill her and find a replacement spy weighed heavily on her mind. She briefly wondered which would be worse: being killed and reborn in a random hell dimension? Or being sent to the First Circle of Hell? Giada held her breath and waited until she heard the footsteps resume their pace. Then she continued following. She was even more careful with her distance and footing this time.

The Countess arrived at the other Hell dimension and entered the sacrifice room. Giada positioned herself behind a cluster of rocks, close enough that she could see the inside of the room. The Countess strolled around the room, occasionally stooping to peer into a jar before standing up straight again. After a few minutes, Giada heard more footsteps and voices. She recognised the gruff male voice she'd heard the first time she'd been here with Motsumi. She peeked through a crack in the rocks. It was Vassago. He was accompanied by a retinue of what Giada assumed were advisors, servants and guards. One of them wore a long white coat, which looked like either a lab coat or doctor's gown. This man, a demon, wore glasses and had strawberry blonde hair and a ruddy complexion.

"I'm confident that this time it'll work my Lord," the man said as he adjusted his glasses.

"It better, I'm running out of scientists to execute," Vassago replied.

The man laughed nervously prompting the demon prince to stop and give him a look of pure malice as he asked, "why are you laughing, Ratu?"

The man immediately wiped the smile off his face and went slightly pale as he adjusted his collar. Beads of sweat rolled down the sides of his neck. After a minute of silence in which the demon prince stared at him menacingly, Vassago swept into the room and his retinue scurried behind him. Vassago and the Countess greeted each other like old friends. She could've sworn she heard the Countess do 'air kissing' noises. Giada found this nauseatingly fake. The Countess had never cared about impressing anyone. Giada concluded that Vassago must be giving the Countess something she wanted badly for her to be sucking up to him like that.

Vassago touched a panel to his side and the entire group disappeared through a secret door in the wall. The patch of rock then rolled back into place. Giada waited until it looked safe to approach. She took out her contact lenses, putting them into their little plastic container before she slipped them into her back pocket. Next, she walked behind more rocks, making it appear as though she'd approached from the opposite direction. Two male wicked spirits stood guard outside the room.

I hope this works

Giada kept her chin up in the same haughty manner in which she'd seen senior demons acting and approached the men calmly.

"Stand aside" she ordered.

The men looked at each other, a puzzled expression on their faces.

"Well, what are you waiting for?" Giada said.

Still the men looked confused. Giada rolled her eyes and put her hands on her hips. "Don't tell me that you didn't get the message?"

"What message?" one of the guards said.

"Vassago told me to come right away."

"Who are you?" the other guard asked.

Giada fixed him with a lukewarm version of the demon death stare and the man grew pale. "That is on a need to know basis and I am certainly not going to tell a lowly ranked servant such as yourself. Now, are you going to let me through or do I have to get Vassago and have him punish you for insubordination?" She raised her eyebrows and leaned forward, glaring at them. The man hurriedly ushered her through and Giada strolled inside, stifling her smirk until she was out of their view.

ONCE INSIDE, the first thing she noticed was that some of the sacrifice jars were now empty. She walked over to the patch of wall that she'd seen Vassago touching and placed her hand in the same spot. The door rolled open and she walked inside. The tunnel was lit on both sides by blue fluorescent lighting and she heard voices up ahead. Her plan was to get close enough merely to hear what was being said. In addition to voices she heard a whirring sound, as if there was heavy machinery or some kind of boiler room nearby. Giada looked up and saw that the ceiling was a metal grid. She could see more light above it and realised that there was another level. It looked like it would be possible to get up there. As she walked further she came to a glass door, leading to a type of laboratory. The room was empty so she quietly entered.

Inside the room, a metal staircase led to the upper level she'd just seen. She crept stealthily up the steps, then held her body snug against the railing, as she looked down at another room below. Inside the room sat the Countess, Vassago, Vassago's retinue and the scientist-doctor guy she'd seen earlier.

What did Vassago call him again? Oh yeah, Ratu.

THEY SAT in front of a machine which looked like a large laser gun with lots of buttons and levers. It was directed at a stone bed, of the type minions slept on. The bed had straps for the arms and legs and forehead. A pair of goggles hung from a hook at the side of the machine. Behind the machine was a series of compartments cut into the stone covered by glass. Each one contained a human body part. Giada held her hand up to her mouth as she felt her nose wrinkle in disgust.

"Now, I will show you how it works," Ratu said. He clicked his fingers at a minion servant who had entered with Vassago. The minion, a short, elderly man, with pale papery skin, shuffled forward on shaking legs. Giada gulped down nausea as she realised that the man was terrified. What horrors was she about to witness, she wondered?

Vassago sighed, "get on with it, we haven't got all day," he barked.

The minion lay down on the bed and Ratu strapped his arms, legs and head down. Then he put the pair of goggles on himself. He turned around and opened one of the glass cabinets. From it, he retrieved what looked like a handless forearm. He dropped it down a shoot as he pressed a few buttons. The machine came to life, fizzing with blue light whilst it let out a loud whirring noise. Ratu put one hand on the lever and counted down.

"Three, two, one," he pulled the lever and a blue laser shot out and hit the minion in the chest. The minion let out a scream of the most blood-curdling variety that Giada had ever heard. She winced as she imagined the pain the man was in. Vassago's eyes were alight with manic joy and excitement. He perched on his chair like a sprinter, about to leave the starting blocks. Giada looked back at the minion, his body was bubbling and peeling under the blue light but then she saw a change. It appeared that the man's body was fading in and out of existence.

"You will observe," Ratu shouted over the whirring machine, "that the minion's body is now exiting our dimension and going to Earth."

Giada watched, transfixed, as the minion's body disappeared completely. Ratu immediately made a whooping sound as he punched the air. The rest of the audience clapped. All except Vassago who snarled, "it's about time. I was beginning to think I'd been lied to."

The Countess, who sat next to Vassago, turned to face him. "Congratulations Vassago." Then turning back to the front to address Ratu, she asked him, "Tell me, will the minion survive on Earth?"

Ratu laughed awkwardly, "I'm afraid we have yet to perfect a means by which to ensure permanent residence on Earth. We can get damned souls there but they die upon arrival. Our trusted acolytes on Earth have informed us they last a few minutes before disintegrating."

The Countess furrowed her brows. "What good is it to get damned souls to Earth if they die as soon as they get there?"

Vassago looked at her. "This is just the start Countess, we are so close now to realising our vision. You just have to be patient."

The Countess bristled, Giada knew that patience was not her strong point.

Vassago gave her a placatory smile, barely registering her discomfort, before moving onto the next subject. "We cannot risk word of this getting out before we have achieved our immediate goal."

The Countess replied, "I understand and I am ready. The defence shields will be down on Thursday as promised. Your forces shouldn't face much opposition. I anticipate it will be a straight forward change of administration."

"It better be, for your sake," Vassago's lips curled into a taunting smile but the Countess didn't flinch. For a second, Giada almost admired her but she had more important things to think about. The Countess and Vassago were planning their coup for two days time. And perhaps even more importantly, they were close to getting damned souls to exist on Earth without human hosts.

Giada studied her emotions and was surprised to find that she no longer yearned for Earth. There'd been a time not so long ago when the idea of going back there filled her with joy and hope but not anymore. She'd come to a place of acceptance in her damnation. She belonged here, in Hell. And Earth had to be protected from damned souls with villainous intentions. She had to get back to tell the Chancellor everything she'd learnt. She didn't know if he would be interested in stopping the Countess and Vassago's plans to get to Earth. Perhaps Motsumi had already told him after their last visit? At any rate, if the Chancellor didn't stop them going to Earth, Giada would. Even if she died trying.

GIADA LEFT her vantage point and started to creep back towards the metal steps but as she did so she heard the Countess say something that made her blood run cold.

"Did you hear that? I think there's someone there." The Countess pointed up towards the viewing gallery. Everyone in the room looked up towards Giada. Ratu pressed a button on a remote control. As he did so bright lights lit up the gallery where Giada stood, frozen to the spot. She felt her eyes go wide with fear as she was caught red handed. She was trapped in a secret room, with her greatest enemy, a load of hostile demons, and no way out.

27

GIADA

~

Giada tried to open her eyes but they were badly swollen. Vassago's henchmen had roughed her up pretty badly. Then they'd strapped her into the realm teleporter machine and left her there for the Countess to question. The Countess, who had watched the beating with a smile of satisfaction on her face, now walked forward.

"Thank you Jameel and Igor, you may leave us," she ushered the two burly demon bruisers out of the room and turned her attention to Giada.

"So Giada," the Countess clapped her hands together, "you thought you could spy on me and report back to the Council did you? Who put you up to this? Oh don't bother answering. I know it was the Chancellor, he's always had it in for me. And I can see he's even granted you demon powers. These will be entirely ineffective against me." She circled around Giada's stone bed like a cat assessing a mouse it was about to taunt before mauling it to death. The Countess shook her head as she tut-tutted, her eyes large with exaggerated faux sympathy. "I had such high hopes for you Giada. You showed such promise but you will insist on indulging in fantasy. This redemption nonsense..." The Countess sighed. "Now you've proven yourself untrustworthy, which means you've outlived your usefulness. I have to kill you."

Giada bucked against her restraints. Her thoughts raced as she desperately thought of a way to get out of the hole she was in.

"However, fortunately. Or unfortunately, from your point of view. Your death will not be in vain. It will further the cause of science." The Countess' eyes had a zealous sheen as she looked into the middle distance.

Giada's heart sank as her mind jumped to the only possible conclusion.

The Countess continued pacing around Giada's bed, hands on hips. "That's right, you know what I'm talking about. The realm teleportation machine. I'm going to send you back to Earth and we'll video the experiment just in case you survive. It hasn't happened before but there's always a first time for everything." The Countess mocked her by raising both fists into the air in celebration. "You're going home, Giada!"

Giada desperately searched her mind for a way to convince the Countess not to harm her. "No wait! I know things... things that could be useful to you."

The Countess bore down on Giada, slapping her hard across the face. "Stupid girl! Do you think you can manipulate me? Do you think I'm that easy? Do you?!" She roared. "I wrote the book on manipulating, I've been pulling people's strings since before you were a twinkle in your papa's eye." Then the Countess bent down so her face was inches away from Giada's. A smile of utter cruelty crept onto her face and her red eyes blazed with triumph. "In fact, I manipulated you whilst you were still alive."

This made Giada's heart rate jump as an uneasy feeling crept into her belly.

What does she mean?

The Countess continued, "yes, I sin-baited you when you lived in Rome, with your Mama... and your Papa... and your little brother,

Roberto." The Countess looked at Giada's face and cocked her head to the side as she said the name 'Roberto'. She was enjoying the psychological torment she was inducing.

"Ah Roberto, such a sweet little boy, so loveable, so spoilt. You hated him, your hatred was like fine modelling clay - so easy to work with. All you needed was a little nudge... and I delivered it." Her eyes blazed, "it was me Giada. I sin-baited you into watching as your little brother strangled himself to death. His little hands reaching out for you as you ignored him. Watching as he turned purple and then his lifeless body hung from the chord, circling round and round. It was my greatest masterpiece. And you know what? I achieved demon status from that outstanding piece of work."

Giada screamed at the Countess; an animalistic scream of pure, unadulterated rage and hatred. She bucked at her restraints, trying desperately to get free so she could tear the Countess to pieces.

"You evil BITCH!" she shouted.

This only seemed to make the Countess more excited. Her eyes shone deep red and a look of ecstasy mixed with passion adorned her seamless features.

"Good! Good! Now you're becoming the demon I've always known you could be. Harness that anger Giada. Use that hatred, let it consume you. You see, that's why I was always so insistent on having you as my minion servant. You're mine. I made you what you are today and I'm still shaping you. You should thank me. I'm more of a mother to you than your pathetic drug-addled depressive birth mother ever was."

Giada was now so angry and frustrated that she felt her lips fluttering. Her breath came out in rasping gasps as her chest shuddered. She hated herself for showing such weakness in front of the Countess. Especially as she knew how much the demon enjoyed watching people suffer emotionally. But Giada was beyond being able to control herself. The Countess had indeed won. She was trapped here. Yet, desperation led her to try one last thing. "Please don't kill me. I can help you.... With your plans for the Seventh Circle." Giada could always wriggle out of whatever it was she promised later on.

The Countess threw her head back, cackling. "Oh don't be so silly Giada - you would say anything to save yourself. We've just been through this. You are no longer useful to me. Don't demean yourself by begging."

Giada felt her lips begin to flutter as she realised she was out of options. She was about to die, right here, right now and there was nothing she could do to stop this from happening.

The Countess busied herself with turning on the machine. She worked methodically, devoid of emotion. After switching a few buttons and levers, she put her hand to her head. Giada saw a rare crease disturbing the perfection of the Countess' forehead as the demon said.

"Oh dear, I can't seem to get this thing to work. I'll have to go and get Ratu to help me."

The Countess looked at Giada one last time, savouring the look of despair and helplessness on her face before she turned on her heel and walked towards the exit. She stopped at the door of the room and leant closer to one of the wicked spirit guards on the way out. "Don't make conversation with her. She's very slippery that one, don't allow yourself to be conned by her." Then she turned her head one last time to smirk at Giada before she left.

Giada was left alone in the darkness save for the two wicked spirit guards. She tried talking to them but they ignored her. Surely there was something within her demon powers that she could use to escape? Demons had superhuman strength. She tried with all her might to pull her hands free of the metal restraints but it was no use. They had clearly been engineered with the strength of demons in mind. Next she tried delivering a demon death stare to the guards but it didn't work. She must've been too far away to make proper eye contact. She didn't know what she would've done once they'd passed out anyway. At best it would've bought her a few extra minutes but she'd still be locked into the metal restraints. She rattled her restraints again and again, determined to release herself but it was no use. After several minutes of futile struggle, the Countess reappeared with Ratu. The scientist carried a video recorder and flipped a few more switches. As he did so he showed the Countess, "you see you missed these ones here. It's quite simple once you know how." He smiled graciously at the Countess.

What a psychopath Giada thought.

Ratu continued, "You don't want to switch all of these on at the same time as that will blow the whole thing. It wouldn't matter too much if that happened. I have the blueprints to build another one in my lab next door."

Giada looked at the switches he was pointing at, reflecting how arrogant he was. He was so sure that she was about to die. He didn't care that he'd just told her how to destroy the device and also where the blueprints were kept. Giada's heart sank as she realised the machine was ready. Her mind raced through the events of her life since arriving in Hell. She thought of her friends in Sinners Anonymous and she thought of her mama. Her poor mother would never know what had happened to her and this made Giada feel the most desolate of all.

Ratu put the video recorder to his eye and aimed it at Giada. Then he started a countdown. His voice boomed out in a tone reminiscent of a boy waking up on Christmas morning, "three, two, one, go!" The machine whirred and a blue laser beam shot out and hit Giada. She screamed as a pain worse than any she had ever experienced gripped her body. She started convulsing. The pain was so great she could've been held by that laser beam for seconds or hours. She felt her body shifting in a way that she couldn't explain and her vision started to distort. As she looked at the Countess and Ratu, they began to fade and in their place was what looked like a human home. She saw furniture and she smelt fresh air. In spite of the extreme pain that she felt, a tiny voice of euphoria rang out in her head. It echoed the Countess' taunts but Giada's joy was real.

I'm going home!

28

NALEDI

~

Naledi awoke to the sound of a cockerel in the neighbouring village. She rubbed her eyes and turned to face Tau. He was still sleeping. She carefully peeled his arm off her chest and sat up. Perching on the side of the bed, she leaned forward, putting her head in her hands. She had to go back to Hell today. As much as she so desperately wanted to stay in Marula, doing so meant risking her life. If she died, there would be nobody to kill the Countess or protect Tau from her vengeful attacks. Tau stirred and nuzzled into the space where her body had been. Noticing her absence, he turned to look at her. "Hey beautiful. How did you sleep?"

Naledi smiled and cocked her head to the side. "As well as can be expected. How about you?"

"The same."

Tau sat up and shuffled over next to her, interlinking her hand in his as he kissed her forehead. Naledi bit her lip as his expression turned from caring to smouldering. He leant forward to kiss her deeply and she melted into him. She savoured the taste of his hot, soft lips as his hands cupped her face. Ripples of pleasure coursed down her spine as she forgot the conversation, losing herself completely in his embrace. His hands worked their way down her top, and back up the inside of the fabric. Naledi felt her breathing increase as his hands moved around towards her breasts.

Naledi groaned, "Tau, we mustn't." She'd told him countless times that she had to remain a virgin or else she would lose her breacher powers completely and forever.

He removed his hand from her breasts but continued kissing her neck. "Oh Naledi..." she smiled with pleasure as she saw his eyes close in an expression of ecstasy. "You make it so hard for me."

She pushed him gently away. "You knew what you were signing up for when we got together. You knew what being with me meant."

Tau sighed, putting his head into his hands. "You're right but it's just... is this all we're ever going to have?"

"Isn't it enough for you?"

"Is it enough for you?" Tau challenged.

Naledi bit her lip as she felt her brow furrow. It was true that it was getting harder and harder to resist the desire she felt for Tau. The temptation was unbearable and sometimes she wondered why she was holding herself back. Would it be so bad if she lost her powers? She'd have to kill the Countess first of course, so that she could reverse the spell she was under but what about afterwards? Would losing her powers mean that she could live a normal life? Motsumi would no longer be interested in training her. He'd already told her that when she first started training with him. The binding ceremony would be null and void. Perhaps that was the answer? Simply lose her virginity and all her problems would be solved? How different her life would be if she was just normal.

Coming out of her reverie, she turned to Tau. "It won't always be like this. One day we will be able to be together, properly, like normal people. But for now, I need my powers to defeat the Countess. She won't stop until she kills us both. I have to kill her first."

Suddenly they heard a strange sound coming from the living room. It was a kind of rustling, like the sound of wind through trees.

Almost as if someone had just opened a window. Naledi also smelt a familiar scent: sulphur mixed with ash. It smelt a bit like... Hell? But how could it be? Tau's brow furrowed as he looked at her. His expression was tinged with fear and his shoulders had crept up towards his neck. Naledi could tell he was thinking about the tulpa again. Had the creature come back to kill them?

"I'll go," Naledi started.

"No we'll both go. Come on." Tau held Naledi's hand as they walked quietly into the living room. He kept his body low, ready to attack whatever monsters they were about to find. When they got to the living room Naledi couldn't believe her eyes. Giada stood in the living room. She was completely naked and her eyes were wide with fear. She stood, trembling as one arm covered her breasts and the other covered her nether regions. Her skin was very red and smoke emanated from it.

"Giada!" Naledi gasped and ran to her, taking a blanket from the sofa and throwing it over her.

"What are you doing here?" Naledi asked

"Is this someone you know?" Tau looked at Naledi.

"Tau, you know her too, sort of. This is Giada - remember? She's the one I told you about who sin-baited you into committing suicide in order to stop Sehloho's resurrection."

Tau's eyes widened. "Giada! Wow, it's great to meet you but... how are you here?"

Giada drew the blanket around her body. She was still shaking and Naledi wondered what horrors she'd experienced.

"It was the Countess. She used the realm teleporter machine on me and sent me here. It was part experiment and part death sentence. She caught me spying on her and knew that I was planning to report her to the Chancellor. He's running the Seventh Circle right now so it would mean banishment and demotion for her."

Naledi broke into a grin, "but Giada, isn't this what you've wanted since you arrived in Hell? You're back on Earth. You have a second chance now!"

Giada shook her head sadly, "I won't last here. They haven't perfected the technology yet. I will disintegrate within the next few minutes."

As she said this Naledi noticed her red, smoking skin get even redder before it burst into flames. Smoke poured out of Giada's body and she started screaming. It was the scream of a wounded animal as it lay dying from its injuries. Tau ran to the kitchen and got the jug of water. He poured it over Giada and the flames died down. He smiled but his smile dropped when he saw that the effects lasted for only a few seconds before the flames reignited. It was as if the fire was coming from within Giada's skin.

Naledi looked at Tau. "I've got to try and save her life. I'm going to breach a portal back to Hell."

Tau nodded and kissed her forehead quickly before stepping back.

Naledi closed her eyes and steadied her breathing. She tried hard not to be distracted by the smell of Giada's burning flesh. She knew that damned souls could regenerate quickly in Hell. All she had to do was get Giada back there before she disintegrated and she'd recover. Naledi breathed a sigh of relief as she found the threads of reality and tore them back to open a portal to Hell. The familiar sulphurous smells and heat poured into the room. Naledi rushed over to Giada.

"Come on!" she shouted. She grabbed Giada's hand, ignoring the searing pain of the fiery flesh as she yanked her friend over the threshold into Hell. Giada collapsed onto the floor as the flames instantly went out. Naledi closed the portal behind her and then went to see to Giada. Her skin was badly burnt. She was barely recognisable. Naledi felt a great wave of pity surge through her. She leant over Giada, being careful not to touch her charred flesh. "Is there anything I can do to help you?" she asked.

With what seemed to be a great deal of effort, Giada lifted her head towards Naledi's ear. She could barely open her lips, so badly burnt were they. Naledi crouched lower so she could hear what Giada was trying to whisper. Her voice came out in an urgent rasp.

"Kill the Countess!"

She collapsed her head back down onto the ground. Naledi

gritted her teeth and looked into Giada's eyes. She transmitted an unspoken promise in her gaze as she nodded.

Her resolve was now stronger than ever. She would kill the Countess. In that moment, her path seemed crystal clear. All confusion and doubt was gone and in its place was simple, resolute determination. She had finally reached her breaking point. She was fed up of being the omega to the Countess' alpha. She had had enough of cowering and watching the Countess score point after point. As she sat in that moment, a plan formed in her head. It was quite simple but all it required was unshakeable faith in her own abilities. She would go back to the pool of vitality and this time she would defeat her adversary and when she did she would become invincible. Then she would annihilate the Countess.

NALEDI CREPT through the undergrowth in the shadow realm. In her hand was her fighting staff, which she used partly to navigate the dense undergrowth, which led down to the pool of vitality. Above her an owl hooted in a pine tree. She heard crickets in the long grass and up ahead she saw the waters of the sacred pool glistening in the light of the moon. She stalked slowly, every muscle in her body tense. As the cool wind caressed her skin, the hairs on her arms stood on end. She was even more scared than she had been last time and yet this time she was certain she would not fail. Last time her adversary had had the element of surprise. Now Naledi knew what she faced. So determined was she to succeed that she hadn't told Motsumi or any of her other friends in Hell of her plan to return. She had to do this alone. She suspected that the safety net which Motsumi's presence had provided last time had contributed to her failure. If there was nobody there to save her then she would have no choice but to win - or die trying.

Over her shoulder was slung a cloth bag, inside which was a flask, in order to take the water back to Tan Ti Han. The witch was the only person who knew she was here. She'd gone back and told her she was returning to challenge her adversary and this time to win. Naledi didn't know why she'd wanted to tell the witch. She could've simply given the water to Tan Ti Han after completing the task so why tell her before? It may have been so that someone would know where she was. The witch could witness her death and pass on the news if it came to that. However, it was more likely that the shame of her earlier failure still haunted her and she wanted to prove herself. Tan Ti Han hadn't believed she could do it. Naledi had seen it in her eyes when she'd first met her and she was determined to prove her wrong. She would not only match her demon adversary, she'd defeat her.

As she arrived at the pool Naledi decided to calm her mind with a quick meditation. She kneeled on the ground with one foot forward in a kneeling lunge so that she could spring up again instantly. Clasping both hands around her staff, she leant her head forward until her forehead touched the staff and then she closed her eyes. She focused on every sound around her one at a time. First the loudest sounds of the crickets, then the insects buzzing around her, then the pounding of her own heart. As she did this she took her attention inwards, steadying her breathing as she got an image of her adversary in her mind's eye.

In the quietness of her contemplation it occurred to her that she was different than she had been the last time she'd been here. She was now more demon than human and she felt the accelerated strength and stamina that came along with this. Was this what the witch had meant by telling her there was 'opportunity within her affliction'? It didn't make sense. What could be the Countess' motive in increasing her strength? Surely it wasn't in her interests to make Naledi stronger? She felt she was just on the cusp of some kind of epiphany when she heard a twig snap and her eyes flew open. Her adversary was here.

This time Naledi waited until she heard the demon directly behind her. Then she sprang up, twirling her body in mid air as her leg powered forward to deliver a crunching kick to her adversary's face. The demon staggered backwards, a look of surprise on her face. Naledi used the opportunity to leap towards her, aiming the point of her stick towards her eye. Her adversary dodged out of the way just in time and Naledi fell forwards and lost her balance. The demon jumped on top of her, clawing at her eyes as she made deep grunting noises. Naledi felt a tsunami of rage build within her chest.

Oh no! You will not best me again. You will not!

She roared with anger and rolled the demon off her. Then she jumped to her feet. As she stood she felt heat radiating throughout her body. She looked at her forearms and steam rose off them. She was momentarily shocked at how demonic she was becoming and her adversary used this millisecond pause to deliver a powerful right hook to Naledi's nose. Blood spurted out of her nose and ran down her face. The blood shocked Naledi into action. She held up her fists and rained a barrage of super-speed punches onto the demon. Her adversary's eyes opened wide as she staggered backwards then fell onto her back. She looked up at Naledi and all at once she thought she detected a hint of regret and even sadness in the demon's features.

As Naledi looked at her adversary, time seemed to slow down and she felt that she was at a crossroads. She saw one version of her life in which she failed and died here and another version of her life in which she was victorious but the means to get to that vision of glory still evaded her. She recalled her first interaction with Tan Ti Han. The witch had accused her of being blinded by bigotry. Of failing to see the spectrum of good and evil which exists in all realms.

And all beings? She inwardly questioned.

She cast her mind back to the exact words Tan Ti Han had said.

You must embrace your shadow.

All at once Naledi knew what she had to do. She took a deep breath and threw her stick to the ground. Then she stepped forward and offered her hand to her adversary. The demon looked at it with suspicion. Then slowly, Naledi's adversary accepted her helping hand and stood up. Naledi was acutely aware of the pounding of her own heart. Her blood pumped through her veins with such speed and strength she was sure that her adversary could hear it too.

On shaking legs, Naledi stepped closer to her adversary and put her arms around her, hesitantly at first and then with more conviction. As she did this she heard a popping sound and the creature started sinking into Naledi's flesh. As she and her adversary submerged and became one, Naledi entered a state of euphoria. It was as if she'd been carrying a heavy sack of potatoes around on her back her entire life and someone had just come along and offered to take the load for her. So many memories rushed through her head. Times that she'd spent in church and times that she'd spent learning about the old traditional African ways with Nkhono. She had thoughts of her strict Christian upbringing and the realisation that she'd allowed her love of God to twist into hatred for herself and for who and what she really was. She was a sangoma. God had given her her sangoma gifts. He'd made her a breacher and He didn't make mistakes. This was her destiny and it was perfect - she was perfect, even with all her flaws. She could be both a Christian and a sangoma, fully in command of her powers and fully accepting of her path.

As Naledi had this realisation tears of joy streamed down her face. For the first time in her life she was no longer scared. She finally knew herself and what she was supposed to do with her life. She looked up at the moon, threw her head back, opened her arms wide and laughed. She felt herself standing in the ecstasy of God's grace and it felt so good.

Bringing herself back to the task at hand, she walked towards the pool of vitality. It had previously been impenetrable behind some kind of magical force field. But now she walked effortlessly forwards and crouched down to touch the cool water. She looked at her reflection in the pool. She looked different: older, wiser and happier. Naledi reached inside her cloth bag for the flask. Dipping the flask in the ice cold water, she filled it, screwed the lid closed and then put it back inside her bag. As she stood up she heard her ancestors singing songs of praise all around her. Then she saw a vision of a procession of aunties. She didn't recognise any of them but they had the familiar Makwetla features. They must have all died before she was born. She watched as they danced in a line, singing and clapping. One of them made ululations and spun her around. The visitation filled Naledi with joy and hope. She had defeated her greatest adversary. And it had not been the Countess. It had been the forces within herself that stopped her from accepting her sangoma mission and attaining her full spectrum of powers. She was stronger than she had realised. This journey had been about more than paying her debt to Tan Ti Han. Now that she had defeated her adversary, there would be no stopping her. The Countess had better watch out because she was coming for her.

29

NALEDI

∽

Naledi strode along the ash swept streets of Hell Central like an avenging dark angel. Every muscle in her body was primed for violence. Her senses were heightened. She was aware of the tiniest sounds and movements around her. Perhaps an effect of her new powers gained at the pool of vitality? Or maybe this was another symptom of her demonification? Either way it didn't matter. After today none of this would matter. She was on her way to kill the Countess and she didn't care who knew it. In fact, let there be spectators for all she cared, the more the better. She was going to win. It would make her victory all the sweeter to see the Countess crushed in front of her entire community.

As Naledi walked she observed the furtive glances and curious expressions of those around her. Her irises were now thickly rimmed red, giving her the appearance of a senior wicked spirit. However she didn't act like a wicked spirit, she didn't give deference to any demons she passed and in fact ignored them. She was single-minded in her intent. She cared only about locating the Countess. She'd guessed that the demon would live in the most expensive part of town. Aaron had taken her there during the tour when she'd first visited Hell. A teenage minion boy stood gawping at her with a mixture of awe and bafflement on his face. She half smiled and stopped in front of him.

"Tell me where the Countess lives." She didn't bother with politeness. She had neither the time nor the patience for it.

The boy lifted a trembling hand and indicated further up the road. Naledi looked in the direction he pointed. There were several grand looking houses, any of which could belong to the Countess.

"Which one is it?" she asked the boy.

"The one with the white marble balcony and gold door knocker."

Naledi nodded her thanks to him as she walked off in the direction of the house.

Arriving at the front door she lifted her hands and focused her intention on opening it. The door immediately flew off its hinges and crashed to the floor. Naledi lifted one eyebrow - her new powers were certainly impressive. Now to see how they fared against her foe. Striding into the house, she was met by the sight of white marble floors, walls and ceiling. A minion maid was sitting on her haunches holding a toothbrush. Her mouth was slack as she stared at the stranger who'd just dared to force entry to the Countess' house. Naledi's eyes flicked to the toothbrush in her hand, briefly wondering if she'd been cleaning the floor with it. The young woman seemed terrified and confused in equal measure. Her eyes darted first to Naledi and then left and right, as if looking for escape routes, and then back to Naledi again. Evidently she'd settled on getting more information before fleeing.

"Who are you?" the maid asked.

"My name is Naledi Makwetla. I am a sorcerer of immense power and I have come to kill the Countess. Where is she?"

The maid bit her lip as worry lines appeared on her forehead. She was clearly weighing up which would put her in greater danger: giving up her boss or refusing to answer Naledi's question. Her face softened with relief as she heard the sound of the Countess' heels clacking along the upstairs corridor. Naledi's gaze followed the sound to a grand staircase just as the Countess appeared at the top. The

Countess stretched her arms wide, a huge smile spread across her face.

"Ah Naledi! You've come at last. But why did you have to go and destroy my door? There was no need for such theatrics."

Naledi sniffed as she felt her lip curl in contempt. "I'm not here for conversation. I'm here to kill you." Keeping her face as serious as an undertaker's, her eyes met the Countess'. The demon evidently wasn't taking this as seriously as she was however. She started laughing before starting a slow clap.

"Oh very good! That's the best laugh I've had in ages. You think that *you* can kill *me*? Naledi, Naledi, you've been spending too much time around Giada. Her tendency towards fantasy has started to rub off on you."

Naledi's patience was wearing thin. She didn't bother responding but merely shook her head and leapt into the air. With her new powers, she easily cleared the staircase in one bound and landed in a crouch in front of the Countess. Looking up she smirked as she saw the merest flicker of surprise trouble the Countess' features. Just as quickly as it had appeared however, the demon corrected her expression and straightened her jacket. Naledi stood up and held up her hand. With a quick flick of her wrist, a lightning bolt shot out of her hand. The Countess' own hand whipped up and caught the bolt, crinkling it into nothingness in her fist.

"Is that the best you can do?" The Countess taunted her

"Oh, I'm just getting started."

"I'm sure you are but wouldn't you prefer we skip the hors d'oevres and head straight for the main course?"

"Excuse me?" Naledi had no idea what any of that meant.

The Countess sighed, "oh yes, I sometimes forget you're only fourteen and have never been to a proper restaurant. Such metaphors are wasted on you. Naledi, there's no reason for us to fight. In fact, we should be on the same side."

Naledi could hardly believe what she was hearing. "Are you out of your mind? You've spent the last two weeks trying to kill me."

"What makes you think that?"

"Um, let me see, perhaps the fact that it's true."

"You're not talking about that incident outside the akashic realm are you? That was just a little tiff between me and Motsumi. You know how strained the relationship between student and mentor can be. How is Motsumi by the way? I hear you've taken up with him again although I doubt you need him anymore now. You've come into your powers so spectacularly."

"Stop trying to change the subject. I'm talking about bewitching me so that I start turning into a demon. I'm talking about sending your tulpa twice now to kill me and Tau."

A look of genuine confusion crossed the Countess' face. "Tulpa? I didn't send a tul... oh... oh wait. I see what's happened here. My poor child you've been manipulated."

For a second Naledi faltered then she clenched her fists. "Don't you dare lie to me."

"I'm not lying. I admit it's hard to believe. But let me lay out to you what I think has happened." The Countess put her hands behind her back and incredulously, began pacing from left to right in front of Naledi. She was either suicidal or she really didn't believe that Naledi would kill her. She waggled her finger as she theorised. "I believe that Motsumi sent the tulpa to kill you."

"Why would he do that?"

"My dear it's obvious. To get you to come to Hell and train with him again. Think about it, what is in it for him? What does he stand to gain by you being here? If there's something in it for him then it's him, no question."

A cold feeling spread across Naledi's chest as she reflected on the Countess' words. Motsumi did stand to gain from her being here. He'd told her himself that if the Countess was killed then he would be promoted to demon. He couldn't kill the Countess himself. He needed Naledi to do it for him. Then when he'd sensed that her resolve was wavering, he'd sent the tulpa back to attack Tau.

He used me!

She couldn't believe she'd been so naive as to fall for it yet again. Naledi felt her resolve crumple just a little bit. If she had been wrong about Motsumi, what else had she been wrong about? Was the Countess even the villain here or had it been Motsumi all along? As she wrestled with these thoughts, the Countess took a step closer to her and Naledi immediately clenched her fists.

"Stay back, demon!"

The Countess rolled her eyes. "Really Naledi, where do you think we are? Seventeenth century Salem? 'Demon' isn't an insult here, in fact it's a compliment."

"Not to me it isn't."

"Well your perception of reality has been distorted by the Christian church. Even you can accept that by now."

Naledi was feeling more and more confused by the second. This was not at all how she'd expected this to play out. The Countess really didn't seem to want to kill her. If she didn't want to kill her then what did she want?

"What do you want from me? Why did you put the spell on me to turn me into a demon?"

"Ah, yes, I did do that one. I can admit to that - not the others."

"Why?"

"I wanted to focus your mind on coming back here to talk. I turned you into my homing pigeon and look now you've come home to me."

"Couldn't you have just asked?"

"Would you have come?"

"No."

"Well then…"

"Okay, I'm here now so talk."

"My proposition is quite simple really. I want you to become my right hand woman."

Naledi's jaw dropped open. "Absolutely not."

The Countess strode towards her so that her face was a foot away from Naledi's as she grabbed both her wrists. "Think about it Naledi, we want the same things. Security, prestige, power."

"You don't know what you're talking about, I've never been interested in power."

"You're lying to yourself. Even now you enjoy the feeling of magic at your fingertips. You yearn for it when it's not there. You're like an addict, a dry drunk who craves the next drink yet abstains for the purposes of propriety. Yield to me and I will make you a goddess. Join me and together we will take over first Hell, then Earth, then the Universe. Two women of power, standing side by side."

Naledi couldn't believe her ears, this woman was delusional. "I would never join you. You must be crazy."

"I've never been more sane. Stop denying your true self Naledi. We're more alike than you think. The only difference between you and I is that I have accepted who I am and made peace with my nature whereas you live in a constant state of conflict. You walk close to the dark side but you never embrace it. Embrace it now and you will find the quiet life you're so desperately seeking."

Naledi looked at the Countess in disbelief. The demon honestly thought she stood a chance at persuading her to switch sides. What could have given her this belief? This confidence in herself. Naledi had never even hinted at any possibility that she might switch sides and it had been offered to her before. Her mind roamed through the encounters she'd had with the Countess, looking for clues as to what had made this demon think she was corruptible. That the Countess was offering her this worried her greatly.

What has she seen in me that I haven't seen in myself?

Naledi shook the thoughts from her head. The Countess was toying with her. She was playing games in order to better her chances of survival and it was working! Naledi gritted her teeth and yanked her wrists free as she shouted, "never!" She raged at the Countess. "I have been living a quiet life and still would be if it wasn't for you."

"Correction - if it wasn't for Motsumi. He was the one who pulled you back into this. I merely saw the opportunity in your return."

The Countess put her hands behind her back and began pacing

again. "You know, I remember being like you. A young girl in Lesotho, all alone, and vulnerable with nobody to show me right from wrong. I worked it out for myself in the end but you don't have to. Your whole life you have been lied to. There is no right or wrong, only choices and repercussions: action and reaction. It's all karma. That's all there is. What's the point of living a life of servile boredom when you can live a life of greatness. You can really make a difference. Whatever is wrong with the world - you can change it. You can change the Universe. I know you want to make the world a better place. Somewhere safe for your sisters to grow up in. Imagine, a world without poverty?" She turned to look Naledi in the eyes. "Imagine a world without disease, a world without AIDS? You could even bring your parents back if you wanted to. Once the Universe is ours, we can do whatever we like. I know you've often questioned God's judgement. His actions don't always make sense, do they?"

The Countess was right. She'd read Naledi like a book and she was right about all of it. Naledi had spent countless nights, staring up at the ceiling as she wondered why God would create a world with such suffering. Why God had created a world with AIDS and why God had inflicted her parents with it. As she searched her heart, she felt like crying but instead of tears coming to her eyes, her lips began to flutter. She realised with horror that she was no longer able to cry. She was close to becoming a demon - perhaps she already was one.

Is it already too late?

30

GIADA

~

Giada walked through the Deeper Depths inspecting the last of her wounds. Although her journey to Earth had been agonising, she was glad that she'd been. It had made her realise that she no longer yearned for home. The joy that she'd felt on realising she was going back to Earth had been fleeting. Once there she'd felt out of place, like an alien on a hostile planet. She no longer belonged on Earth. She'd fully accepted Hell as her home now and as she walked she felt relief that she'd healed within a day of arriving back. Her near death encounter had strengthened her resolve to confess to her mother. Now that she was on the Countess' hit list, it wouldn't take long for word to get back to the demon that she was still alive. And when it did, the Countess would try and kill her again.

As Giada had unexpectedly survived, she was now the only person in the Seventh Circle who knew how to destroy the realm teleporter machine. She'd decided to go back and do it, even though she risked death by going back there. Sure, she could tell the Chancellor but she wanted to do it herself. This was her way of making amends for the shitty things she'd done whilst alive. She'd never entirely make up for her sins but if she could live a better life now, she'd at least feel better about herself. Protecting Earth from demons was part of that.

Arriving at the laundry room, she entered and walked to the back where her mother normally worked. However when she got there her mother was nowhere to be seen. She called up to the wicked spirit overseer who stood on a metal ledge. He was holding a whip as he looked down on the workers below.

"Where is the woman who was here the last time I came?" she asked.

Giada no longer feared reprisals from the wicked spirit overseer. Being a demon, she now outranked him.

The man caressed the whip in his hands as he spoke, "the new one? She got mouthy with a demon and was taken to the skin-flaying room." He said this as nonchalantly as if he were commenting on the weather. Indeed to him this would be a commonplace occurrence. The effect on Giada could not have been more different. Her entire body went rigid and it felt like all the wind had gone out of her lungs. For a few moments she forgot to breath before she realised and started coughing violently. She almost choked on her own saliva in the process. The wicked spirit looked at her strangely but he didn't question her further. He simply sniffed and went back to glowering at the workers. Giada didn't bother engaging the man any further. She rushed out of the laundry room, still coughing and spluttering.

Mama! I have to get her out of there!

Giada raced along the rough stone streets, barely registering who she was brushing past in her desperate haste to reach her mother. As she walked she felt her heart beat faster and faster until it felt like reality was spinning around her. She remembered her first time in the skin-flaying room. The pain was beyond description. It was the kind of pain she didn't think she'd ever recover from. She did recover but she had to spare her mother from that. In spite of everything that had passed between them, this woman had given birth to her. She'd adored Giada and comforted her when she'd scraped her knee as a young child. She'd tended to her when she'd been sick. She couldn't leave her to languish in a torture room, surrounded by braying demons, getting off on the thrill of witnessing her pain.

GIADA REACHED the torture room in moments and pushed past the doorman. She was vaguely aware of him opening his mouth to ask her a question. However, she glared at him with such violent intent that he abruptly shut his mouth and stepped out of her way. It was more than his job was worth to question an enraged demon. She raced through the dimly-lit rooms. Each room was painted red. Condensation dripped down the walls and the smell of blood and fear permeated every surface. Giada felt herself gag but pushed on. She opened and closed the door to each room, feeling worse and worse with each scene of depravity she witnessed.

Finally she came to a room right at the end. When she opened it, and saw the scene inside, she felt her legs buckle. She went in and collapsed against the door, closing it behind her, with her body weight. Her mother was alone and suspended from a chain attached to the ceiling. Her entire body had been stripped of skin all except for the face. Her eyes were closed and Giada suspected she'd passed out from the pain. Giada put her hand to her mouth. She heard garbled cries coming from somewhere. Giada realised the noises were coming out of her own mouth. Her blood pounded through her veins and time seemed to stand still. She felt dizzy. Her lips started quivering.

"Mama!... oh Mama... what have they done to you?" Giada walked forward and carefully placed a hand on her mother's cheek.

Her mother's eyes fluttered open and she attempted to smile before wincing. "It's alright, it's not as bad as childbirth." She tried to laugh and again winced. Then she opened her eyes a little wider and Giada saw the shock of recognition upon seeing her red eyes.

"No Mama, it's not what you think..." she held her hands out as she shook her head.

"So what is it then? Are you a demon now?"

"I am but it's temporary. I'll explain later." Giada was eager not to get side-tracked. "Mama, who did this to you?"

Her mother sighed. "Mephistopheles. I hear he has quite a reputation."

"He does... How long have you been here?"

"Hours... days.... I'm not sure."

Giada nodded. She understood. Time had no meaning when you were in that much pain. She looked at her mother and longed to hold her hand to comfort her but she knew that would be too painful so instead she stroked her cheek again. "Mama... there's something I have to tell you. But first, let me get you down from there."

Giada reached up and tested the restraints, pulling on them slightly. Then, with her demon strength, she easily snapped the iron chain. Her mother slumped to the floor in a heap.

"Is that any better?" Giada asked.

"A little," her mother croaked. Then with what appeared to be a huge amount of effort, she sat upright and opened her eyes fully to look at Giada. Not for the first time Giada realised how strong her mother was and where she got her own determination from.

"Come on, let's get you out of here." Giada offered her hand to her mother but she said.

"Wait, I'm in too much pain. Just give me a minute."

"Okay." Giada sat down next to her. Her mother gently put her hand in Giada's. The feeling of her raw flesh felt unnatural to Giada and she recoiled slightly. But she felt happy to have her mother's hand in hers and she left it where it was. After a few moments of silence, she bit her lip as she realised the moment had arrived.

She looked at her mother and took a deep breath before continuing. "I'm involved in something dangerous - it's official Seventh Circle work but the thing is..... I might get killed."

Her mother's lips began to flutter. "Have you come here to say goodbye before you die, is that it?"

"No!... it's something else. It's more important than that." Giada felt her pulse rate increase. Her stomach was doing somersaults but she had to do this. She looked at her mother.

"You asked me why I'm in Hell. You wanted to know if I had any idea what got me here?"

Her mother nodded slowly.

Giada looked up at the ceiling. She would do anything to be able to turn back the clock and not have to have this conversation. If only she could go back and not do the awful thing she did. The pain of having to confess to her mother what a terrible person she was. The grief she knew she would feel when her mother looked at her with the disgust that she deserved. Giada could hardly bear it but still she continued. Ignoring her fluttering lips she forced herself to speak. "I was there when Roberto died."

Her mother looked confused, "yes I know you were there. We were all in the apartment together."

Giada looked her mother in the eyes. "No. I was *there*. In the room. When he died."

Giada's mother took her hand out of Giada's hand and put it up to her mouth. "No... no... Giada don't." Her mother started trembling.

"Mama, I have to. I have to tell you." She took a deep breath. "I came into the sitting room. He was still alive. His neck was caught in the curtain chord. He was struggling to get free." Giada took another deep breath and closed her eyes. When she opened them again she said, "he reached out for me to help him.... and... and I stood there. I did nothing except watch as he strangled himself to death. I saw him take his last breath. Then I went back into my room and I pretended that I had been there reading the whole time."

Giada felt an avalanche of pain and regret sweep through her as she looked at her mother, waiting for the reaction she knew was coming. She didn't make any excuses, didn't give any reasons for why she'd done it. She didn't want her mother to think she was trying to dodge the blame. She'd done this unforgivable thing, to her own blood and she deserved her mother's condemnation.

Her mother looked at her and said very quietly, "I think I always knew. Deep down. I suspected at least but I didn't want to face it."

Giada looked at her mother. She looked older than normal as her face sagged with grief. Giada's heart leapt out to her. "Mama, I'm so sorry… I wish I could go back and change what I did. I'm a despicable person. I'm the lowest of the low. What I did was indefensible. I deserve to be here."

Her mother held up her hand and shushed her. "Giada don't…". She stood up unsteadily and turned her back to Giada. Standing up, Giada reached out her hand towards her mother's back but then dropped it. She wasn't sure what scared her more: touching her mother's flayed flesh or the rejection that might come with it. The silence that followed felt like it lasted an eternity. It was a silence weighted by all the many things that had been left unsaid. When her mother spoke again her voice was slow and gravelly, as if coming from a place of emotional destitution.

"When you first came into our lives I was so happy. You were the baby girl I'd longed for. You were so much like me. You looked like me and as you grew older you talked like me and you thought like me."

Giada smiled at the unexpected compliment. Then she dropped her smile as her mother continued.

"I hated myself. Looking at you was like looking in a mirror. All of my best and worst features, both externally and internally, were reflected back at me in your image. The older you got the more you resembled me. At first I was just harsh with you. I was overly critical and mean, hoping to drum your personality out of you. But it didn't work, you just became more and more like me. Eventually I could hardly bear it. I took it out on you. It wasn't fair and I'm not proud of myself. When Roberto was born I thought. *Here is my second chance. Here is a son. A child who will never turn out like me.*

So I simply stopped paying you any attention. I think I hoped that I could erase your existence but I couldn't. I created you, every part of you. I created your hatred for Roberto." Her mother turned around and grabbed Giada's hand. She seemed numb to the pain her flayed flesh must have felt. Or maybe the physical pain was a relief as it drowned out the emotional pain. She looked deeply into Giada's eyes. "You don't deserve damnation. I do."

Giada felt her face contorting with the agony which she felt in her heart. Her whole body shook as her lips fluttered uncontrollably. She wanted to hug her mother. She wanted to feel the comfort of a mother's unconditional love so badly but would she get that from her mother? Was her mother even capable of such an act? As Giada pondered this, lost in a sea of grief and abandonment, her mother reached forward. She hesitantly reached her arms around Giada's torso. Giada was so shocked, she froze, not knowing how to react. Her mother had trapped both of her arms beneath her embrace. Slowly, Giada wiggled her arms free and tentatively patted her mother on her back. Her mother's back was already starting to regenerate and her new skin felt as soft as a baby's. The embrace felt awkward but it also felt liberating. Giada had wished for this kind of relationship with her mother ever since Roberto had been born. It had taken being damned for an eternity in Hell for her to get it.

Releasing herself from her mother's hug she leaned back and asked, "so what happens now?"

"Now... I would like us to repair our relationship if you think that's possible?"

Giada gushed, "Mama, I would love that!"

"Perhaps I could come to your Tuesday SA meeting? I know that those meetings are important to you."

Yet again, Giada longed for the release of human tears, denied to damned souls. "Yes, I would like that." She looked down at her shoes before asking the next question. "Mama?"

"Yes?"

"How is Roberto? You said he is in Heaven?"

Her mother's face lit up in the way it always did whenever she talked about Roberto but for some reason this didn't hurt Giada as much as it had done in the past.

"Yes he's in Heaven. He misses you. He's waiting for you."

Giada's heart sank, "he'll be waiting a long time."

"But don't you believe that redemption is still possible? Isn't that what those Tuesday night meetings are about?"

"I don't know, on good days I believe, on bad days I don't. This isn't exactly a good day."

Her mother nodded then paused before she said. "Giada... I'm glad we had this talk. Thank you for telling me. You're a brave girl, a fighter and a survivor... just like me."

Giada smiled at her mother and her mother smiled back at her. This had gone entirely differently from what Giada had expected. She'd expected this discussion to heal herself, to cleanse her from her regrets and force her to face the consequences. She'd expected to face her mother's hatred. Indeed it had cleansed Giada but not from regret, it had cleansed her from self-hatred and she realised that it had cleansed her mother too. In the course of trying to heal herself, she'd also healed her mother.

31

GIADA

∼

After confessing to her mother, Giada was even more determined to destroy the realm teleporter. She set off for the other hell dimension that same day. Walking towards the Deeper Depths, she passed Aaron on rock collection duty.

"Hey Giada, how did it go with your Mom?"

Giada smiled, momentarily forgetting her mission. "Really well. Much better than I expected. I'll tell you about it later."

"Why, where are you off to?"

Giada looked down, unwilling to meet Aaron's gaze. She knew that what she was planning was reckless and Aaron wouldn't approve. Her guilty expression told him enough.

"You're not going back to the other hell dimension, are you?"

Giada held her hands out in protest. "Aaron, I know how to destroy the realm teleporter. I have to go back."

"You got real lucky last time. If they catch you again and send you to Earth, this time Naledi won't be there to rescue you. You will die."

Giada clenched her jaw before she spoke. "I know the risks Aaron."

Aaron raised his eyebrows, "well, at least take someone with you. Take Motsumi. His magic is a powerful weapon. He's on rock collection duty today too. He's about five minute's walk in that direction."

Giada considered this. She'd softened in her opinion of Motsumi since she'd first met him. Yes, he had his faults. He was certainly manipulative and pompous and arrogant but he was trying to become a better person and she could relate to that. Plus he used to be the Countess' acolyte and that meant he knew her weaknesses better than anyone.

"Alright, I'll ask him to come."

Giada started walking in the direction in which Aaron had pointed before he called out to her one more time.

"And Giada?.... Good luck." He looked at her with the type of sombre expression of a father sending his son off to war. Giada's stomach somersaulted as she realised that Aaron was saying *goodbye*. He didn't think she was coming back and the icy grip of fear in her belly told her that maybe he was right.

GIADA AND MOTSUMI crept up behind a cluster of rocks from where they had a good vantage point of the sacrifice room. Motsumi had performed a cloaking spell on Giada and altered her appearance. It would fool the guards but the Countess would easily see through the magic if she got close. They had to be sure she wasn't around first. They spent half an hour watching the entrance and then decided that, knowing how impatient the Countess was, if she'd been inside she would've left by now. Creeping further along behind the rocks, they came to a point at which they could exit and make it look like they'd been walking along the pathway. As they approached the guards, Giada recognised the one on the left from the last time she had been here. He wouldn't recognise her with her altered face but she would have to vary her method so as not to trigger his memory. Strolling up to the guards, Giada put on her poshest voice and said.

"Good day. I've come to take an inventory of the sacrifice room."

The guards exchanged glances.

"Where's your ID?" the guard on the right leaned closer to her.

"I lost it but I can assure you that my audit has been authorised by Vassago himself."

"Then you won't mind if we wait until he arrives, will you? He's on his way here now."

Shit!

Giada forced herself to keep her face placid. "No, of course not." She laughed somewhat nervously.

"Hey, do I know you?" the guard on the left asked, narrowing his eyes as he studied her face.

"No, I don't believe so," she turned away slightly. Rubbing her nose she made eye contact with Motsumi. He understood the signal immediately. She turned back and as she did so she made a fist and socked the guard on the left square in the jaw with the full force of her demon strength. His head snapped backwards, making contact with the stone wall with a thud. Then his eyes rolled around involuntarily and he slumped to the floor. The guard on the right looked aghast. His mouth opened and closed in outrage. Grabbing a whistle around his neck he brought it to his mouth but it never reached. Motsumi made a quick hand movement over his face and said, "sleep". The guard instantly slid to the floor next to his colleague.

Giada nodded thanks at Motsumi and they rushed into the sacrifice room. If Vassago was on his way, they possibly only had a few minutes to destroy the machine. They made their way to the room which housed the device. Motsumi easily subdued the two guards inside the room using the same sleeping spell that he'd used on the guard outside. Giada moved swiftly around the machine, flipping the switches that she'd seen Ratu indicate. She remembered Ratu saying it would cause the machine to blow up. She hoped it wouldn't cause a massive explosion and kill them both. At any rate, it was too late now, if they were blown to smithereens so be it. The machine started beeping as she flipped the switches and the beeping increased in pace with each switch that she flipped. Once all the switches had been flipped it started vibrating violently. She looked at Motsumi, widening her eyes.

"Run!"

They dashed for cover and just made it to the corridor before they heard a *Boom*. For a few seconds everything went silent as Giada flew through the air. She hit the ground with a thud and grimaced at the force of the impact. There was dust, smoke and ash everywhere and she coughed and sat up, waving her hand around to try and clear the smoke. She heard a high-pitched whistling. Then her ears recovered from the noise of the explosion and normal function returned. The crackle of fire came from the room which had housed the realm teleporter. The smoke was so thick she could barely see. She squinted trying to see Motsumi. When she eventually did spot him panic seized her. He was passed out on the floor.

Is he dead?

Giada stood up too quickly and immediately felt dizzy. Staggering over to where he lay she rolled him over and checked his vitals. He was still alive. She said a silent prayer for her demon powers as the strength they afforded would allow her to sling Motsumi across her back. But first, she had to find those blueprints. Leaving Motsumi where he was, she hurried inside the lab room and started looking around. There was a metal cabinet over by the far wall. She walked over and opened each drawer one after another. Inside each drawer were miscellaneous pieces of lab equipment. No blueprints. There weren't any other cabinets and for a moment she was out of ideas. Then she spotted a computer on a table in the corner of the room. Perhaps the blueprints were electronic? She could just destroy the whole machine but then she'd never know if the blueprints had been on there or not. She'd attended a few coding classes one summer and one of the other kids had shown her how to hack into a computer. The hard part was figuring out the password and without knowing Ratu, it would be even harder. She walked over to the computer and started trying a few common combinations.

Just as she was deep in thought, her entire body tensed up. Was that the sound of someone entering the corridor? She crept to the door and peered out just a fraction then whipped her head back inside. Adrenaline coursed through her body as her heart thumped. Motsumi had gone! Had he regained consciousness and simply left by himself? It seemed unlikely. Surely he would look for her before leaving. There was only one other possible conclusion. Someone else - probably Vassago, had arrived and taken him. Giada thought quickly. If Motsumi had been taken, that meant they were seconds away from taking her. Now was her last chance to destroy the blueprints. She was out of time to check if they were on the computer. She had to just hope that they were and destroy the machine. She rushed over to the cabinet. The last drawer contained bottles of chemicals. She opened it and picked up bottle after bottle, scanning each label until she'd found one that she knew would be effective: hydrochloric acid. Opening the bottle, she walked over to the computer and poured it over the hard drive. It made a satisfying sizzling noise as the plastic and components inside melted. Giada coughed as a nasty, pungent smell filled the air. She covered her eyes as they started to sting and blur. Putting the cap back on the bottle, she headed for the door. She'd almost made it when the door opened. She jumped with fright as there, standing right in front of her, was Vassago. Giada's jaw hit the floor as her eyes widened. Her stomach felt like it had turned to liquid. On either side of him stood a demon bodyguard the size of a ox. How was she going to get out of this one?

Giada thought quickly. She could try fighting but she'd be no match for the principal demon or his henchmen. All three of them would be stronger and more powerful than her. Her best bet was to try and talk herself out of it but from the look on his face, he wasn't in the mood to negotiate.

"Um... it was an accident?" Giada's voice rose, with the inflection of a question, in the manner of a toddler caught with her fingers in the sugar bowl. Vassago crossed his arms and raised one eyebrow.

"You blew up my realm teleporter and poured acid over my computer - by accident?"

Giada bit her lip. "Let's call it a misunderstanding then?" she tried, knowing how weak this sounded.

Vassago looked at his henchmen, "take her". The muscular demons lunged at her.

It's now or never she thought. She rushed forward, elbowing one of them in the ribs as she tried to squeeze through the gap between them. Her attempt at escape was futile. The men looked like they'd played for the NFL whilst alive, athletic and built beyond belief. One of them had biceps the size of her thighs. He wrapped his arms around her, lifting her off the ground effortlessly. She wriggled furiously, kicking her legs as she growled.

"Let me go!"

Vassago chuckled and tousled her hair, "I love it when they fight. It makes the torturing so much more fun." Then without warning his expression turned dark and he head butted her.

Everything went black.

GIADA AWOKE to find herself shackled to the walls of a dungeon. Taking quick stock of how she felt physically, she was relieved to find that she hadn't been tortured yet. Vassago had probably knocked her out so that she wouldn't know where she was being held. But as demons enjoyed watching their torture victims in pain, he'd most likely waited until she regained consciousness to begin having fun with her. It was dark in the dungeon but she could make out enough of her surroundings to see that she wasn't alone. Another person was shackled to the wall opposite her but she couldn't make out who it was.

"Hey you," she called over.

The figure raised his face and said, "Giada, you're awake!"

She recognised Motsumi's baritone African accent immediately and was surprised at the comfort she felt in having him there.

"What happened to you? Have they tortured you?" Giada asked

"Not yet, they wanted to wait until you were awake so that you could watch. They're really sick bastards."

"Can't you use magic to get us out of here?"

"No, they've put us in an etheric protection chamber. Magic doesn't work in here. That can mean only one thing - the Countess is advising them. How else would they know that I can do magic."

"Unless it's a precaution they take with all foreign hostiles?"

"Perhaps but I guess it doesn't make much difference. We're in deep trouble here whether she's around or not."

Giada tried using brute force to rip her hands out of the shackles but even with her demon strength, she couldn't do it. Then her ears pricked up as she heard what she thought was the sound of heels clicking across stone floor.

"Do you hear that?"

"Yes, it sounds like...."

Motsumi didn't get to finish his sentence as the door swung open. Light from the corridor outside flooded into the room. The Countess entered, she was wearing a long, fitted military style coat and knee high leather boots. She stood at the doorway, with her hands on her hips.

She looks like a member of the Gestapo - how fitting, Giada thought.

The Countess had a particularly smug, triumphant look on her face and as she stepped into the room Giada saw why. Trailing behind her, with her head down, was the last person Giada expected to see.

Naledi?!

32

NALEDI

~

Naledi tried not to look at Giada and Motsumi as she entered the dungeon where they were being held captive. She told herself it was because she didn't want them to try and influence her but deep down she knew it was because she felt guilty. The truth was she was tired of having to be strong all the time. She'd had enough of shouldering the burden of saving the world all the time. It was exhausting and the more time she spent in Hell the more she asked herself if the world was really worth saving.

"Naledi?! What are you doing here?" Giada asked, forcing Naledi to meet her gaze at last.

Naledi opened her mouth to explain but found herself at a loss for words.

The Countess helpfully stepped in. "Naledi has finally seen sense and realised she is better off on my side."

Motsumi looked at the Countess with a mixture of incredulity and disgust. "I cannot believe that. You've performed some kind of mind control on her. I demand you reverse the spell."

The Countess looked at him as if he was something she'd just scraped off the bottom of her shoe. "Excuse me? You're in no position to demand anything from me, Motsumi."

Motsumi switched his gaze to Naledi, leaning forward as far as his shackles would allow. "Naledi, whatever she's told you, she's lying. Don't trust her, don't listen to her."

The Countess strode towards him and grabbed him around the jaw with one hand, squeezing his cheeks hard so that his lips puckered. Fixing him with her ruby red gaze she raged. "Now you listen to me you worthless piece of shit. Naledi has seen through your lies. She's seen through your abuse. You've used her for the last time."

She dropped her hand and stood upright, smoothing down her coat as she said. "Naledi is with me now. Get used to it."

Giada shook her head as she looked at Naledi. "Just tell us why? Why would you go to her? Was it magic?"

Naledi bit her lip, "no. I've spent so much time trying to protect Earth. For what? It's not worth saving. There's so much sadness and poverty and sickness. Now that my powers are limitless, I can recreate the world and make it perfect. I can make it better - we can make it better."

Naledi caught Motsumi's eye and his face was drenched in disappointment.

"Oh Naledi... I never thought I would ever see *you* seduced by power. Me, maybe but not you." He paused then added, "you do know that she's just using you, right? As soon as she's used you to get the universe, she'll find a way to destroy you to take it all for herself."

The Countess scoffed, "That's rich coming from you. You used Naledi to try and kill me. You manipulated her by sending a tulpa, in my image to Earth to goad her into training with you again and all so that you could get a demon promotion."

Giada's mouth dropped open as she gave Motsumi a look of horror. "Is that true?"

Motsumi's eyes widened with the shock of discovery as his head flicked from Naledi to Giada and back to Naledi again. "Yes, it's true but I did it for you, Naledi. I knew you yearned to complete your training but your Christian conscience prevented you from following your heart."

The Countess interrupted, "see, he's at it again. Even now he's trying to manipulate you. He just can't help himself. And I'll tell you something else too. The reason why I didn't kill him outside the akashic realm was because he bargained with your life to save himself."

Naledi shot Motsumi a look of death as her jaw hit the floor.

That evil bastard!

The Countess continued. "That's right. He told me that he would lead you to me when the time was right. It turns out he didn't have to as you came to me of your own accord but he gave you up Naledi. He's a double-crossing snake."

Beads of sweat were now rolling down the side of Motsumi's face. "I lied to her Naledi! I was never going to lead you to her. I just told her that so that she wouldn't kill me. I'm on your side Naledi. You have to believe me. I admit, I've made some mistakes but I've always had your best interests at heart. If that wasn't the case, why did I insist on getting you out of the akashic realm first. I wanted to make sure you were safe."

Naledi felt her heart crumpling inside her chest. He'd let her down again and again. Each time she trusted him, he lied to her. How could she have ever been taken in by him. He was just a conman in a flashy suit and shiny shoes.

Motsumi began to look desperate. Evidently he saw that he was losing her so he tried harder. "Naledi, remember when I told you that you're the daughter I never had but always wanted? That's still true and it always will be. We're bound together and nothing can come between us."

"Erm... until such time as she fully qualifies as a sangoma," the Countess butted in. "She's now come fully into her powers. You can't deny that. She is no longer an initiate. She is an adept, more than you will ever be. Release her from her bondage to you."

Motsumi pursed his lips and lifted his chin. "I will not. Not if it means she gets bound to you. I have a duty of care to..."

The Countess interrupted again, "a duty of care which you have abused again and again for your own selfish ends. Anyway, we didn't come here to bicker. Naledi has made up her mind. You've lost and I've won. Deal with it."

"What did you come here for then, to gloat?" Giada asked.

"No we've come to escort you to Vassago for execution."

Giada's face turned red. "Any of Vassago's other lackeys could've escorted us - so you did come to gloat."

The Countess shot Naledi a glance and Naledi realised that Giada was right about one thing. They didn't need to be here so why had the Countess brought her?

She's testing me

The Countess needed to know Naledi was truly on her side and the best way to test this was to see her turn her back on Motsumi and Giada. Well, it was a test she would easily pass. The more she'd learnt about Motsumi's lies and treachery the more certain she'd become about the choice she'd made.

Naledi set her lips in defiance. "Let's go" she said as she turned to leave.

The Countess smiled at her and then smirked at Motsumi and Giada before turning to the guards. "Release them, then follow us."

One of the guards had a set of keys hanging around his neck. He walked over to Motsumi and unlocked his restraints. Motsumi rubbed his wrists once his hands were free. "You're just going to abandon Dineo and Puleng, are you?"

Naledi wheeled back to face him. "I'm doing this for them. I don't want them growing up in a world with such sadness and injustice and disease. I want them to have an easier life than what I had."

Motsumi shook his head, "you're running away from your responsibilities. Abandoning them, just as you abandoned me when I was a boy."

"Don't you dare! Don't you dare try and guilt trip me into changing my mind." Naledi put her hand to her forehead, "you're unbelievable."

The guard walked over to Giada and unlocked her shackles. She didn't take her eyes off Naledi. "All this time I've been in Hell, I've been desperate to be on Earth. I would've done anything to change places with you, just to smell the fresh air of home and feel the sunshine on my face. You have a choice and you've chosen this." She brought her arms up and then dropped them at her sides, shaking her head in disbelief as she looked around. "You know your eyes are almost completely demonic now. Once they are pure red there'll be no turning back. You'll spend the rest of eternity regretting your decision." She took a step closer to Naledi, imploring her with her eyes. "Naledi, I know what it's like to live with regret. Believe me, you don't want this. I wouldn't wish it on my worst enemy, least of all my friend."

The Countess rolled her eyes, "oh pur-lease! Don't listen to these bleeding heart liberals. Hell is the best thing that ever happened to me Naledi and it will be for you too." She clicked her fingers at one of the guards. "Tyler, put a gag on each of them will you, they're giving me a headache. I trust you have some to hand?"

The guard opened his mouth as his face went red, "I'm afraid not Ma'am."

The Countess tutted as a look of irritation creased her face. "Why ever not? Now we'll have to put up with their incessant gabbing until we get to the execution pit."

Naledi felt a rumble of guilt course through her belly. The thought rose unbidden within her

If I feel guilty, surely that means that I'm still human?

And it was accompanied by a feeling of hope. She scowled and exorcised the rogue thoughts and emotions from her mind. She had to be strong and not allow sentimentality to take over. She looked at the Countess for reassurance but the demon had moved onto the next task.

"Time to go," the Countess said cheerily as she clapped her hands together.

The guards pushed Motsumi and Giada roughly out of the dungeon and along the stone lined passageway outside. Naledi had been fully briefed about the plans for the execution. Motsumi and

Giada were to be taken to Vassago for decapitation. He took pleasure in performing executions himself which was why Naledi had been surprised he would choose such a quick method. Surely death by lava melting, in their equivalent of the Deeper Depths would be slower and far more satisfying?

It was clear that the Countess was right, Motsumi in particular was not about to give up his campaign to get Naledi to switch sides again. He said to her, "You know, that's why she put the spell on you, don't you? She infected you with her demonic nature because she knew that was the only way she could get you to abandon God and side with her. You've actually allowed yourself to get seduced by a demon."

Tyler, shoved Motsumi. "Shut up and walk faster, minion," he barked.

Naledi felt her breathing increase as Motsumi's words twisted her conscience like a knife in her gut. The problem was that she no longer believed in what she'd been taught. She still believed in God but she no longer believed in the Christian church. She realised so much of what she'd been taught all her life had been lies. Witches could be good or bad. Damned souls could be good or bad. Even demons could be good or bad.

Giada took over the campaign from Motsumi. "You don't know this Naledi but the Countess is the reason why I'm in Hell."

Naledi wasn't having any of this. "That's a lie. You're in Hell because you sinned."

"Yes but the Countess sin-baited me into doing something unforgivable. I watched as my younger brother strangled himself to death on a curtain chord. I could've saved him but I didn't because I was jealous of him."

Naledi looked at Giada with curiosity. She found it strange that Giada was able to recount this incident with such a lack of emotion. She was either a psychopath or she was lying. Naledi decided she was lying. "Nice try Giada. The Countess told me you were a smooth liar."

"It's true! It's taken me months of work to get to the point where I'm even able to admit what I did. Now I've made peace with my damnation. I belong here, I did a despicable thing. I'm not blaming the Countess for my actions. I accept responsibility but she enjoyed sin-baiting me and she earned her demon status from my damnation. Is that what you want for your future? Is that the kind of person you want to partner with? The kind of person you want to become? My little brother was only six years old. I was only twelve. She manipulated a child."

Naledi felt her body stiffen as she walked. Giada was now getting more emotional. If this was a lie, Giada was an even better liar than Motsumi. Naledi looked at the Countess but she didn't make eye contact or reveal anything at all. For the first time that day, Naledi wondered if she was making a big mistake.

33

NALEDI

~

The execution pit was a large amphitheatre with a circular stage and rows of seats arranged in concentric circles around the outside. The seats were filled with what Naledi could see were a mixture of demons and wicked spirits. There were also a few minions who were there as servants to their demon masters. The air was filled with the excited buzz and chatter of a crowd about to be entertained. Naledi heard people laughing and others arguing. A few opportunistic salesmen were walking around selling torture devices, whips, chains, razors and the like. In the front row were the elite members of this society. Naledi recognised Ratu, who she'd been introduced to as the senior scientist in charge of the realm teleportation programme. Vassago sat on a large metal throne in front of a block of wood. He held an axe in his right hand. Naledi could see that the axe hadn't been cleaned and the blood of its former victims stained the rusty blade. They approached down a set of central steps leading to the stage. Vassago lifted his head and raised his hand, urging them to quicken their pace.

"Let's not keep our audience waiting," he shouted up at them.

In spite of the heat, Naledi felt a chill course over her skin and the hairs on her arms stood on end. She tried to steady her breathing and was surprised to find that her hands were shaking. This wasn't lost on Motsumi who whispered to her. "You don't want to do this, I can tell. It's not too late to change your mind you know. Your powers are limitless. You could take out this entire arena with just a few flicks of your wrist."

Naledi gritted her teeth and tried to ignore him.

They got to the stage and the guards handed Giada and Motsumi over to Vassago then stood to one side. Vassago stood up, hoisting up his leather trousers as he did so. He flexed his colossal biceps. "You first" he said, pointing his axe at Motsumi. Walking slowly over to the wooden block, Motsumi gave one final pleading glance to Naledi and then kneeled down, placing his head in the groove on the block. The arena hushed as every head turned to watch the spectacle. Vassago raised the axe then waited for a few seconds. He was getting off on creating the dramatic suspense. The arena was now so silent, Naledi could hear the bubbling of lava in the pits further down. With a mighty swing, Vassago brought his axe down. Then all at once, Naledi saw a flash of something come from the side of the stage and push Motsumi off the block. The axe hit the wooden block as Motsumi rolled safely to the side. Naledi's eyes shot to the source of the disturbance and she found herself looking into her own eyes. Her eyes stared back at her and shook her head with a look that spoke volumes of regret and warning. It was her, she'd stopped the execution! As quickly as Naledi recognised herself, the second Naledi disappeared through a portal which she closed behind her. Naledi's thoughts raced. She needed more time to work this out.

If only I had more time

As soon as she had this thought everything went silent and completely still. Vassago was as still as a statue, his face frozen in an expression of confused annoyance. Motsumi too was unmoving, the entire arena was suspended in time.

"Of course! Wish fulfilment - the most advanced of the sangoma skills." Naledi whispered to herself. She'd wished for more time and she'd got it. Now she had to make use of it. She thought quickly. She must've been looking at a future version of herself. If she'd regretted the execution so much that she'd travelled back in time to stop it, it meant that it was a mistake. It also meant that she was still human as she still had her breacher powers. The confusing part was that her eyes had been brown?...

Naledi closed her eyes and imagined how she would feel watching Motsumi's head roll off his body. She felt herself start to tremble and gasp. Grief wrenched at her heart and she felt her legs go weak. She remembered how she'd first felt after the binding ceremony. It was a feeling that she would never be able to explain to anyone. Motsumi and her had become a family unit during that ceremony. They were bound together by magic but they were bound together by something stronger than that: destiny. Motsumi had been right. All this time.

The memory of Motsumi as a boy flashed into her head. The first time Naledi had seen him, he'd been running across a field. He was being pursued by demons and he'd implored Naledi, with his eyes, to save him. Bringing her mind back to the present, she walked over and looked at his eyes now. She could still see the little boy in those eyes. The same little boy she'd been so instantly desperate to protect that she'd disregarded her own safety and the wrath of God's archangels to rescue him. How could she have considered abandoning him now? How could she have considered abandoning Tau and her sisters? And God?

She realised that the Countess wasn't going to create a perfect world. She was trying to seduce Naledi by promising a world of absolutism, perfect in every way but the universe wasn't absolute. There was light and dark. The Countess knew this and the fact that she was promising an end to the darkness proved that she was lying. The dark had to exist to cause destruction so that the light could cause renewal afterwards. It was karma, a never-ending cycle of death and rebirth, perfect in every way. The Countess had said that karma was all there was but she'd got it twisted. Karma didn't mean not caring about hurting people. It meant accepting the constant cycle of good versus bad whilst still striving to be good. It was infinity in action. As the epiphany washed over her, she realised what she had to do. She had to end this madness, right here and now and do what she'd come to do. She had to kill the Countess. She walked over to where the Countess stood, studying her angry face. She could just open a portal and push her out right now. But she somehow felt that the demon at least deserved a few seconds warning. Naledi opened the portal and then closed her eyes and wished for time to start again.

The Countess jerked her head back in surprise at Naledi having instantly appeared in front of her face. Naledi cocked her head to one side, smiled and pushed her through the portal. But the Countess dove under her legs and back into Hell with lightning speed and agility. Motsumi, realising the tide had turned, scrambled to standing and started making for the stairs. But one of the wicked spirit guards grabbed him by his collar and hauled him back again. Naledi raised her hands and magically lifted the Countess high into the air. The Countess lowered her hands with her fists balled and the magic disappeared as she landed on the floor with a thud. Giada glowered at the wicked spirit guards, putting the full force of her ill will into the demon death stare she was delivering. It worked and the guards collapsed onto the floor. Vassago growled and strode towards Giada but she leapt into the air, soaring over his head and landing behind him, next to Motsumi. Picking herself up, the Countess flicked her wrist and a lightning bolt flew towards Naledi. Naledi didn't move but raised her hand and grabbed the lightning, hurling it back at the Countess with greater force. The demon dodged it effortlessly.

"Think bigger Naledi," Motsumi shouted before diving behind Giada as Vassago approached them. Naledi flicked her glance at Motsumi and was torn between saving him and Giada and killing the Countess. She decided he had to save himself and she turned back to the Countess. But the second of indecision had cost her dearly. The Countess grabbed her around her neck and lifted her off the ground.

"You can still be my acolyte Naledi - this is just damnation jitters. It's totally normal. In any case, all mentors and mentees fight. Let's just put it behind us and carry on with our plan."

Naledi didn't indulge her by replying. She knew the demon was trying to manipulate her again. She felt her lip curl into a snarl as she tensed her chest and flung her arms out to the side. As she did so she flew into the air and hovered there for a few moments. She looked down at the Countess and then considered Motsumi's advice.

Think bigger

Closing her eyes she wished for a hoard of monsters to manifest and do her bidding. She opened her eyes and hundreds of ghoulish hell hounds appeared. They were huge black dogs, the size of rhinoceros' with multiple clusters of eyes and rows of serrated fangs, dripping with oily slime. They poured like a tsunami over the stage and through the arena. Naledi heard frenzied screams as the audience fled, trampling over each other in their haste to get out. A hound launched itself at the Countess. She flicked her wrist and the creature's neck snapped. It fell to the ground, dead. However, there was another beast behind it and another behind that. There were hundreds of them and they were swarming over the Countess and Vassago. Naledi raised her hands and Motsumi and Giada floated into the air as if carried by a tunnel of wind. Naledi looked at Motsumi and grinned. "Pretty cool, huh?"

Motsumi nodded, smiling back at her. "Yes Naledi, it is indeed... *pretty cool.*" The modern phrase sounded awkward on his lips.

As the Countess was kept busy subduing hell hounds one at a time, she was unable to defend herself from the other threat of Naledi. Now Naledi simply raised a hand and made a pushing gesture. The Countess screamed as she went sliding back through the portal. Naledi saw her skin begin to blister on Earth. The Countess shouted back at her. "Naledi, you fool! We could've made the world perfect - we still could!"

Naledi looked at her and said, "The world already is perfect, just the way it is."

She kept one hand outstretched to keep the Countess in place and with her other hand she lifted Vassago up and pushed him out of the same portal. Then she closed the portal. She turned around to see where Ratu was and found him being eaten by a group of hell hounds. He was definitely dead. He'd be reborn in another hell dimension of course but without his blueprints and status, it would be some time before he'd be in a position to begin his realm teleportation work again, if ever. Naledi closed her eyes and willed the hell hounds back into the realm from which they'd come. When the last of them had left, she gently lowered Motsumi and Giada to the floor before floating down herself.

Giada grinned at her. "Your eyes are brown again."

Naledi couldn't see herself but she smiled.

Giada continued, "What made you change your mind?"

What had made Naledi change her mind? It was too complicated for her to explain so she merely shrugged and said, "I just came to my senses."

Motsumi dusted himself down and said. "I'm sure seeing yourself save my life must've had a profound effect on you." Then he stared into the middle distance with a look of concentration on his face. "But if you've now stopped my execution... you won't have been there in the future to stop my...." His eyes widened, "Naledi, you have to go back in time right now and stop my execution!"

Naledi smiled and closed her eyes, summoning her powers once more...

34

GIADA/ MAUREEN

∼

It was Tuesday evening and Giada was at the Sinners Anonymous meeting as usual. This time however, her mother sat next to her. She looked at her mother and smiled. Her mama squeezed her hand and smiled back. Their relationship was now everything Giada had always wished for. She couldn't believe it had taken so long for them to get to this. All they had needed was honest communication.

After the Countess' death, the Chancellor had offered Giada the chance to remain as a demon. She'd get to live in a grand house in Hell Central - maybe even the Countess' old house, if she wanted it. She'd get minion servants, access to VIP events and all the other power and privileges that came along with being a demon. Giada would be lying to herself if she didn't admit she was tempted. But she nevertheless turned him down. She didn't need or want demon status. She wasn't interested in climbing up the hierarchy of Hell. She now had a sense of belonging and completion, which she'd never felt even whilst living on Earth. She'd once heard that home was wherever a person's mother was. Now that her mother was with her, and she knew that she was loved, she felt at home in Hell. Sure it was still Hell but she felt at peace. She could make it here now.

The Chancellor had asked her what else she might want instead and she'd requested to be put on permanent rock collection duty. That way she'd be able to see her pet parasite, Lucky, often. She could visit her mother whenever she wanted and she'd be around the other SA members. They often volunteered for the unpleasant task in order to escape the tyranny of their sadistic demon masters. Now that Giada had grown to a point of acceptance in her situation, she wanted to give back to newer SA members. Most of them were in the same deep pit of despair she'd been in when she'd first arrived in Hell.

Giada turned her thoughts back to the meeting. A young man called Paul was sharing about how he'd defrauded the charity he'd worked for out of a small fortune. He'd thought he'd gotten away with it until he'd been hit by a bus whilst cycling home one day. He had woken up in the newly-damned waiting room. There were sympathetic nods from some of the other members. Giada had learnt that greed was a very common reason why people ended up in Hell. As Paul's testimony came to an end, Aaron looked around the group and asked if anyone else wanted to share. This time Giada didn't hesitate, she stood up and smiled warmly around the room.

"Hi, my name's Giada and I'm a sinner." The rest of the group murmured a greeting in reply. "I've been coming here for several months now. Many of you have heard my story but for the benefit of the newcomers I'll briefly recap the big sin which I believe got me here." Giada was surprised to find that there was none of the maelstrom of emotions which normally overcame her whenever she started to talk about this. The emotions were still there but she was able to observe them as if from a distance. Putting them into a compartment on one side of her mind whilst talking about the experience on the other side. She continued, "I was jealous of my younger brother Roberto. It was more than just sibling rivalry. I hated him. I wished he would die. The reason was simply that I believed my parents loved him more than me. One day whilst he was playing, his neck got caught in the living room curtain chords. I found him being strangled. He reached out for my help but I ignored him and actually watched as he died." Giada paused and looked around the room, meeting the eyes of the other members. The newer members who hadn't heard this story before looked shocked.

Giada was aware that her delivery perhaps seemed cold and callous so she explained further. She looked down and softened her voice, a rue smile playing at her lips. "It took me a long time to get to the point that I was able to admit what I did. Longer still to talk about it and only now am I able to talk about it without completely breaking down." She looked back up and smiled shyly. "But I wanted to share with you all tonight. You see this week something happened which changed everything for me. My mother arrived in Hell." Giada turned around and swept her arm out to the side to indicate her mother sitting behind where she stood. Her mother smiled at her and nodded slightly for her to continue. "Most people wouldn't see this as a good thing necessarily but for us - well... It's allowed us the chance to finally talk, honestly, for the first time ever. I've admitted my sin to her and she's admitted to me her mistakes as a mother. We now have the kind of relationship I'd always wanted and... it feels strange to say this in Hell but I feel happy." Giada felt her lips fluttering as her emotions overcame her. "Not just for the first time in Hell but probably for the first time ever. I now realise this was what was missing from my life on Earth. If I'd been happy before. If my heart had been full of love in the way that it is now, I never would've been capable of doing what I did. All I ever wanted was to be loved and accepted by my mama and I have that now. It's taken an eternity in Hell to get it but if I'm going to spend the rest of eternity with Mama... well, I don't mind so much."

Giada looked around at the other group members. Some of the newer members looked at her in confusion and disbelief - as if she'd lost her mind. Aaron and some of the other older members smiled and nodded. It was very rare to hear SA members share anything positive. Aaron was the only other person who sometimes did but Giada wondered how much of the time he was bluffing.

She'd finished sharing but something kept her on her feet. A feeling of warmth welled up inside her and her eyes started to tingle.

No! It can't be?... It feels like I'm... crying?!

Tears rolled over her cheeks, real tears. She heard gasps and Paul asked under his breath, "is that possible? I thought that wasn't possible?"

"It's not!" Maureen hissed back at him.

Giada half laughed as the tears continued to flow. "I know it sounds crazy but I'm grateful. I'm actually grateful I'm here. I'm glad I was sent here because if I'd never been damned, I never would've realised that Mama loves me and always has. I see it now, the reason for all my experiences. All the shitty things I did and all the shitty things I felt. How everything led to everything else and how it all had to happen to get me to this point." She felt her face crack wide open with joy. "I wouldn't have it any other way. I wouldn't change a thing. I wouldn't even change the terrible thing that I did. Am I sorry I did it? Yes, of course I am but it worked out for the best in the end. Roberto is in Heaven and Mama says he's waiting for me and I believe now. I truly believe that I'll meet him there some day."

As she said these words, Giada felt a tingling sensation ripple over her body. It felt like the way she'd remembered feeling when she'd been very young and her mother had looked at her like she was the most precious thing in the world. It felt like love. As she felt this, the entire room was filled with bright light. A beam of what looked like golden sunshine descended over Giada's head. She heard the sound of a beautiful chorus of angelic voices, singing the most perfect melodies she'd ever heard. She also heard Paul, the newly-damned charity defrauder, saying,

"Can everyone else see and hear that? It's really happening right?"

Aaron nodded and looked at him, "yes Paul, it's really happening."

Giada's mother stood up and went over to her and they embraced. Giada felt like her heart was going to explode with love. She looked down and felt her eyes widen as she saw that both she and her mother were levitating. The beam of light was carrying them off the ground. It continued raising them upwards. As she travelled, Giada saw the scene of Hell begin to disintegrate around her. First it became pixellated, like an online movie where the internet connection is too slow. Then it started fading until it had completely disappeared. In its place was a scene of lush green fields and a queue of people standing in front of a middle aged man. Giada was still wiping tears from her face. She looked at her mother in disbelief and confusion. Her mother on the other hand was laughing and crying tears of joy as she explained to Giada. "This is Heaven - this is the line to be let into the heavenly gates. We've been redeemed Giada. We'll finally all be together: you, me and Roberto!" Giada wept with joy once more. Her long journey was finally over.

BACK IN THE SA MEETING, Maureen sat with her mouth wide open. She stared in stunned silence as Giada and her Mother were carried upwards in a golden beam of light before disappearing in a poof of smoke.

"Holy Shit! Redemption is real!" she said.

"I told you," Aaron replied.

35

NALEDI

∽

Naledi put her hand up to her forehead, to shield her eyes from the sun, as she looked out across the valley in the direction of the next village. She smiled as she reflected on the events of the past few days. The Countess was dead. She'd watched as the demon had burnt up and then disintegrated, blowing away as dust in the mountain breeze. After Naledi had killed the Countess, Motsumi had agreed that she was ready to graduate. They performed a special ceremony together after which Naledi could call herself a qualified sangoma. He told her that the effects of the binding ceremony would no longer be felt and she was hence free of him permanently. She wasn't sure how she felt about this. He had his faults and they were many but he'd also become the closest thing to a father that she had. Would she remain in his life by choice? Would she continue to visit him in Hell as he had visited his mentor, the Countess, in Hell before the breakdown of their relationship? She wasn't sure yet. But for now she was clear that she wanted a simple life. She was looking forward to concentrating on her schoolwork and living the life of a normal teenager with her friends and family and with Tau.

There was something else she was looking forward to and her smile widened as she saw someone crossing the valley on foot. As the figure got closer Naledi walked downhill to greet the girl. It was Thato, her new student who she'd now accepted as her initiate. She'd be the first of many. Naledi planned to open a school to train other ithwasa-inflicted young people to become sangomas. Thato showed promise and had a lot of natural ability. Naledi decided it was her duty to mentor her. She didn't want Thato being vulnerable to exploitation by dark forces or another powerful sangoma who wanted to use her for the wrong reasons. Naledi knew what it was like to be used in that way and although ultimately things had worked out well for her, she wanted to protect Thato from the dangers she had faced.

Thato walked up to her, taking her hand in both of her hands and shaking it vigorously. A look of boundless enthusiasm and joy was on her face.

"Dumela Naledi - or should I call you Teacher?"

Naledi giggled. "No, no, Naledi is just fine. I'm glad you wish to be respectful towards me but it just feels too weird - I'm only a couple of years older than you."

Thato giggled back, "I'm glad you said that, it would feel a bit weird to me too."

Naledi suddenly realised she hadn't really planned this through at all and now she felt a bit awkward. She noticed that Thato looked slightly anxious. She was probably even more nervous than Naledi was. Naledi wrapped her arms around her own elbows and shrugged as she half smiled. "How about we just get to know each other for today? How does that sound?"

The tension seemed to leave Thato's body immediately and she smiled with relief. "That sounds great."

Naledi continued, "at the end of today's meeting we can discuss when we should get together next. I'll perform the binding ceremony at that next session. Okay?"

"Perfect" Thato grinned and looked towards Naledi's house. "I understand that used to be your uncle's house, right? How did he come to leave it to you?"

Naledi blew out air from her mouth with a slight whistling sound. "That is a looong story. Let's go inside, I'll make us a cup of tea and tell you all about it."

As they walked towards the house, Naledi realised that she no longer felt scared about the future. Even the idea of death no longer bothered her - she knew for certain that it wasn't the end. Her faith in God was now stronger than ever but it was enhanced by her faith in her own abilities. God had made her the way she was. He'd given her her powers and it had taken her time but she'd come to realise that accepting her powers was another way of honouring Him. It didn't have to compete with or eliminate her Christian faith, the two things could complement each other. As Thato talked to her, sharing details about her background and family life, she saw herself in her position. Thato was the girl she had been just a few months ago but that girl was gone and in her place stood both a Christian *and* a sangoma in full possession and acceptance of her powers.

***

READ on for a sneak peek of Chapter 1 of World Breacher: Book 3 'Called by the Redeemed'.

1. GIADA

Whack!

Giada's face hit a puddle, splashing dirty rainwater all over her face and top, as she went crashing to the ground. She picked herself up, wiping her face with her hands, as she scowled at the girl who'd just tripped her up. Of all the things that Giada had been expecting from Heaven, being bullied by a bunch of 'mean girls' wasn't one of them. Her first two months had been perfect. She'd met her younger brother, Roberto again. A smile crept onto her lips as she recalled their reunion. Little Roberto running across the lush grass field outside his house. His beaming face as she swept him up into her arms and nuzzled him with her nose. His look of adoration as he stretched up to put his fingers in her hair and giggled. Roberto had barely been able to believe that she was in Heaven. He'd waited so long for her to join him. He didn't seem to harbour any ill will towards her for not preventing his death. Her younger brother simply idolised her. How had she never noticed before how sweet he was? How much he loved her? Giada sighed.

So many wasted years.

She'd decided right then and there that she'd make up for it. She spent every spare waking moment after that with Roberto. They played together. They went for long walks and had long conversations. Giada felt they were finally having the relationship they should have had as children on Earth. They were not just siblings; they were best friends.

After those blissful first two months, she had to sign up for Redemption School, as all newly-redeemed souls had to. That's when her problems started.

She scowled and shook her head as she brought her thoughts back to the present. She owed it to Roberto to make it work here but it was almost like she was being pushed to fail. Hadn't she already suffered enough in Hell?

The mean girls had verbally attacked her on her very first day. Queen bee, Rika was at the helm, followed by three other blonde-haired beauties. Giada had never been bullied at school and she'd always thought it was because she was attractive but in the presence of these supermodels, she felt like a frumpy librarian.

On her first day, archangel Gabriel had explained that one of the functions of Redemption School was to help them adjust to the radically different conditions of Heaven. The only thing Giada had adjusted to so far was being bullied for the first time in her life.

Giada dragged her feet along the white pebbled pathway as she headed towards the Redemption School hall. Up ahead she saw groups of angels sitting and talking in the grass surrounding the school.

Giada looked at the groups of angels with a pang of longing. She felt like the new kid at school who had arrived mid-year to find everyone else already in friendship groups. Giada would love to be an angel. They were the cool kids who everyone wanted to be. They got given a whole range of powers, flying, healing, manifestation, telepathy plus they got to fight demons! Even though Giada had been redeemed at the same time as plenty of other damned souls, there were few who were her age. Giada sighed. As a newly-redeemed soul, she had a long way to go before she'd even be considered for angelic promotion. She'd have to complete Redemption School first and the way things were going so far, she'd probably be here for a long time.

Arriving at the school, she looked up at its glittering crystal walls and dome-shaped roof. She walked up the grand steps and through the large, arched entrance into the assembly hall. The hall had a central lectern surrounded by rows of ascending benches, all made of crystal. Giada slumped down on one of the benches. Rika's gang sat across the room, twittering and giggling as they gave her stink eye. Giada's heart sank at the prospect of another day dodging abuse from them. How was it even possible that such mean-spirited souls could get to Heaven anyway? Surely, they should still be in Hell?

"Look who it is: Italy's biggest loser," Rika called over at her. Giada felt her blood pressure rising.

Ignore her, ignore her.

She couldn't help herself though, "at least I don't need a group of lookalike fembots to back me up."

Rika's eyes narrowed, "what did you just say?"

"You heard..."

Rika stood up and clenched her fists as she glowered across the room. Giada's heart pounded as she readied herself for another beating.

But the fight never came. They were interrupted by archangel Gabriel, their teacher for the morning's lessons. She swept into the room in a shimmer of white floaty fabric, coppery skin and glittering afro hair tips. Her feline eyes danced with light and amusement. Her entrance was accompanied by angelic choral music which followed wherever she went.

Archangel Gabriel, or 'Gabi' as she liked to be called, carried a trumpet which she now blew into. The chatter in the room immediately went silent and all eyes turned to face her. "Good morning class."

There was a murmur of greeting in reply, the tone of which was less enthusiastic than her own. Her smile dropped, "you don't have to sound so disheartened about it. Today we have arranged a special tour. We are going to take you to the creation vault."

There was a chatter of excitement from the room. Giada felt her brow crease. What was the 'creation vault?' She turned to ask the person sitting next to her and did a double take, inhaling her breath sharply at the shock. He was the most beautiful boy she had ever seen. His high cheekbones descended into a strong jaw and full lips. Her gaze hovered over his lips for a moment. She watched as his tongue wet his lips enticingly. She forced her gaze upwards and her heart skipped a beat as she met his large, soulful brown eyes. He looked at her quizzically as he cocked his head to the side. His eyes displayed a sublime mixture of innocence and wisdom which made her feel almost dizzy. Flicking his floppy brown fringe out of his face, he half smiled at her. Giada felt her cheeks grow warm as she looked back away. Her throat suddenly felt very dry and she coughed. She'd entirely forgotten what it was she wanted to ask him. Was he still looking at her? She daren't look back again so she forced her attention back onto Gabi.

"For those of you who don't know, the creation vault houses the spark of creation. An eternal source of power which has the ability to build or destroy worlds. The entirety of creation came from that spark and it continues to be an endless source of power which the Almighty uses according to his infinite grace." Gabi bowed her head and joined her hands together in a gesture of prayer. A few of the other students copied her. Giada shook her head slightly and smiled at the fakeness of these sycophants. A few weeks ago, they'd all been in Hell and now they were falling over themselves to act like the most saintly beings who'd ever existed.

Giada's eyes slid to the side. The boy lounged on the bench with his gangly legs askew. He looked about her age or a little older. His gaze was fixed on Gabi and he sat up, adjusting his jeans as he brought his hand up to clear his throat quietly. His movements had the grace and precision of a thoroughbred stallion.

Who is this boy and how have I never noticed him before?

Giada flicked her eyes back onto Gabi's introduction.

"Archangel Michael, who you've already met, is in charge of security. He will take you down to the vault. He will be here shortly but first I have another announcement to make." Gabi smiled as she looked around the room. "Over the next two weeks you will each be given your graduation mission. Indeed, some of you, those who have been here longer, have already been given a mission. This mission is unique to each person. Since your arrival, we have been watching you and assessing what your special talents are and this is the basis on which we will assign the missions. Completion of the mission means that you will graduate from Redemption School and will then be given your eternal assignment."

Gabi paused as if considering whether to add anything further. She opened her mouth then closed it again before looking at the ground, deep in thought. When she looked back up, she smiled brightly. "Does anyone have any questions?"

Giada's hand shot up. Gabi looked at her and nodded. All eyes turned to look at Giada and she gulped. "Erm, what happens if we fail to complete the mission?"

"You won't fail to complete it. We give missions based on what we know you are capable of achieving."

Giada wasn't at all satisfied with this response. "But, hypothetically, if someone did fail the mission... what would happen?" She had a mounting feeling of dread in her stomach as she anticipated Gabi's response. There was only one reason she could think of why Gabi had been reluctant to answer the first time. It was confirmed as the archangel replied simply.

"You would be sent back to Hell."

A gasp went up from the room followed by a low murmur as the students chattered amongst themselves.

Gabi patted her hands up and down as she tried to regain order. "Settle down, settle down. You have nothing to worry about. It is extremely rare that anyone fails."

Extremely rare but not unheard of.

This was just getting worse and worse.

A hand shot up from another corner of the room. Gabi nodded towards the bald, pot-bellied man who wanted to speak.

"If we get sent back to Hell, would it be eternal damnation?"

Gabi nodded, "you only get one chance to redeem yourselves. If you blow that chance it doesn't come again."

The room erupted in chatter once more. Giada felt her eyes blur with tears. She turned to look at the boy next to her. He seemed unfazed by the announcement. Almost as if it didn't concern him. Giada couldn't prevent her brow from furrowing briefly in confusion at the boy's lack of anxiety. Maybe he'd already been given his mission and it was dead easy? She turned back to the front. Gabi was taking more questions from others, but Giada struggled to listen. Her thoughts rushed from one scenario to the next. She could be back in Hell and this time with no way out. At least before she'd had an unproven and shaky belief that redemption might one day happen. If she returned, all hope would be gone. Memories of the torture rooms flashed into her mind. The agony. The smell of blood sweat and fear. She'd witnessed and been victim to the kind of sick depravity that would haunt her for the rest of eternity. She shuddered as she thought about the absence of sunlight. Her nose wrinkled at the memory of the constant smell of sulphur. She could almost smell it now and she gagged. She couldn't go back; she'd do anything to escape that fate. Whatever her mission was, she'd make damn sure she completed it.

Click here to buy World Breacher: Book 3 'Called by the Redeemed'.

Did you enjoy this book? If so, please write a review on the store front of your choice and Goodreads now and tell all your friends about it.

If you want to stay updated about my latest book releases, join my VIP list! Visit www.jalihenry.com, enter your email address and you'll be the first to know when the next book is released. I'll also email you with exclusive offers of giveaways and promotional deals.

Please come and join my facebook reader group https://www.facebook.com/groups/3128187757251090
Or follow me on Instagram https://www.instagram.com/jalihenry/
Or on TikTok @jalihenryreadsfantasy
Or on Twitter @jalihenry

ALSO BY JALI HENRY

Cursed Charm, Arcane Witches #1 (New Adult Dark Urban Fantasy)

"He's had centuries to master this game and he is very, very good at it..."

One minute I'm a regular Londoner – overworked, underpaid and living in a flat the size of a shoe box. The next minute I'm doing magic and hunting vampires. You see, it turns out that I'm an arcane witch. Never heard of them? Neither had I until I got attacked by a vampire while trying to make a food delivery. Ok, that wasn't all bad. It did get me through the doors of the sexiest doctor this side of the Thames. The trouble is he's hiding something. I know it's something BIG but I just can't work out what it is...

Now the other arcane witches want me to join their crusade. They say if we don't hunt vampires to extinction, the blood-suckers will take over the world, turning humans into cattle. I tell those crazy witches to get lost, but that's a mistake. The vampires know about me. They know that I'm special and they won't stop until I'm dead.

I soon find myself locked in a battle of wits against the most devious vampire in existence. I'm in way over my head, but the biggest fight may be the one for my own soul...

For fans of Annette Marie, Linsey Hall and BR Kingsolver. If you love sassy heroines, villains you love to hate and unputdownable chapters, you'll love this fast-paced urban fantasy book.

Content: Contains language, violence and mild steam.

Lightning Source UK Ltd.
Milton Keynes UK
UKHW010114031121
393296UK00001B/244